LOVE & OTHER MUSHY STUFF

Book 1 in The Professional Player's Series

LYNDSEY GALLAGHER

ISBN: 9781916251519

CHAPTER ONE

ABBY

I've never been to a fortune teller before. I am a realist. Not for a single second do I believe a 'gifted' stranger has the power to divulge my fate, how many children I'll have, or if there's a man out there that I'd be mad enough to consider marrying. When my best friend Karen pleaded with me to go with her, I had ten days to formulate any number of wild and weird excuses, yet, I failed to come up with even one.

As the familiar Georgian buildings of Dublin City blur in my periphery, Karen negotiates four lanes of Monday evening traffic. Her erratic driving is something I've become dangerously accustomed to over the course of our four-year friendship. I wonder for the millionth time how this lunatic next to me assumed the role of my best friend. The simplest explanation is that she advertised for a flatmate and I applied. The long-winded version entails serious bonding over copious amounts of tears and wine.

'She's supposed to be the best in the country, although she'd want to be, for a hundred and fifty euro.' She performs a last-minute lane change, forcing a neighbouring yellow Nissan to brake hard and beep furiously.

'I'm in the wrong profession.' I tut at her words, not her driving and blow a stray strand of hair from my face. My roots are in dire need of attention, but I'd rather spend my Saturday mornings at the park run than in a sweltering salon sipping watery coffee.

I flick on the ancient radio to accompany us, locating Ireland Today 97.5 FM, the station that employs me. Miraculously, I landed myself a job as a national radio presenter. My show's called Ask Abby. It airs on weekdays from eleven a.m. until two p.m. Though I detest the phrase 'agony aunt', that's precisely what I am. If it weren't so ironic, it might be funny.

To me, it's still hilarious that people seek my advice, considering my track record. Not that I advertise the teeny tiny insignificant fact that when it comes to love, I am beyond hopeless. On paper, I'm the perfect candidate for the position, with a master's in journalism and a second degree in psychotherapy. The fact that I needed the psychotherapy qualification to primarily counsel myself is a very private matter. One which, funnily enough, I never discuss on the radio.

Sally's Soul Show is currently on air. The problem with Sally is that she has no soul. She sold it to the sea witch somewhere along the line. Thank God for the music.

'I listened to your show on Friday.' Genuine enthusiasm affects Karen's tone.

'What did you think?'

'Savage,' she declares, taking a sideways glance at me. I worry when she takes her eyes from the road. Her black blue bob, complete with a scarlet headband, flicks back to the centre, to my relief. I'm not ready to die today. If we did die en route, would the fortune teller ring Karen to see why we hadn't arrived? Or would she already know what had happened?

'I couldn't get over that woman who phoned in to confess her undying love for her next-door neighbour. It wouldn't have been so bad if she wasn't already married to his brother!' Karen reminds me.

A flashback of a brash forty-year-old woman with a strong Donegal accent springs vividly to mind.

I think I managed to talk her out of it, though no amount of hand muffling over the handset would have disguised that voice.

'And then that gay guy who explained how difficult it was to find a partner in Mayo nearly broke my heart.'

'I know. Some of the rural counties aren't as forward-thinking as the city. It must be hard,' I sympathise.

'The cities aren't even that forward-thinking, to be honest.'

'You never know who might have been listening.' I hold a lot of hope when it comes to other people's love lives.

'You set for Friday?' Karen asks.

We're booked into Carton House, a five-star hotel in County Kildare, boasting one of the best spas in Ireland. I can practically taste the cocktails already.

'Yep. Looking forward to a night away. Who else is coming?'

'Kerry and Emma.'

Kerry and Emma are Karen's old school friends. Though I didn't join the clique until much later, they welcomed me with open arms, adopting me into their circle.

'Where the hell is this place, by the way?' It felt like we'd been in the car for hours already.

'Only about another forty minutes away, if you trust Google Maps,' she replies.

'Forty minutes? These are hours of my life that I'll never get back.'

'Ha! Let's be honest, Abs, it's not like you've got a lot to rush home to on a Monday night,' she teases.

'Thanks for reminding me.' It's the truth. I live alone, I eat alone and I always go to bed alone, and I'm happy that way.

Google Maps is uncannily accurate. Forty minutes later, we arrive outside a crumbling cottage in the arse end of nowhere. The sky rages red against the Wicklow mountains. There's zero sign of life. I'm not superstitious, but a chilling shudder rattles along the length of my spine. I'd rather be anywhere else in the world right now.

Sparse scatterings of gravel crunch sharply under my flat leather boots as we follow the pathway towards the paint peeled front door. Withering baskets of purple pansies, dying a slow, painful death, swing lifelessly in the evening breeze. How can a woman, who can apparently predict the future, not predict that her plants will die if she fails to water them?

Karen places her shivering fingers round the rusty brass knocker and bangs loudly. The hollow sound of slow footsteps approaches and the door opens with a low groan. A lady in her late sixties stands expectantly before us. She's frail, both hands crippled cruelly with arthritis, and she relies on a wooden stick for support. Her thinning hair is fastened at the back of her head in a tight grey knot. She wears a mustard coloured jumper and brown slacks cover her bowed legs.

'You must be Karen.' The formal tone of her voice reminds me of an old schoolmistress.

'That's me. And this Abby.' Karen links her arm through mine, her bright eyes gleaming in nervous excitement.

'Excuse the state of my hanging baskets.' The woman raises her eyebrows at me, shooting a knowing look. 'My arthritis has been shocking. It's months since I could grasp the watering can properly.'

I shake my head, briefly perturbed, before dismissing her statement as a weird coincidence. We're led into a large drawing room. A wooden dreamcatcher sways in front of a single-glazed bay window. Slatted, once white blinds are layered with dust.

'Sit, please.' The lady gestures to a worn leather couch. I realise I don't know her name.

'Sorry, I'm Esmerelda.' She introduces herself to both of us but looks at me intently once again. Ok, this is creeping me out now.

'Who wants to go first?' Esmerelda breaks the silence, looking between us.

Thankfully, Karen jumps at the chance, still absurdly excited at the prospect of handing over a hundred and fifty quid for a ten-minute stab in the dark at her impending future. The enormous sapphire engagement ring on her finger states the obvious. I could offer more of an insight, and I'd happily do it for free.

'Come.' Esmerelda leads Karen through another doorway into a small study.

Half an hour passes, I know because I check my watch fifty times, wondering what on earth could take so long. Eventually, the study door opens. Karen emerges with tear-streaked cheeks.

'Are you okay?' Adrenaline surges within at the sight of my normally vivacious friend.

'Be truthful with yourself.' Esmerelda issues her parting advice, with a meaningful finality.

I hesitate in the doorway.

'Don't just stand there, dear, come in.' Her patronising tone is one that only a woman of her age can get away with.

Inside the room, two mahogany armchairs face each

other. Esmerelda places a small bottle of water on the table between us. I realise wryly, it's the most expensive bottle of water I've probably ever had.

'Sit.'

I do as I'm told, grateful there's no crystal ball.

'You're sceptical.' Her bony hands struggle to pull in the handles of her chair to draw her withering body closer to the table.

'I'm not really into this stuff,' I admit. 'Would you prefer to leave it?'

I'm tempted to flee. But a newfound niggle of curiosity stirs in my stomach.

'I'm here now.'

Esmerelda takes my hands in her cold decrepit fingers. She scrutinises and squeezes without uttering a single word. Does she do this to everyone, or is my future particularly worrying? My clammy palms stick to hers.

'This is your heart line. It's broken badly.' She traces a curled-up finger over the curve of the first line across my palm.

What a cliché. Who hadn't experienced some sort of heartbreak at the age of almost thirty?

'The fact that it's feathered at the end indicates that you are a very passionate lover.' She smirks.

I'm unable to prevent the laughter that explodes from my lips. I knew this was a load of bollocks. I haven't had a lover in four years. Not since Him.

'Laugh now, but you'll see.' Her confidence is unwavering.

She's wrong. There's no way I'm letting anyone in again. My parents haven't gotten over the shock of my last disaster. Besides, I don't need anyone. My life is perfectly full. I rely pleasantly and reassuringly on only myself. There's more chance of Donald Trump having a sex change and moving to

Mexico than me taking a new lover. I bite my tongue out of politeness and allow her to do her thing.

The gentle ticking of a small antique clock above the grimy unlit fireplace is the only sound, bar my own ragged breathing. The water remains untouched in front of me, even though my mouth is as dry as the Sahara. It's wine I need, not water.

I imagine running from this eerie little room, free from this unusual and unconvincing little woman.

'I've ascertained three things that might interest you. Not all from your palm. I get feelings about people. I'm never wrong.'

I might believe her had it not been for the 'passionate lover' remark.

'Tell me,' I beg, eyeing the closed door longingly. 'An opportunity will arise at work.'

Huh. It could be an opportunity to go for a pee mid-show, which is a rare chance in itself.

'Secondly, someone close to you will pass.'

My heart sinks. I only hope her predictions are as inaccurate as I suspect.

'Thirdly, he's called Patrick.'

'The person that's going to pass?' I ask, despite claiming I'm a non-believer.

'No, that was number two,' she reminds me. 'I don't know the name of that person, but it's definitely there. Try not to overthink it.' She barely attempts to reassure me. Is this woman for real? No wonder Karen looked emotional.

I scrape my chair back and toss three crumpled fifty euro notes across the table.

'Patrick's the man you will marry. You will have a ring on that finger again – before the year is out,' she declares with unquestionable certainty.

A hundred hairs prick on my neck. I pretend not to hear

the word that she couldn't possibly have known – again. The tell-tale tan band, long since faded.

'Ready?' I ask Karen. The two of us bolt from the drawing room together. I've never been happier to plonk my backside in Karen's tatty passenger seat.

Neither of us utter a single word until we reach the motorway.

'Karen O'Connor, I am telling you now, if you ever do that to me again, I'm going to have to seriously reconsider being your bridesmaid next year. Either that or I'll tie you naked to a lamppost in Amsterdam at your hen party.'

'I only hope she's wrong. Or there will be no wedding for you to be a bridesmaid at!' Karen's practically hyperventilating. She winds the window down and gulps the cool evening air.

'Of course she's wrong.'

'You probably thought the same though, before everything?' She refers to the subject I deliberately evade.

'That was different.'

Only later, when I'm lying in bed alone, does it occur to me that He Who We No Longer Discuss, is actually called Sean Fitzpatrick.

Coincidence, I remind myself.

CHAPTER TWO

CALLUM

As I sprint the final lap of the track, I overhear two teenage boys, tormenting a smaller third boy. 'Keep dreaming, fatty. You haven't got a hope in hell of getting that green jersey.'

The younger boy is a little heavy in truth, but sometimes in rugby, weight can prove advantageous.

Carton House has been our training ground for four years. We always attract spectators; it's not every day you get to see the Irish rugby team training in the grounds of the hotel you're residing in. Most of the time I smile and move quickly on to the showers, but something about the defeated acceptance in the young boy's eyes reminds me of myself at his age, under the constant scrutiny of my brothers. It strikes a chord buried deep within, resonating so much so that I'm unable to ignore it.

I wasn't born a professional rugby player. I spent my childhood questioning my self-worth, hoping I'd make it.

The boy looks up to what I assume is his older brother, deflated by his words.

'The only thing you'll be good for is flipping burgers in Supermac's. Even then you'll probably eat more than you sell.' The torment continues. Tears well in his eyes, and he turns his back to the grounds slinking away, like a dog with his tail between his legs.

Instinctively, I jog towards him and pat him on the back. 'Hey, buddy. How are you?'

'Callum Connolly?' Surprised eyes light up in recognition.

'That's me.' I grin, delighted to be able to make a difference to this kid's day.

'You were awesome in the Scotland game last month! What a try! You're my absolute favourite player.' The boy scrambles around in his coat pocket, searching for his mobile phone and the bravery to ask for a photo.

The two teenagers watch from five feet away, debating on whether to approach. I beckon them over.

'Lads, do me a favour? Take a photo of me and my friend here.' It's an order rather than a question. I extract my mobile from my kitbag and throw it to the boy who spoke the cruellest words. He drops it, but that's my intention.

'You'd want to work on your game.' A discreet reminder of what it feels like to be found lacking.

The boy stoops to lift the phone and mumbles an apology.

'What's your name?' I whisper to my new young friend, staring at me like I'm some sort of hero.

'Martin McAndrew,' he stutters. I wrap my arm around him and pose for the picture.

'Are you on Facebook, Martin?' I ask him. He nods shyly in a starstruck response.

I thank the teenager, simultaneously imparting a warning look and share the picture on my social media, tagging Martin in the post.

'Thank you so much. You honestly are my favourite player.' His sincerity would melt the coldest of hearts, mine included.

'One more thing...' I call to him as he waves goodbye.

I remove my training jersey and throw it to him. 'It's yours.'

Martin whoops in delight. I hit the showers with the rest of my teammates feeling unusually good about myself for once. The warm fuzzy feeling is one I don't often get to avail myself of. The boys are mid-conversation, discussing a kick that had been missed from the halfway line. I listen, peeling off my muddy shorts from my sweaty thighs.

'You were a tank out there today, Callum. Great work. Keep it up.' Coach slaps me encouragingly on the back as he passes.

'Thanks, Coach.' I don't elaborate that my aggression stems from the fact that I'm overflowing with frustration, desperate for a release, and not one that I'll find on the pitch.

After a quick shower, I dry myself off in the locker room. My legs burn, a combination of fatigue and a dirty tackle from my best friend and fellow prop, James. The Six Nations may be behind us, but training stops for no man. It wasn't our best year, and I'm reluctant to admit that it might also be my last.

Tucking the plush white towel around my waist, I scrape my fingers through my wet hair and glance around at my teammates in various states of undress. We'd be lucky if we manage to escape this afternoon without Eddie demonstrating his 'helicopter' impression for the thousandth time.

'Who's up for a pint on Friday night?' We don't drink during tours or championships, but the odd night out's well-warranted off-season.

I need to pull more than just a pint; it's been ages since I've shared a woman's bed, and I'm getting irritable.

'I can't, man,' Marcus answers first. He's our team captain

and the best fly half this country's ever seen. 'I promised the girls I'd take them away for the weekend.' He shrugs, blissfully content in his role as father and husband. His wife Shelly almost died during the birth of their second daughter. She arrived six weeks early, and we were playing France in Paris. I thought he'd swim the Channel himself in his rush to get home to her. In all the rugby tours we've embarked on in the last seven years, he's never even glanced at another woman. And there has been ample opportunity, there always is. Despite his admirable loyalty to his family, he's a pain in my ass most of the time.

'I'm up for a couple of quiet ones.' Eddie's voice resounds mischievously across the tiles. He's the team joker and our resident hooker, on and off the pitch. Hard to know if he's referring to pints or women. Either way, we're on the same page. I give him a fist punch in solidarity as he passes by me in the direction of the shower.

James chips in from behind a long section of lockers. 'I'll go for a couple, but I need to get back to Dublin for Nadine's dad's sixtieth.' James is my best friend, but lately, I've had to share him.

'Man, what is it coming to when I'm getting ditched for a geriatric birthday party? Fucking hell, dude.' I pretend to be pissed, though I understand.

Fuck it, if he invited me, I'd probably go for the craic. But three's a crowd these days.

'Got to keep the old man sweet if he's going to allow me to marry his daughter in a few short months.' James shrugs.

'Why you want to get married is beyond me.' Selfishly, I'm worried about losing my best mate. I've already lost him as my favourite wingman, but marriage's a whole different kettle of fish. Change is looming. On and off the field.

'Have you seen my girl?' James delivers a sharp dig to my ribs.

'Ouch! She's a looker alright.' I can't disagree.

Nadine's an underwear model for a high-end clothing catalogue. James regularly brags he's going to turn her into a maternity model the second he gets that wedding band on her finger.

'About time you found yourself a good woman, by the way. You're not getting any younger, Connolly.' Marcus throws on his long-sleeved green top with the Irish crest on it.

'Ha! You've got to be kidding.' I will him to shut up. I hate this line of conversation.

'Why not, man?' Marcus stares at me inquisitively.

Just because he has his perfect wife and beautiful family, it doesn't mean we all crave the same.

'You know me, lads. Never looking for the one, just the next one.'

'What about that girl in the paper a few weeks ago?' Marcus pipes up.

'It was a couple of dates, that was all.' I brush off his questions, hoping he won't remember the heading of that particular article.

'What did the tabloids call it? Callum Connolly's Latest Touch Down.' A snigger follows. 'You're not getting any younger, Callum. You'll have to grow up sometime.'

Smug marrieds look at a single status as something to be sympathised with. As though I'm somehow lacking if I don't have a wife.

Eddie slaps me on the back encouragingly. 'Callum has no problem with women. They flock to him like flies around shit. Makes him a terrible wingman.'

I don't like his analogy, but he's right, I don't have a problem attracting women.

'No one is saying he can't get a woman, you douche bag. We're saying he can't keep one.' James punches Eddie lightly on the shoulder.

'I can keep a woman. I just don't want to,' I insist. 'Who wants to eat the same dinner every night anyway?' I'm oddly compelled to defend myself from the implication that I'm somehow lacking. It's a direct insult to my masculinity. Why do I need a woman to prove myself as a man?

'What if it was the most succulent meal that you ever tasted? And the thought of someone else indulging in that very same delicacy made you want to rip their head off?' Marcus stirs the pot as usual, resting an enormous shoulder on the closed red locker next to mine.

'It hasn't happened, but if it does, I'll work it.' I pull on jogging bottoms and a hoody.

'Prove it,' James challenges me cockily.

'Prove what exactly?' I don't like where this conversation is leading, but the competitive streak in me refuses to shut up.

'That you can keep a woman for more than a week,' James persists.

'If you insist, tough stuff. I'll send you a photo if you like? I'll even smile so you can frame it.'

'Put your money where your mouth is.' Marcus bets me, that cool smug look he sports when he thinks he's right instantly raises the hair on my neck.

If there's one thing about Marcus, he'd gamble with his own mother if he thought there was a chance he might win something.

I can't back down, despite an increasing sense of impending doom.

'What is it precisely that you eejits want me to do?' I sigh deliberately, emanating an air of boredom.

'Here's the deal. The next girl you go out with, you have to keep interested long enough to bring her to my wedding,' James dares me.

'That's three months away!' I can't hide my shock. It's a

lot to ask of anyone, especially me. They know what I'm like. Either I'll have to stay away from women until the week before or try to put up with the same one for months. Neither option is particularly appealing.

'Exactly.' Marcus snorts.

I've never dated the same girl for more than a week, a fact they're all well aware of. I'm not a relationship type of guy. Never have been, never will be, and I certainly don't pretend to be. My semi-functional family have long since given up any hope of me bringing a girl home.

'He can't do it. He isn't capable.' Marcus shakes his head, the low whistle that escapes his midline diastema pushes my buttons in an irritating manner that only he can achieve.

'Does your snoring drive them away?' James teases.

'Do you wet the bed?' Eddie chips in, apparently forgetting he's meant to be on my side.

'Can't get it up?' James bends his baby finger, emasculating me further.

'Or do you still cry for your mamma in the night?' Marcus hammers the final rusty nail into my coffin.

The guys are on a roll, it might be funny, if it weren't me on the receiving end of it. Marcus's last remark cuts close to the quick.

'Fuck off, you mad bastards. It was Ollie Quinn that pissed in the fucking wardrobe the week we were in Edinburgh.' I pray they'll take the bait and head off in a different direction.

'Yeah and considering that, even Ollie can keep a woman,' James says, laughing as he remembers.

'Actually, he can't,' Eddie informs us. 'The Mrs gave him the p45 last month. Maybe he'll be up for a few pints on Friday night? He might be ready to get back on the horse and I'm just the man to give him a leg up.'

The lads can feck off with their romantic notions, but if I play along for now, maybe they'll forget in a day or two.

'Fine. I'll bring the next girl I date to your wedding.' Anything to get them to shut up.

'That doesn't mean you don't date anyone until the week before.' Marcus is quick off the mark, snagging my plan.

In all honesty, I can't wait three months, I'm horny as hell and looking for some female company ASAP. I'll just have to be discreet about it for once.

'Fine. But this little wager you insist on making better be worth my while. You morons know I don't do relationships. If I bring the next girl I pick up to James's wedding, I want your Audi, Marcus.' I cross my arms over my chest and stare intently at him.

That Q7 has been his pride and joy since he first slid his fat arse into it four months ago, it's his fourth baby. Never, in a trillion years, will he agree to a bet where he risks losing it.

'You've got yourself a bet, man.' He grins, sticks a hand out and shakes mine firmly. I mask my shock with a well-timed cough.

Either Marcus is exceptionally confident that I can't keep a woman for three months, or he has a new car on order. I'd like to think it's the latter but can't be certain.

I tie the laces on my runners, scanning my mental black book for female acquaintances who might be convinced to play along. I'm competitively compelled to restore my reputation amongst the lads. Or I'll never hear the end of it.

'One more thing, buddy...' James says, as we exit the changing rooms into the fresh air.

'What?'

'We get to pick her.' My heart sinks.

CHAPTER THREE

ABBY

The Ireland Today building overlooks St. Stephen's Green, offering spectacular views of the greenery and the tourists who frequent it. I stroll into the radio station around ten o'clock, grasping a cup of chai tea from a nearby Starbucks.

I love being a radio presenter. There are nights I spend hours replying to some frankly bizarre emails, but I want the women of this country to have a friend in me when they have nobody else. The prospect of aiding the heartbroken or sad, somehow helps validates my own heartbreak. A reminder that it at least served a purpose.

Today's show is entitled Ten Signs of Infidelity in a Relationship. Titles like this one always provoke a great deal of interest from the listeners.

'Hey.' Aoife, my assistant and occasional co-host greets me in the corridor. She's pale-looking this morning, her shoulder-length brown hair hangs lankly behind her pierced ears. We walk and talk simultaneously. 'Candice's looking for you. She has a bee in her bonnet about something,' Aoife warns me. 'Like a good bee shagging a flower or more like a wasp hovering around shit?' I roll my eyes.

'Neither.' She laughs at my analogy. 'More like a bee bursting to get something off her chest. Speak of the devil...' Aoife trails off as our producer, Candice, approaches our recording studio, one of six studios in the building.

'Oh my God, girls, wait until you hear what I have to tell you.' Excitement glints in her topaz eyes. We heavily rely on Candice's eyes to decipher her mood, because the rest of her face barely twitches thanks to her unhealthy penchant for Botox.

I suppress a giggle as a vivid image of a queen bee, resting leisurely on a luminous sunflower springs to mind. Candice thrives on drama. I wonder who might be having an affair. For a brief second, I hope it's Sally, but squash that train of thought immediately, not wishing to be unkind.

Candice launches herself into the black leather chair on the far side of the desk, the iMac and recording equipment sits between us. Her short platinum hair's styled into its usual trendy spikes. Black wet-look jeans cling to her shapely legs, and a tight-fitting pink T-shirt bears the slogan, If You Think I'm Cute, You Should See My Girlfriend. Unethical T-shirts are her trademark. She crosses her legs and picks imaginary fluff from her trousers, drawing out the suspense for as long as possible.

'Put us out of our misery please.' It could be lunchtime and we'd be none the wiser.

'There's an opportunity.' She hunches forwards conspicuously, her impeccable eyebrows lift a fraction.

She loses my attention with the use of the single word opportunity, which rings freshly through my mind from less than twenty-four hours earlier.

I take a large mouthful of the chai tea, squeeze my eyes shut tight and count to five.

'Do your ears need cleaning or what, Queenan? I said there's an opportunity,' Candice says.

This is officially creepy.

'What kind of an opportunity?' I'm immediately suspicious, not to mention borderline disappointed at the absence of an affair.

'The powers that be are looking to up the station's overall ratings. They've announced a competition. But get this – the competition is not for the listeners, it's for the DJs for once.'

'What? That's crazy.' The competitions are always aimed at listeners – prize money, holidays, cars, gig tickets, backstage passes. You name it, we've tried it all in an attempt to surpass our competitors.

'The show that secures the highest national ratings over a three-month period wins an all-inclusive trip for two people to New York. But that's not the best bit...'

Well, it sounds pretty good to me. I've never been to New York, but it's top of my bucket list.

'So, what is the best bit then?' Aoife asks.

'You won't believe it. The winner will be the first to interview M.O.D.E.R.N. exclusively.' The words burst out of her mouth. In her excitement, she forgets it's supposed to be top secret.

M.O.D.E.R.N. are the latest man band to top the charts in America. With three consecutive number one records under their low-hanging belts, they've so far been too busy, or too drunk, to be interviewed exclusively.

The entire music world is alight with curiosity about these four, self-made Irishmen that smashed their way into New York City on the back of a YouTube video that went viral. Word has it that they haven't been sober since. No wonder their manager hasn't wanted them too close to the press. Whoever breaks that interview will make a name for themselves that won't be forgotten. It's one hell of a prize.

'Holy feck.' I exchange a pointed look with Aoife and push the knowledge that Esmerelda had predicted this to the back of my mind for now at least.

'My thoughts exactly. The rest of the staff will be briefed before the end of the week. Keep it quiet until then.' Candice manages a wink. She must be due a trip to the salon. 'I can't enter, but I'll give you all the help I can. Anything to make sure Sally No Soul doesn't win, or we'll never hear the end of it. She's after my job, I can feel it in my water.' She pouts like a child instead of the forty-year-old professional that she is.

I imagine myself lazily stretched out in first-class clutching a glass of my favourite champagne, en route to meet the most intriguing act to emerge from Ireland since U2. We need to win. But how?

During the show, there isn't a single second free to formulate a plan. I alternate music with the ten key points that have been highlighted for us: Has your partner started to dress differently or act differently of late? Are you noticing extended periods of unexplained absence? Are there unusual or unexplained expenses within your joint finances? Some of them are so painfully obvious I cringe internally as Aoife and I tackle them in a light-hearted fashion. We're in perfect sync with each other. I wish she'd consider fulfilling the co-host role permanently, but she point-blank refuses, insisting it's too stressful.

With today's topic at the forefront of my mind, I wonder for the umpteenth time if I'm the right woman to be doling out advice on this particular subject, given my own past.

Impostor syndrome creeps in before I remind myself that I'm the precisely right woman to be offering advice because of my past.

Hundreds of WhatsApp messages fly in with tales of 'honey trapping' and fake Tinder accounts. I prepare myself for the first live caller.

'Who do we have on the line?' I grin across at Aoife, both of us aware of the potential for all hell to break loose as the women of Ireland begin naming and shaming their cheating partners.

'Hi Abby, its Kara.' Kara sounds about thirty-five with a distinctly unpolished Dublin accent.

Rightly or wrongly, I conjure an image of a woman with heavily pencilled eyebrows and a copious amount of lip filler. Kara sounds like the classic example of a woman scorned. Candice offers me a thumbs-up from the other side of the glass window, encouraging me to roll with it. I place my hands over my enormous headphones and adjust them as she begins.

'My husband...' She pronounces the word husband though it was the filthiest word to ever roll from her tongue. 'My husband told me on Saturday morning that he was going fishing for the day, but who showers and shaves before they go fishing? I suspected he was lying. While he sat shovelling a greasy rasher sandwich into his big fat gob, I crept out and checked the mileage on his car. The lake's a forty-kilometre drive. I wrote the current mileage on the back of my hand in a permanent marker.' The tempo increases with every word. Kara's on a roll now.

It's decidedly more tragic than humorous, but her dramatic tone and delivery prove hilarious.

'Sure enough...the cheating man-whore was gone for the entire day! When he arrived home, all smug thinking he'd got away with it, I slipped out the back door in me dressing gown and checked the mileage again. Low and feckin' behold, he'd barely done twelve kilometres. I told him there and then he's a dirty lying cheating bollocks and to get out me bleedin' house!' She peaks, approaching her finale.

'We are live on national radio, Kara, just to remind you.'

'Sorry! Sorry. I forgot meself for a second there. Talk

about mileage, the feckin' mileage was up alright, but he'd clocked it up in other ways surely.'

I place my hand over my microphone to muffle my snorts. Kara's a legend; relatable and hilarious. The women of the country will love her.

'You want to know the best bit about the whole bleedin' lot?'

'Uh-huh.' I just about manage to compose myself again.

'When I went back in the house to confront him, what did he smell of? Feckin...'

Aoife scrambles over the table and cuts straight over her with an ad break and the two of us howl with uncontrollable laughter. Even Candice is doubled over outside the glass window, hanging onto the wooden door frame for support.

'That was brilliant. Make a snippet of Kara for an advertising jingle.'

'If Kara wasn't such a loose cannon, I'd have her on as a guest.' I push my glasses up onto the bridge of my nose, unable to cope with my contacts every day of the week.

'A guest speaker with an exceptional insight might be a brilliant idea for the ratings, you know.' Candice places a hand on her hip thoughtfully.

'Yeah, but it'd need to be someone seriously high profile to drum up enough interest,' Aoife says.

'Someone that you'd never expect to talk about love and other mushy stuff,' Candice suggests.

'Wait, I've got it! We need a man,' Aoife exclaims.

'Oh my God. That is an absolutely brilliant idea. The women of the country will go mad for a man's opinion. I'll see who might be available.' Bubbling excitement simmers within. I'm determined to win that trip to New York, be it fair or be it square.

As I leave the studio, I ring Mam and Dad. They live in Carrick, my picturesque hometown on the River Shannon. A horrible sense of uneasiness edges in, even though I claim to be a non-believer. If Esmerelda's first prediction came true, there's a chance her second might.

Mam answers on the first ring, her only complaint is that next door's cat is repeatedly shitting in her rose bush. She informs me that my sister Alicia has a new boyfriend. Dad doesn't approve. I wonder if I'll get the chance to meet this one. Alicia and I aren't exactly close, not anymore. As I bid her goodbye, I exhale a weighted sigh of relief that everyone is healthy and make a mental note to avoid any Patricks, just to be on the safe side.

CHAPTER FOUR

CALLUM

A recurring cruciate injury has been troubling me since the Six Nations. Thirty-three isn't old in the real world, but it's pushing on for a sporting career. I can't complain. What a career it's been, but that's exactly why it is so hard to accept its inevitable conclusion. My chest tightens at the thought. I put it down to stress and attempt to relax. The steam room, jacuzzi and massages are my favourite way to do so after a week on the field. Some Friday afternoons, half the Irish rugby team could be found lazing between the pool and the jacuzzi at Carton House.

'Callum. How are you?' A pretty spa therapist called Hannah greets me warmly. I know most of them by now – not like that. I love women, but even I try not to shit on my own doorstep. Coach would kill me, apart from anything else.

'Glad it's Friday,' I answer truthfully. The reprieve from training is a welcome relief.

I sling my bag into a free locker, don my swimming shorts and hang the hotel-issued white fluffy robe on a free hook outside the eucalyptus steam room. I place my towel on the wooden bench and seek some much-needed solitude in the swirling steam, replaying today's training over in my mind. Next year will more than likely be my last season. If I can even get that far with this damn injury. It's perfect for weeks on end, then bam – before I know it I'm floored again.

The solitude is short-lived, as the condensation-blurred glass door is thrust open against the wall, allowing a gust of cool air to sweep in. I had hoped to reflect on the situation, maybe even wallow a little. But Eddie and his youthful athletic energy put heed to that for now.

'Hey, man. I thought I'd find you here. We still on for a pint later?' He takes a seat opposite me, shaking out his floppy hair like a damp dog.

'Sure. Let's eat here, then head back to Dublin.' As one of the few remaining singletons, we often dine together.

Fuck the boys and fuck their bet. I'm on the prowl for a woman tonight. It's been four weeks. My needs are consuming me. The last woman turned up at training three times in one week, despite my crystal-clear declarations from our very first encounter. Coach had to ask her to leave, much to Marcus's amusement. She sold her story to the press, resulting in the touchdown remark. She was too much. I prefer my women the same as my cars; sleek, fast and low maintenance. It's easier that way.

'Heading for a swim, I'll meet you in the bar about seven, yeah?' I stand to leave.

'Grand.' Eddie nods.

Sweat trickles the length of my tired muscles as I towel off the excess water and reach for the robe I left on the hook. A tall exquisite blonde, sporting nothing but a cerise bikini, stands deliberately blocking my access.

'That's mine.' She reaches for my robe.

I glance briefly over her slim, exposed body. She's seriously hot, literally and metaphorically.

'Actually, it's not.' I'm one hundred per cent confident that this particular robe's the one I left here, not twenty minutes earlier. But if she wants to get technical about this, it actually belongs to the hotel.

Her porcelain jaw sets in a hard line of determination, and ferocious flames ignite in her rich brown eyes. Confidence oozes from her every pore. She shows absolutely no sign of backing down. If I offer to share the damn robe with her, would she take me up on it? How would her toned sweaty body feel sliding underneath mine? I'd love the opportunity to find out.

She folds her arms over her prominent chest, conscious that I'm blatantly admiring her semi-naked state. Subtly isn't my strong point, especially when it comes to something I want. And I always get what I want, primarily because I'm willing to work for it. Unable to prevent the smirk from sliding onto my face, I put all thoughts of wallowing aside and opt to have a little fun.

Arched eyebrows continue to challenge me.

'Check the pocket,' she insists. 'You'll find my keycard in the right-hand side.'

'Is that an invitation?' I tease, knowing full well it's anything but.

'It most certainly is not. It's proof of identity. Of ownership of the towelling robe!' she corrects me, furiously articulating every word.

A slow blush creeps up over her make-up free face. Blonde messy hair secured on the top of her head exposes a decidedly kissable slender neck. Despite her obvious femininity, she's openly fierce, possibly even liable to snap if I push her much further. Yet, I can't help myself.

I snatch the robe in question from the hook before she

can, wrap it around myself and hold it open suggestively. 'Room for two.' I wiggle my eyebrows at her and motion for her to climb inside with me. Laughter presses tightly inside my chest, though clenched fists highlight her lack of amusement.

'You must be the most chauvinist arrogant man in this entire estate. Check the pocket and be done with it.' Tiny goosebumps ripple across her exposed wet flesh, she's freezing following the heat of one of the many saunas.

I glance at her bikini top, to check for symptoms of her chilly state elsewhere, earning a sharp, but unsurprising slap on the arm. At least it wasn't my face. And even I have to admit, I'm asking for it. I can no longer restrain myself, devilish laughter escapes my chest, echoing throughout, yet she refuses to crack a smile.

As much as I'm enjoying the sight of her semi-naked body, I don't relish the thought of her perishing. It's a shame to cover something so beautiful, but my chivalry wins out in the end.

'Okay, okay, have the damn robe.' I slip it off and hand it to her, holding my hands up in defeat.

She fastens it around her, securing the waistband tightly in position before slipping a hand into the right pocket. Wrinkled fingers search for her keycard, one that I'd already ascertained isn't there. Her body visibly sags. The earlier blush develops into a burning crimson fire, illuminating her cheeks. She struggles to meet my grinning eyes.

'You're welcome...' I momentarily enjoy her embarrassment.

'S-sorry...' she stammers. I watch in an unusual fascination as she reluctantly appears to contemplate removing the robe. As much as I'd love to see that fantastic body once again, I've wound her up enough for one day.

'Keep it. I'll get another from the desk.'

'I could have sworn…' she trails off, patting her hair self-consciously, an attempt to regain some kind of composure.

'You could always take me for a drink, by way of an apology?' Ever the opportunist, I'm not prepared to let this one slip past me.

A scowl forms on her face in response.

'Okay, I'll buy you one, if it makes you feel better.' I'm fighting an uphill battle with nothing to lose and everything to gain.

This alluring beauty is not one bit interested in me. Why it bothers me, I have no idea. There will be plenty more opportunities in Dublin tonight. Maybe I'm just unused to the word no.

At the risk of sounding like a complete twat, I wonder if she knows who I am, though it wouldn't probably make a difference to a woman like her. She radiates an aura of class, every single square inch of her body screams independent and unavailable. It's probably half the appeal – the thrill of the chase. That and those full breasts and tiny waist.

'I've taken up enough of your time already.' She turns on her heel and stalks through the archway into the main swimming pool.

Attempting not to look like a stalker, I follow her to the pool area, keeping my distance and dive into the crystal-clear water. All I wanted was a little peace, a little solitude to wind down, yet my encounter with the glaring ice queen has me more wound up than I was before. Thirty lengths aren't enough to prevent my mind imagining the contents of that hot-pink bikini. I head back to my room for a shower before I explode with frustration.

CHAPTER FIVE

ABBY

With no idea of the whereabouts of my original dressing gown or who is now in possession of my key, emblazoned with the room number on the cardboard sleeve, I'll have to go to reception and deactivate it.

'Abby, over here,' Karen calls from a jacuzzi adjacent to the pool.

'Sorry, I got distracted.' You would have too if you'd seen the arrogant godlike creature in his ripped pectoral glory.

'Whose robe is that?' Kerry asks, furrowing her brows like a squirrel squinting at an acorn.

I'm mortified, made doubly worse by the fact that not only was I practically naked, but also in the wrong. The enticing abs and his enormous physique had thrown me, and don't get me started on those smouldering eyes. I devote my life to avoiding men like him.

'We brought yours with us when we left you in the sauna, in case you had anything valuable in the pocket.'

At least I don't have to worry about some random man

sneaking into my room in the middle of the night... although if he looked like the arrogant athlete that just dived into the pool, even I might be hard pushed to boot him out. He's obscenely attractive, but my God does he know it. Broad shoulders give him a tank-like appearance, powerful and strong, contrasting a narrow waist. The definition of his abs carved like a Roman sculpture. He must live in the gym.

I shake my head, dismissing the memory of his semi-naked body from my sex-deprived mind. I'd quiet my unruly hormones with copious amounts of cocktails in the bar later. Until then, I attempt to keep my eyes from the distinct and delicious masculine outline perfecting his butterfly stroke not twenty feet away.

'Get in, Abs,' Karen urges. 'You're gawping with your mouth opening and closing like a fish.' How is she not gawping too? How could anyone miss that? Even I couldn't deny his appeal, and I wouldn't notice Jamie Dornan if he were standing immediately in front of me. I know for a fact, because it happened once on Grafton Street. Aoife almost fainted on the spot.

I sink into the endless flow of bubbles next to Kerry, positioning my back in front of a fast-flowing jet. Kerry's a dote, she's only five foot two but what she lacks in size she makes up for in personality. Her infectious laugh can be heard countrywide. In contrast, Emma is tall with jet black hair, emerald coloured cat shaped eyes, and a figure that most women would kill for. She owns multiple hair and beauty salons, seems to know exactly what she wants in life, and isn't afraid to pursue it. She's also the angel that did my highlights at short notice earlier this week, and the coffee in her salon was to die for. I don't know why I haven't been into her before.

The girls resume their conversation about Karen's lack of wedding planning.

I came close to walking down the aisle myself four years

ago. It obviously didn't end with the traditional 'and they lived happily ever after'. I vowed never to repeat the situation again.

Mr Hot Robe Guy pulls himself out of the pool in an indecent show of strength and suppleness, and shoots me a meaningful wink as he passes. I pointedly look away in exaggerated distaste. I refuse to be the next notch on his bedpost, regardless of the indecent indentations leading directly to his groin.

Later in my hotel room, my thoughts return to that precise image as I wrap a fresh towel around me, hoping not to destroy it with last night's hastily applied tan. Using every inch of willpower, I force his picture-perfect image from my delinquent brain and prepare for dinner, carefully blow-drying my freshly highlighted hair. I colour my heart-shaped lips with a shade described as fire engine red, barely recognising the sultry woman staring back at me from the steamy bathroom mirror. Almost ready, I step into a red slim-fitting dress and curse, realising I'm unable to reach the zip myself.

Two sharp raps on the bedroom door startle me, although I'm expecting Karen. Not only does she speed on the road, she races impatiently around all aspects of life. And when dinner time approaches, she waits for no one.

'Two seconds.' I slip my feet into gold pointed stilettoes and douse myself liberally in the Chanel perfume that Candice coerced me into buying on one of our infrequent trips to Brown Thomas.

'Thank God you're here. I can't reach my zipper.' The stiff bristled matt wedges under the door, and I fight with it for a second before it's forced open from the other side.

A low chuckle sends a ripple of alarm through the length of my spine.

'Allow me...' Mr Hot Robe Guy pushes the door effortlessly towards me.

I take a step back to find myself, once again, face to face with this flirtatious stranger. He stands a foot in front of me; navy slacks and a slim-fitting white shirt hug his muscular frame. His top two buttons are undone, and a flash of tanned supple skin hints at the perfection that lies promisingly beneath the thin cotton.

I have no words. Not a good trait for a radio presenter. I press my lips together to mask my surprise. Large insightful pupils demand my attention, examining every inch of me, scorching me from the inside out.

'Turn around.' He twists one finger in a simple demonstration.

Mute, I accept his assistance, seeing as he's here. Gentle fingers brush against my bare skin. Tiny fine hairs at the base of my neck prickle in a betraying state of arousal.

'I came here intending to undo your dress.' His warm breath seductively tickles my throat. I dart away from him the second I'm certain the zip's secure.

'Does that line usually work for you?' I stare at him pointedly, hands on both hips.

'In all honesty, yes.' He closes the distance between us again, a blatant refusal to respect my personal space.

'It's wasted on me, I'm afraid.' Could he be any more arrogant?

'I hoped we might at least have a drink together.' He raises a bottle of Moët in his left hand.

'I don't drink,' I lie.

'Neither do I,' he says solemnly, crossing his heart in a boy scout-like gesture. 'Actually, I'm not usually allowed,' he confesses, running a hand through his dark crew cut.

'I can see why, if this is what you're like sober.' I smooth my dress down. He stares with an unhealthy interest.

'One glass won't hurt either of us.' He pops the cork swiftly before I can decline again.

'Us' sounds so natural rolling from his tongue. He's good, I'll give him that. Clearly, he's had a lot of practice.

Thankfully I'm an expert in resisting male advances. Though I've never been so physically tempted this way before. I know nothing about him, and what I do know I don't even like, but there's something astonishingly appealing about his abhorrently caveman-ish approach. Despite the arrogance, he exudes the most infuriating sex appeal of any man I've encountered.

I'm painfully aware of the proximity of the king-sized bed. As is he, since he glances at it twice while I reluctantly search for a couple of wine glasses.

What am I doing?

I've lost the plot. His pheromones are driving my ovaries insane. His subtle masculine scent taunts my nose, sharp cinnamon with wooden undertones.

'One drink. Then you're leaving.' I hand him the glasses.

'Most women say thank you when a man arrives at their door with champagne.' He gazes intently over my trembling body again, unashamedly undressing me with electric eyes.

'I'm not most women.' I take a step back again, aware that there's only three more steps that I can take before I land on the bed.

'So I gather. Tell me.' He bends forwards, pouring the foaming liquid. 'Who are you exactly?'

Does he already know? I could be alone in a hotel room with a crazy stalker who likes to wear women's clothing and jerk off to my show. I scoff at the implausibility of it. I can't imagine this man being stuck for female company.

'I'm Abby,' I tell him as Esmerelda's words replay in my head. Her remark about me being a passionate lover doesn't seem quite as funny now. If Mr Hot Robe Guy reveals his name is Patrick, I might literally keel over and die.

And if I did, that would come fairly close to ticking all three of Esmerelda's boxes.

'Abby's a beautiful name.' He clinks his glass against mine. 'I'm Callum.'

Relief and disappointment seep into my skin, washing over me like a tidal wave. I exhale the breath I'm unknowingly holding.

'Are you here alone?' My curiosity around Callum piques.

'Careful now, Abby, that sounds suspiciously like a pick-up line,' he warns with a suggestive wink. Even I have to laugh at that. He's charming and funny, no wonder he's unbearably arrogant.

'I can assure you of one thing with complete and utter certainty. I am not trying to pick you up. Or any man for that matter.' There, it's out in the open. Now I can enjoy my drink.

'Are you spoken for?' He glances pointedly at my ringless fingers.

'Is it that hard to believe that a woman just doesn't want you?' It's harsh even for me, but delivered with a smile. I don't mean to be a bitch, but I can't afford for him to get the wrong impression here.

'Don't hold back, hey. You ever seen a grown man cry?' He places a huge hand over his heart in mock offence.

'It's not you. I just don't date. I haven't in years.' I admit more than I intended.

'I'm not asking you on a date... More like an experience, I suppose we might call it. A private tour? It could be our little secret?' He eyes the bed again suggestively. I slap him playfully on the arm for the second time today. Instead of being offended, I'm stupidly flattered.

His bicep's rock-solid beneath my fingers, which linger several seconds longer than necessary. It doesn't go unnoticed. My mouth says one thing, but my defiant body screams another. I need him to leave.

'Absolutely no chance. You've already outstayed your welcome.' I sink the last mouthful of Moët and usher him pointedly towards to door. Secrets never remain a secret for long.

'Not even a kiss?' He chances, playful outrage etches onto his eternally hopeful face.

I admire his persistence, like a teenager out for the shift. 'No.' I'm firm, though surprisingly secretly tempted. Maybe it's being in this beautiful hotel, the fact I'm away from every part of my normal life or the idea it could remain our secret. This is the closest I've come to wanting to kiss a man in years, and it has to be a man-whore of all people.

He hovers in the doorway before finally accepting defeat. 'Nice to meet you, Abby.' His tone's tinged with regret.

'Enjoy your night, Callum.'

'I intend to.' He saunters arrogantly down the corridor.

His effortless ability to embark on the next conquest stings. And that's precisely the reason I don't get involved with men. They tend to hurt me.

CHAPTER SIX

CALLUM

Abby is a beautiful name, but one I'll have to forget. I was under no illusion she'd fall at my feet. She's far too classy for that, but, unable to forget her, I'd been compelled to at least try to penetrate the hardened wall of her cool exterior. Reluctantly, I accept her big fat resounding no. A pity, but not to be.

Eddie and James are already propping up the bar and Marcus kept his word, landing in for a short while before embarking on the journey home to his family. Ollie appears at the same time as me.

'There you are,' Eddie states the obvious.

'We were beginning to think you'd wimped out of the bet.' James takes a sip of his Heineken Zero.

I'd forgotten about the bet, preoccupied looking for 'the next one'. An image of Abby in that indecently decent dress sweeps regrettably through my mind. Why is the allure of the unavailable so much more enticing?

'Don't be daft. That Audi is mine. Fake it until you make it, right?'

These lads have seen me at my best and my worst, yet my private life is something I can't share. The concept of being judged, or worse, pitied is unbearable. It's far easier to be a player for the sake of being a player. Besides, not everyone craves the deep and meaningful.

'Tonight's the night, buddy,' Marcus warns me mischievously.

It takes a second to register. They can't seriously mean to pick out a woman here?

'Here? You've got to be fucking joking.'

'Why else do you think I'm hanging round here with you losers when I could be at home having a drink with my gorgeous wife?' Marcus pokes me firmly in the chest.

'This place is full of skirt.' James glances around the busy room. Women dominate the numbers, sipping wine and drinking gin from enormous fruit-filled chalices.

A ripple of nerves flickers through me as they eye up potential candidates for this stupid gamble. I consider inventing a fake girlfriend, but the trouble is then I'll have to produce one.

'Eddie and Ollie can pick later, there will be loads to choose from in the club.' I'm stalling for time.

'You're not backing out already, Connolly? I won't be in the club. Let's do this now,' Marcus insists.

'Your Audi's fairly safe, by the look of it.' James twists the knife.

Smug bastards. And these are my so-called friends. I can't give in. I'll never hear the end of it.

'Very well. Do your worst.' I take a swig of my pint as the guys scour the place for an unlikely candidate.

'What about her?' James points out a heavy lady in her eighties sitting with two other pensioners.

'A bet's a bet,' Marcus says with a snigger.

'That might float your boat, fellas, but I prefer my women with a heartbeat.'

'What about her?' Eddie nods towards a 'lady' sitting alone, six metres away from us. An oversized sequinned dress hangs from her. Heavy foundation cakes the lines of her face. Her shoulders are bigger than mine, and I'm fairly sure there's a possibility it's not the only part of 'her' anatomy that's bigger.

'The bet is, I can't keep a woman, not pick the most questionable one you can find,' I remind them. 'I have to bring this girl to James's wedding. He's going to be looking at these photos for the rest of his life.'

'He's right,' James concedes.

'I have her,' Marcus announces triumphantly. His voice a daring edge to it.

I dread what my eyes might land on next.

He confidently nods towards the corner of the large room where four women are engrossed in animated conversation, the food menu unopened on their laps. 'The one in the red dress.' Marcus crosses his burly arms over his chest. 'If you can pull her, there's no way you'll be able to keep her.'

My pint catches in my throat, choking me. James claps me hard on the back.

I'd recognise that figure anywhere.

Abby sits sideways, offering a discreet opportunity to examine her profile. With full red lips and a button nose, she appears delicate and feminine, reinforcing the old saying – never judge a book by its cover. She may look sweet, but she possesses the ferocity of a lioness; I experienced it first-hand today, twice. She's beautiful, no doubt. But she's also distinctly uninterested in me.

Fuck.

I contemplate my options, thrumming my fingers on the

bar. A bet's a bet. I'll just have to work a little harder. A part of me even relishes the prospect. There's nothing in this world quite like the thrill of the chase, be it a ball or a woman. Both came relatively easily to me in recent years. Now it appears I'll be fighting tooth and claw for both again.

CHAPTER SEVEN

ABBY

'How's work, Abby?' Kerry asks before taking a sip of her Pinot Grigio.

'Did you hear the show on Tuesday? Ten Ways to Tell if Your Partner is Being Unfaithful.' I relay Kara's advice about the mileage.

'I heard it. Kara was brilliant.' Emma flicks her glossy hair back from her shoulder and glances at two middle-aged men on the neighbouring table. I observe her subconscious movements in awe. No wonder men flock to her. She claims she attracts all of the wrong ones, but it hasn't deterred her from serial dating in her never-ending quest to find the right one.

'Tell me about it.' The jingle was played every day this week. Kara's voice has become one of my firm favourites.

'The poor woman, but the way she told her story was absolutely hilarious,' Emma says.

'There's actually a competition running within the station at the minute,' I whisper as discreetly as possible.

'Oh.' Karen leans forward in interest. She's one of those

people who luck seemed to follow, forever winning Facebook competitions and random raffle prizes. Last year, she even won ten grand on a Credit Union draw, which enabled her to spend a couple of months touring Europe with a friend called Eve.

'This is one competition you won't win, because you can't enter.' I relay the details, and they squeal in high-pitched excitement at the mention of M.O.D.E.R.N.

'You need to win that prize.' Karen refills our glasses, draining the remainder of the bottle.

'Such an opportunity.' Emma uses the one specific word that I deliberately avoided.

'Oh no.' Karen's face sinks as she realises the first of Esmerelda's predictions came true.

'It's a coincidence,' I say 'Technically it's a competition, not an opportunity.' My words seem to placate her.

'So what do you need to do in order to win it?' Emma leans in attentively.

'Achieve the highest ratings by the beginning of August. I have a little under three months to work it.'

The waitress arrives at the table with her pen in hand to take an order.

'Sorry, can we have five more minutes?'

She repeats the daily specials and leaves again.

'What are you thinking?' Kerry adjusts the strap of her one shouldered top.

'Food-wise?' I look at the menu, hungry all of a sudden. 'No, the show.' Emma rolls her eyes playfully at me.

'Find the most controversial, current topic you can and pull the heartstrings of the nation. That's your forte,' Karen says.

'I was thinking something similar.' I place my menu down in front of me again. 'But I think I need a man.'

'Abby Queenan, you haven't had a man in the entire time

we've known you,' Kerry says in surprise. 'Either that or you've kept him chained to the bedpost.' She sniggers at such an implausible thought.

I've never disclosed the extent of my aversion to men. Karen knows, obviously. But we don't discuss it. No point rehashing the past, the end result remains the same.

'I don't need a man myself. I need one to win the hearts of the nation. A show where women can ring in and ask the male perspective. You know how hard it is to get men to talk about feelings and stuff. It would be momentous if the women of the country had access to the deepest darkest thoughts of one, even if it was for one time only.' I bite my lower lip thoughtfully, before remembering my scarlet lipstick.

'Abby Queenan, that's absolutely brilliant.' Emma clinks her wine glass against mine in a salute. High praise from the ambitious owner of three, soon to be four, hair and beauty salons over Dublin – she doesn't mince her words.

'The only trouble is, I need a man that the women of Ireland will be clawing over themselves to actually talk to. He has to be hot. Young, but not too youthful. Successful, but approachable. It's like looking for a needle in a haystack.'

'You are preaching to the converted, sister. If you find a man like that, be sure to give him my number,' Emma says.

'I never said he had to be single. In fact, his relationship status never occurred to me.'

'It might help. Get all the flustered housewives in a tizzy thinking about him.' Karen nods.

'But who?' I've failed to come up with even one suitable candidate that might consider helping me.

The waitress returns carrying a tray with a chrome wine cooler and four champagne flutes.

'We didn't order champagne,' Kerry says.

My empty tummy lurches at the sight of the Moët being

placed in the wine chiller This is too much of a coincidence. I glance nervously around, scanning the room for any sign of him.

'I was told to bring this over for "Abby and her friends". That is you?' She looks at me for confirmation and places the crystal glasses in front of us.

I nod, pretending it's the most natural occurrence in the world. I eventually spot Mr Hot Robe Guy wedged in at the bar between four other gigantic men. Their shoulders make his look small, and that's no mean feat. I wonder if they're brothers. Reminding myself his name is Callum, not Mr Hot Robe Guy, the image of him in his swimwear rebelliously rises to the forefront of my mind.

'Probably one of your mad fans that listen to the show.' Kerry happily accepts the glass without giving it a second thought. As small as she is, she certainly likes to put them away.

'Oh, you're Ask Abby from Ireland Today,' the waitress says. 'I absolutely love your show. My favourite was the one where the mothers who had their babies taken from them by the nuns got the chance to have their say. Oh my God, I was bawling.' Emotion cracks in her voice as she remembers.

I nod again, lost for words for the second time in one day, uncertain why I'm so uncomfortable with this. The only reason I can conjure is that Callum is the most attractive man I've ever set eyes on, and I've been having explicit thoughts about him ever since I did exactly that.

It's not the first time I've been hit on. I've had practice dismissing advances, become ridiculously good at it. So much so that my colleagues and cronies have labelled me a staunch feminist, which I'm not. I believe in equality, don't get me wrong, but I don't exactly fight for it, content in my own life. I could do a lot more for the cause if I chose to. In fact, I probably should. I know for a fact that some of my colleagues wonder secretly if I'm a lesbian. There had been rumours about me and Candice. Probably started by Sally, again.

Today, and tonight for that matter, should be no different to any other time I've been hit on, but it's not. Callum is infuriating and intriguing, and he's penetrating my pores. He's the kind of man I would have avoided like the plague, even before Sean Fitzpatrick broke my heart.

'Well the Irish rugby team must like your show,' the waitress says with a smile. 'Callum Connolly sent this over to you, and he knew exactly who you were.'

He's a rugby player, for Ireland no less. It makes perfect sense; massive shoulders, overly confident, assertive and accustomed to getting his own way.

I don't watch rugby, and even if I did, I probably still wouldn't have recognised him. I dab the corner of my lips with a napkin in what I hope looks like a feminine gesture, but it's a poor attempt to conceal the tell-tale smile, exposing my foolishly flattered face.

The girls giggle and stare, less than subtly, at the men at the bar.

'Thank you,' I mouth, hoping to convey that the outcome will still be the same.

A boyish grin appears on his face, assuring me that he's far from receiving closure on his indecent proposal. A thousand butterflies flutter intrusively around my stomach. Butterflies that have no right to be there.

It's a generous gesture, but it doesn't change a thing.

'Holy shit, Abby. You're not going to say no to that, are you?' Emma interrupts my thoughts abruptly.

'It's only a drink, albeit my favourite one.'

The same one we'd shared only half an hour ago, in my bedroom.

'Men like him do not just want to buy you a drink,' Karen says with a grin.

'You know my policy on the situation, girls,' I say.

'So you got your heart broken. Haven't we all been there at one stage or another?' Emma shrugs her shoulders.

Karen winces.

'I don't want to talk about it.'

'Callum Connolly's the biggest player going. And I don't just mean on the rugby field.' Kerry tactfully diverts the conversation back to Callum.

'His reputation does precede him.'

'He was dating one of those Victoria Secret models last year,' Emma says.

'Yeah, and before that, he was linked to one of the English Royals. You know the blonde cousin that's always photographed drunk in the nightclubs?' Karen says.

'Apparently, he's a nice guy, as long as you're not looking for anything other than what he's got in his trousers,' Kerry says.

'Well, that's me out,' I tell them.

'Well, if you're not interested, I am,' Emma says, readjusting her cleavage in her top.

Internal flames threaten to scald my face. The pounding of my blood resonates around my rapidly tensing body. Jealousy... What is wrong with me? Emma has every right and I shouldn't blame her in the slightest for feeling that way, when sex personified is standing twenty feet away from us, throwing the wandering eye.

I send up a silent prayer that Callum does not come over here. For some absurd reason, the thought of him and Emma hitting it off makes me feel physically sick. What kind of a friend am I? I don't want him, but I don't want anyone else to have him.

Karen leaps out of her chair in excitement.

'I've got it. This is absolutely feckin' brilliant,' she practically screams. The elderly couple to the right of us flinch at her colourful language.

'He could do it. He'd be perfect,' Karen says.

He is perfect. That's half the problem. It should be illegal to leave the house looking like that. He'd give a weaker woman a heart attack.

I tear my gaze from where he stands with his back to us and meet her eyes questioningly.

'For your show,' she spells it out to me, shaking my arm with excitement.

Realisation dawns on me. If a man like him talking about romance doesn't interest every straight woman in the country nothing would. Hell, he might even convert the gay ones, too. It would be out of this world. Candice would be so impressed that she might finally drop her incessant suggestions of a new co-host for my show. It would blow Sally's Soul Show out of the water.

'Yeah, but good luck with that,' Emma says crushingly. 'There's absolutely no way a man like him will go on national radio to talk about his feelings and all that kind of guff.'

She might have a point.

'He doesn't have to talk about his feelings. All he has to do is offer a male perspective,' Karen says.

'Well, it's not like I've got any other options right now.' A newfound sense of confidence returns.

The prospect of having a legitimate excuse to be near Callum Connolly excites me more than I'm comfortable with, and it has nothing to do with the fact that he plays rugby for Ireland. I have zero intention of becoming the next notch on his apparently extensive bedpost, but I can look and not touch. I'll simply need to keep a tight rein on these ridiculously unruly hormones, which seem to excrete directly to my deprived lady parts, any time his eyes bear heavily into mine.

CHAPTER EIGHT

CALLUM

'The champagne seems to be going down a treat,' Marcus says. 'You better hope she drinks the entire bottle herself before she gets a proper look at you with those fucking cauliflower ears.'

As if his ears are any better. Occupational hazard, unfortunately.

Marcus should've left hours ago, yet he loiters like a bad smell, desperate to witness my certain failure. I push a medium-rare sirloin around my plate across the table from him.

'Everything ok with your food, sir?' a young brunette waitress asks politely.

'Yes. It's perfect. Thank you,' I reply.

'I wouldn't have pegged you for an Ask Abby fan.' She clears the empty glasses from our table.

'What's an "Ask Abby"?' I don't even attempt to mask my confusion.

'You know that radio show on Ireland Today called Ask Abby?' She nods at the four girls across the room. Abby.

So she's some sort of celebrity. Typical. 'Did you know this?' I demand.

'Did we fuck, but she's perfect,' Marcus bellows clutching his stomach with pent-up laughter. 'My Mrs. listens to that show at lunchtime, reckons she's absolutely brilliant. You want to know the best bit?' He sits back from the table and smacks his thigh with utter childlike glee.

I don't really, but he's going to tell us anyway.

'She's one of those women's rights proactivist or something. One of those burn-your-bra type of gals. Women from all round the country phone in with their woes, usually about men. If I recall it rightly, now I could be wrong, but Shelly told me Fabby Abby doesn't date. Ha!' He rubs his hands together in sheer, unconcealed delight.

This complicates things, but at least she wasn't lying earlier when she said she doesn't date.

'I couldn't have actually picked anyone better for you. Two peas in a singleton pod. I can safely say, the heated leather interior of my beautiful Audi, has never been more secure underneath my pert little backside.'

'Well played, man.' Ollie is impressed. 'She looks like a ballbreaker alright.'

'But the bet still stands?' Eddie checks.

'Hell yeah!'

'And if I lose?' I ask.

'You'll be lonely forever, man. We're doing this for your benefit, really,' James says with a wry smile.

For a split second, I wonder if he's telling the truth. Is this how men instigate an interfriendshen? Jesus, I must be in a worse state than I originally thought.

'At the very least, I'll enjoy watching you squirm.' Marcus strokes his stubble arrogantly with his knuckle.

'At the very best, you might find that dating the same girl turns out to be better than you think.' James assumes the voice of reason, his impending vows have gone straight to his head. Where's my mate that used to brag about his aching balls after nailing not one, but two girls in the same night?

Did they hatch this plan because they secretly think I'm a disgusting desperate old man, approaching his peak, on and off the pitch, and the only way now is down?

No, they're not that thoughtful. My eternal singledom's simply a source of entertainment to them. Suddenly, I feel old.

'You know what, guys, I'm going to stay here for another night.' My luggage's been in and out of the boot of my car more times today than a toddler doing the hokey fucking pokey. I can't face another night out on the pull now. Odd, when it's all I'd been looking forward to all week. I've got work to do. If I hang around here, I might just be able to Ask Abby...

The fact that she doesn't date intrigues me. She must have at some point; she's too good looking not to have. Not to mention worldly, if she has enough experience to be dishing out advice to the women of the country on national radio. What happened to her? She's different to any other woman I've encountered, demonstrating more spirit than most of the guys I've met on the field.

For a split second, I consider negotiating a deal with her to get her to come to James's wedding with me to get my nutjob teammates off my back for a couple of months. I can't pursue her under a pretence. God forbid, she broke her rules for me, I'd only break her heart. Ha. Talk about getting ahead of myself. She shot me down loud and clear. Twice. Not that I'd disclose that to the lads, though it offered a head start in some respects. I'm not stupid enough to plough on over like an oncoming freight train, to be knocked back magnificently, as I undoubtedly would be.

No, this needs careful consideration if I'm to wipe that smug smile from Marcus's face once and for all. I'm determined to have the last laugh here. Maybe Fabby Abby could be just the woman to help me.

'You're a man on a mission,' Marcus says with a smirk.

'You have no idea.' Abby might need a hand unzipping that dress after all.

CHAPTER NINE

ABBY

Emma's assertiveness snags us the last free space at the bar. Low lighting and soft jazz are the only distraction from the girls discussing the merits of honeymooning immediately after a wedding or chancing a mini-moon first. I'm bored senseless.

Karen looks bewildered, reality striking with the constant wedding talk. She chews her nails subconsciously, overwhelmed with it all.

There's been no sign of Callum Connolly since dinner. Perhaps he took the hint when I didn't immediately flock to him. An unwarranted surge of disappointment whips through me. It's probably for the best. I'll never give him what he really wants. Although it still leaves my radio show dilemma.

'Are you okay, Abs?' Karen asks, stirring ice around a rapidly decreasing G&T.

'Tired after dinner and the massage.'

'I can't believe the boys didn't hang around,' Emma says.

If there was ever a woman that was made to be a WAG, it

was Emma. Her hair's always immaculate, as are her nails, and I've never once seen her without a full face of make-up, even in the spa earlier. She'd look the business, cheering Callum on from a private sporting box. I should encourage her, but I loathe the thought of it. What is wrong with me?

'Weird how he sent the bottle and didn't even come over,' Kerry adds. 'Maybe he actually is a fan of the show.'

The alcohol's gone to my head. It's bursting out of me, I'm dying to tell someone, anyone about what happened earlier. 'I wasn't going to mention it, girls... but it wasn't the first glass of champagne he bought me today.' I flash a sly smile and smooth my dress down.

'You dark horse, Queenan!' Karen's eyebrows disappear beneath her fringe.

It's too tempting not to continue, to relive the moment out loud, even if it did amount to nothing in the end.

'He arrived at my bedroom door about five hours ago.' I deliberately leave the details abstract.

'It's always the quiet ones.' Karen is practically jumping up and down. Only she knows the significance of me overcoming my own self-imposed boundaries.

'Well, don't stop now, Abby. You're on a revolutionary roll,' Kerry says.

'So, did you?' Emma licks her lips, desperate for details.

'Of course, I didn't. Do I look like the kind of woman that would happily be another notch on that man-whore's bedpost? Good looking though he is, it'd take more than that.' I enjoy the way Kara's term rolls off my tongue.

The rapid widening of Karen's pupils alerts me that something's off-kilter. Emma stands to attention, fluffing her hair at the roots.

I feel Callum's presence before I see him. Heat spreads betrayingly up my neck, rapidly progressing towards my cheeks. Not because of what I called him. I practically said that to his face already. I might have held back on the exact term 'man-whore', but he got the gist.

It's the agonising physical effect he commands that embarrasses me. The way my heart rattles in my ribs. The way that my pulse deafens me.

'Thanks again for the champagne.' I attempt to recover the situation quickly, as though I intended him to hear my harsh words.

'It's a pleasure, Abby, as always.' He doesn't miss a beat.

The simple blue lining of his white shirt emphasises his oceanic eyes. Eyes a woman could drown in. The sheer size of him makes me want to fall into the security of his arms and wrap them around me. The alcohol hasn't helped my mouth or my resolve.

'So, you think I'm good looking?' Callum murmurs, lips brushing against my ear. His masculine scent sends my hormones into overdrive again.

Note to self, order a rampant rabbit before I meet him again, especially if I plan on consuming alcohol. If the chemistry escalates much further, I can't trust myself.

'There's many a good-looking bastard out there.' I quote one of Mammy's wise words of warning to my sister and I before we left for college, smiling again to soften the insult.

'Where are your buddies?' Emma happily accepts Callum's interests are well and truly focused elsewhere.

'Two went home to their wives and the other two went to a club in the city.' He doesn't take his eyes from me for a second. He possesses a dangerous ability to make a girl feel like she's the only woman in the world. Thankfully, pictures in *The Irish Sun* remind us of a different story; one in which others felt that they were the only woman in the world. Obviously, they weren't. And I'm not stupid enough to think I am either. Not least because I refuse to surrender to his advances. If I do, he'd disappear the second he reached his flesh induced peak.

But I do need him for another purpose. He's undoubtedly perfect for my show. How to get him to agree to my proposition's another matter entirely. I decide to grab the bull by the horns, or the hand, at the very least.

'I have a proposition for you.' I hold my body flirtatiously close to his.

Surprise etches the lines of his devilishly handsome face.

'I think I like the sound of that.' No, he likes the sniff of an opportunity.

'Let's go somewhere we can talk, privately.'

Karen's white with shock, having never witnessed this side to me before.

'See you at breakfast.' Emma wiggles her eyebrows suggestively at Callum's perfectly rounded backside.

His hand sears the small of my back as he guides me out of the busy bar. My heart hammers erratically under the heat of his touch, invisible flames lick parts of my body that I've neglected for years. Every single sleepy cell within me jolts vividly back to life at his touch, as he leads me to the elevator.

CHAPTER TEN

CALLUM

It couldn't be this easy. No way. I've no idea where she's going with this proposition of hers, but I'm not stupid enough to believe for a single second that she's going to fall into my arms, or my bed for that matter. She's apparently famous for being strong-minded. I'm missing something here.

'My place or yours?' I allow the charade to play out while I gather my thoughts.

'Yours.' Swirling chocolate eyes stare hotly into mine.

If the boys hadn't given me the lowdown already, I could have been persuaded that Abby genuinely experienced a change of heart. The intensity of her gaze hints that she's at least contemplating losing that little red number for me. My body aches with over-sensitised longing at the prospect.

I remove the keycard from my trouser pocket and insert it into the slot. Abby would only have to glance down to witness my growing excitement.

I hold the door open for her.

'Wow. So this is what being an Irish rugby star gets you.'

Abby heads straight for the sliding doors, which open onto a large patio overlooking the golf course.

If I admit it's a downgrade from my own place overlooking the Liffey, she'll assume I'm a materialistic dick.

I throw my phone onto the table while she scrutinises the accommodations. There's a super king-sized bed and a spacious living area, containing a large charcoal coloured couch and a long oak stained coffee table. Slipping her heels off, she relaxes into the cushions of the sofa, elevating her long supple legs. In a deliberately seductive fashion, she positions her red varnished toes onto the coffee table. If she hasn't come here with the intention of having sex with me, why is it oozing from every part of her? It's the worst type of torture. Yet I don't want it to stop.

'Can I get you a drink?' I assess the selection in the minibar.

I can phone room service if there's nothing here she wants.

What does she want? That's the million-dollar question. I'd love to think it's me, but I'm not that vain – contrary to popular belief. Match tickets maybe? Not likely. Her little brother to be a mascot at one of the Ireland games. More plausible, but I doubt it.

'I've probably had enough for one night...but why stop when I'm on a roll?'

'Good girl.' I nod my approval before remembering she's supposed to be a bra-burning feminist who could well mistake the term girl as patronising.

Abby's face doesn't flicker. Maybe this won't be as difficult as the lads led me to believe.

'I'll have whatever you're having.' She offers a seductive smile across the room, which illuminates her entire face and imprints boldly into the most private part of my brain.

'Are you sure?'

'Give it to me.' She means the drink, but her innuendo is deliberate.

Oh, how I would love to, Abby. You have no idea.

I pour two Jameson on the rocks and hand her the whiskey. She arches an eyebrow. I want to lower her inhibitions, and I'm prepared to play dirty.

She pats the couch next to her, offering me encouragement that I don't need. I sink down and place my feet companionably on the table next to hers.

'What are you doing to me, Fabby Abby?' I groan in frustration.

'Ah, I wondered if you knew about that.' She takes a sip from the crystal tumbler thoughtfully.

'I didn't. Until the waitress enlightened me. Funnily enough, I don't usually need advice when it comes to the opposite sex. Now, if I'd known the host was so fucking sexy, I might have tuned in.'

A coy grin spreads from her mouth to her ears. She flashes perfectly straightened, neat white teeth. 'Funny you should mention that. I was thinking something along those very lines earlier.'

'That if I knew you that you were so sexy, I'd listen to your show? You can't be that desperate for listeners.' Perhaps she thinks dating me will raise her profile.

No, I've got a feeling she's already more high profile than I know.

'Something along those lines, yes.' She glances at the open top button of my shirt, licking her lips. Her mixed messages are sending me dangerously close to the edge. It's all I can do not to kiss her.

'Well, by all means, I'll tune in if it means that much to you.' I take a mouthful of golden liquor and try not to stare at her luminous skin, inches from mine.

I imagine her legs wrapped around each side of my waist

as I lift her up against the shower wall and kiss her full, promising lips. It's the exact image that sent me begging Hannah to find out which room she'd be in.

'So you'll do it?' She lunges forward, excitement pinched over her delicate features.

Distracted by images of her entwined in explicit positions, I have no idea what she'd asked of me. I could be persuaded to agree, when it makes her face light up like that.

'Sorry, Abby, do what?' I take another sip of the whiskey and will myself to concentrate on what she's saying.

'Feature on my radio show?' she repeats casually, as though it's already been decided.

'What? You've got to be kidding.' Yet it explains the reason that a woman who had literally thrown me out of her bedroom only a few short hours ago is here in my bedroom, flashing her brightest smile and a little too much flesh.

'I need a man.' She assumes the persona of a damsel in distress. Oh, she is good.

'I'm right here, honey...' I wink suggestively at her and glance down at my groin.

My last comment earns my third light slap on the arm of the day.

'Oh, sorry I thought you meant...' I know well she didn't, but nothing in this world will stop me trying. The more she shoots me down, the more I want her. I haven't been turned down in years. This is alarming unfamiliar territory and fifty shades of fucked up, even for me.

'Will you help me, please?' She adopts an altogether different tack again.

What man can resist a woman in need of rescuing?

'What would I have to do? Theoretically speaking, of course. I'm not agreeing to anything yet.' Listening to her proposal will buy me time with her at least.

'I need a man, someone that oozes sex and success,

someone who will send the ladies looney, to answer a few callers' questions about love, from a man's perspective.' It rolls off her tongue, as though it were the simplest request in the world.

Her words might have stroked the largest of egos; hot, sexy, successful. Not mine. Alarm rips through me. I'm the one person that can't talk about love. I've never had any real experience of it. If she wants me to talk about one-night stands on the other hand, I could talk for days. But love? No way.

'Abby.' I resign myself to the fact that once she accepts my refusal, she'll bolt out of the door, at lightning speed. 'I honestly don't think I'm the right man for the job.' It's the truth.

'You see, Callum Connolly, that's exactly where you're wrong.' She jabs my torso, wincing as her finger bends backwards in the process. It doesn't deter her from stating her case.

'You're sexy, young enough to draw interest, old enough to have a bit of life experience, successful, yet approachable.' Her flattery knows no bounds when she wants something.

'You think I'm sexy and approachable?' I momentarily bask in her compliments. I've been called a lot of names over the years, but none of them included approachable. Arsehole maybe, arrogant definitely. I sigh deeply and attempt to summon the right words. 'The thing is, Abby, I might have a reputation with the ladies, but I'm definitely no expert on *love*.' I downplay the worst of my front page antics.

'What and you think I am?' She laughs. 'Biggest fuck-up ever, yet because I have two degrees and a bit of compassion, I'm deemed as some sort of guru. Ha. If only you knew...' She knocks back the rest of her drink and holds the glass out for a refill.

I stand but hover nearby hoping that she'll expand on

what she started, but she opts for a different approach once again. She should have considered a career in politics.

'The thing is, Callum, you clearly don't struggle with women. They seem to like you. You represent the kind of man that a lot of women think they want. Your opinion would mean everything to them. You don't have to talk about your own experiences in love, you only have to advise them on their own situations.' She crosses then uncrosses her legs as she talks.

Does she know what she's doing to me? Of course she does.

A lightbulb moment overcomes me. I've been thinking with my dick and completely forgotten that I need her, too. The bet had gone right out of my head.

She notices the change in my stance immediately. I'll have to add 'astute' to her ever-growing list of unexpected traits.

'What?'

She probably expects me to announce that I'll do it, if she has sex with me right now. Tempting though it is, I need her for something way bigger, a matter of my reputation amongst my teammates, my integrity, a question of my masculinity.

'I actually need a woman, too,' I confess.

'I knew you'd put me in this position, Callum Connolly. I won't sleep with you to get you on my show! It goes against everything that I preach every day on air.' She plays with the charm bracelet on her wrist instead of meeting my eye.

At least she didn't say she won't sleep with me because she finds me repulsive.

'I'll make you a deal.' I return to the couch with our refills.

'What kind of a deal?' Confusion clouds her earnest eyes.

'I'm going to lay it out straight. Do not slap me. Bear in mind that I came to your room long before you were picked.' I raise my hands in surrender. Her blackening eyes narrow with each word that leaves my lips. I never was very good at keeping secrets, except my own of course.

'Go on...' Her voice is thick with distrust.

'Marcus Williams bet me that I can't keep a woman long enough to bring her to James's wedding.' It's like telling tales at school again.

'Who is James?' At least she doesn't thump me.

'James O'Malley. My best friend, teammate, fellow prop. Seriously, girl, have you never watched Ireland play rugby?' I'm part curious, part horrified.

'I don't do team sports.' It doesn't surprise me now I'm getting the measure of her.

'They're adamant I can't keep a woman. They bet that the next girl I date, I can't keep interested long enough to actually bring her to James's wedding.' Wincing, I feebly attempt to word it in a way that doesn't make us sound like a bunch of sexist masochistic arseholes, yet that's exactly what it sounds like.

'I see.' Abby blows a stray strand of hair up in the air thoughtfully. 'So, if I agree to come to this wedding with you, you will agree to feature on my show?' Her show's clearly more important than our lowly behaviour. That's something, at least.

'Yes.' I nod. The boys will destroy me for talking about love and that sort of shite on national radio. Coach might even kick me off the team. No, on second thought, he'd think it was great advertising for our sponsors.

She sticks a dainty hand out quickly to shake on it before I can change my mind.

'Deal,' we say in unison.

As my hand envelops hers, a powerful stream of chemistry surges between us. She flinches, physically affected by my touch, and tries to pull her hand back. Sensing her discomfort at being exposed, I deliberately hang on for a few seconds longer than necessary, enjoying the glaringly obvious attraction between us.

'One more thing, Fabby Abby,' I remind her. 'I'm supposed to be dating this girl until the wedding.'

'And when is exactly is that?'

'Three months away. Fifteenth of August, to be precise.' I fight to restrain the upward curl of my smirking lips, I have her over a barrel.

If I can't get her into bed with me in the next three months, then I might as well hang up my boots. Excuse the pun.

'You've got to be joking.' Mixed expressions flit over her face. I can read almost all of them; fear, excitement, and finally – reluctant acceptance.

'What do you want me to do?' The resignation in her voice would be humorous if it wasn't so damning. Am I that bad? 'I'll rephrase that. Here's what I'm willing to do...' She considers it for a few seconds. 'I'll show up at a game or two? We could go out for dinner once?' She sets the bar deliberately low. Scrap the politics, her negotiation skills could secure her a job at MI5.

'One dinner? You'll have to do better than that.'

'We can cement the terms over the weekend. You do realise I wasn't joking when I said I don't date. Prepare for a thousand questions from anyone that knows me.' She glances at the floor hesitantly.

'Neither do I. Hence the bet,' I remind her.

'Just out of interest...what's the prize for this interesting bet? What do you win?' She's curious, yet borderline reluctant to hear the answer.

'Marcus's Audi.' She should hear the full truth from me, rather than anyone else down the line.

'Why me?' Another woman might have been fishing for compliments, but Abby seems genuinely puzzled.

'Because you were the best looking woman in the room. And he said if I could pull you, there was no way I could keep you.'

Surprisingly, she laughs out loud. 'I'm flattered that someone thought so, although this bet goes against everything I normally preach.'

She's nothing like the bra-burning feminist I feared.

Without warning, she stands to leave, handing me her empty glass.

'I'll see you for breakfast.' She pulls a business card from her tiny gold bag, her name and number emblazoned in bold italic.

I'm compelled to try once more. Just because we have a business agreement, it doesn't exclude the possibility of a little pleasure along the way. 'You could stay here for breakfast.'

'I don't think so, Callum.' She places a warm hand on my chest and pushes past me toward the door.

I groan internally as she sways out of the room, leaving a delicate trail of perfume in her wake. She is my new favourite smell.

The knockbacks are torture, but it will all be worth it when I wipe the smug smirk from Marcus William's face once and for all.

CHAPTER ELEVEN

ABBY

Callum caught me by surprise in more than the obvious way. I didn't anticipate his honesty, and begrudgingly, I have to respect him for it. How many men make a bet about a woman and then go and tell her? Even if it is hopefully going to benefit both of us.

Pretend dating has got to be easier than the real thing; no feelings, no expectation and no disappointments. Because it is, after all, only pretend. Thank God his name's Callum and not Patrick. God forbid I'd be daft enough to develop a stupid notion that we're meant to be together. Esmerelda was right about the opportunity, though. I'm approaching the biggest one of my career.

I roll out of the hotel bed and pick up my phone. Startlingly, it rings as I reach for it. A number I don't recognise. It can only be Callum.

'Hello?'

'Good morning, gorgeous.' His smooth voice echoes down the line.

'Cut the crap, Callum. We're only pretending.'

'I'm just practising, you know, roleplay...I suppose you could call it. Do you like roleplay, Abby?'

Why does he have to be so infuriatingly hot? I suppose if he wasn't, it would do nothing for my ratings. I'll have to take this one for the team – or not.

'There's really no need when it's just the two of us,' I insist.

'So how are we going to play this?' He cuts to the chase.

'I was wondering the same thing in bed this morning.' Did I deliberately refer to my bed to tease him?

'Abby Queenan, were you lying in bed thinking about me?' He latches on immediately. 'Did I have any clothes on? More to the point, did you?' His arrogance knows no bounds.

At least he isn't present to witness my flaming face. In truth, he hadn't been wearing a single stitch. Unless I count myself as clothing? Maybe I'd be described as more of an accessory, if anything. I'm sure that's what most women amounted to, with a man of his reputation. And we all know Callum Connolly has never been spotted with the same accessory twice.

I forgot what it was like to want somebody, physically. Of all the men in the world to remind me, it has to be the man-whore. I'm in worse shape than anyone that has ever phoned into my show, because I, Ask Abby, should know better. I'm a challenge, and he's only after one thing. I'd be a fool to think otherwise. I'm doing this for my career.

'Don't flatter yourself, big guy. I'm in it for the prize.' It's not a complete lie. The fact that he's offensively appealing is a plus. Or negative, depending on how you perceive it.

'You want Marcus's Audi?' Bellowing laughter erupts down the phone. 'It's yours, I don't actually care for it, I'm just desperate to see Marcus part with the one thing that he loves as much as himself.'

'Not the Audi. There's a prize for the radio presenter with the highest show ratings. That's why I need you.' I tell him about the trip to New York.

'That blows the Audi out of the window. When are we going?'

'I'll be bringing my assistant, Aoife. It's only fair.' Thank God, because I couldn't handle four solid days in his proximity. He'd get the next notch on the bedpost, and it would be all over the front page of the tabloids when he discards me like yesterday's trash.

'I hope you're decent.' His goading tone indicates that he hopes for the exact opposite.

'Why?' I've got a feeling I know the answer already.

'I'm outside your door.' I swear, I hear him smirking through the phone. For someone I met less than twenty-four hours earlier, I already have a fair understanding of his personality.

'Well, you'll have to stay there. I wasn't expecting company.' I scramble around the room, looking unsuccessfully for something to throw on for now.

'Come on, Abby. It's not like I haven't seen it already.'

'I had a bikini on, that doesn't count.' His remark reminds me of the dressing gown on the back of the bathroom door. I hastily sling it around me and sweep up last night's clothes from the floor. Callum doesn't require an eyeful of my black lace thong.

I run a brush hastily through my hair and rinse my mouth with Listerine before opening the door. He looks effortlessly edible; a green Ireland rugby jersey clings tightly to his broad chest and a low riding pair of jeans hangs from his narrow waist.

'Nothing like a bit of notice,' I grumble.

'You look just as sexy without the dress, in fact...' He

attempts to place a hand on my robe. 'You'd look even better without this too.'

'Quit it, Callum! Or the deal is off.'

'Who are you kidding, honey? You wouldn't dream of missing out on that trip to New York, and we both know it.' His eyes deliberately linger over my chest. He has absolutely no shame.

'I shouldn't have mentioned it. I'm still drunk.' As if the dry mouth and headache weren't enough of an indication. And my head isn't the only thing that's pounding this morning.

Callum makes himself comfortable, sprawling out on my unmade bed, continuing to taunt me.

'Bet you didn't think you'd have an Irish rugby player in your bed this time yesterday.' He enjoys my obvious discomfort.

'I'm warning you for the last time.' I battle to keep a straight face, he is pretty funny.

'Oh, Abby, please. Put me out of my misery.' He pats the bed right next to him.

A weaker woman might cave. Not me.

'I'm going for a shower. I'll be out in five minutes. Do not touch a thing.' I eye my weekend bag deliberately.

'Don't you touch anything either!' he yells cheekily after me.

I stifle a laugh and shake my head in despair.

Returning from the en suite ten minutes later, my hair's dripping wet, but at least I'm clean. Callum's unusually quiet. In the time I've known him, he's never once been stuck for a one-liner. I creep over to where he lies silently on his back, hands cradling his head. His eyes are tightly shut, the slow rhythmic inhalation of his chest suggests he's asleep. I can't help but stare. Even features and full lips gave him a boyish appearance, but the lines on his face reveal a rich history, all man. None of us get this far in life without accumulating a scar or two.

I sigh, unsure if I should wake him. After deliberating for a few seconds, I crawl under the covers next to him, exhausted from spending the night imagining this man in my bed. Now he's here, all I'm fit for is sleep. It's not exactly how my dream had played out. But it could only ever be a dream. I must add a clause into this deal of ours that when the fake dating is done, I'm the one that ends it. I'm happy to go to the wedding with him. Who knows, it might even be fun. But when we've both got what need from this deal, I need to be able to come out of our arrangement with my reputation intact.

I place a pillow carefully between us, separating the two halves of the bed and roll over, pushing all thoughts of any deal away, and rest my heavy eyes.

Pounding fists on the door jolt me from a deep dreamless sleep. I bolt upright, momentarily unsure where I am. Callum lies next to me, beaming from ear to ear. The cat that got the cream.

'Well, at least I can officially tell the lads I slept with you.' He winks knowingly at me.

'You'll do no such thing. A gentleman never kisses and tells.'

'I never claimed to be a gentleman.' He nods in the direction of the door. 'Are you going to open that?'

'Well, you better at least pretend to be a gentleman where I'm concerned. If we're going to keep this charade up for the next three months, we're as well to face it head-on.' I pad towards the door, barely awake and more than a bit peeved at the interruption.

The girls bulldoze in, croissants and pastries under their arms, travel cases dragging behind.

'Tell us everything,' Karen begs in her usual high-pitched

shriek. She looks decidedly more fresh-faced than me with a cerise floral hairband securing her locks in place.

'Did you shag him? Was he any good?' Emma demands details.

The interrogation continues long enough to provoke a low rumble of laughter from further inside the room. The three of them freeze, their expressions priceless. What I wouldn't do for a photo.

'He's still here?' Karen whispers outrageously, hands vaguely attempt to cover her eyes.

'Good morning, ladies.' Callum swaggers over to where they huddle outside the en suite in shock.

Emma's the first to compose herself. 'Callum, how lovely to see you again.' Her voice drips like rich honey. I wish I had one tenth of her composure when it comes to men.

Callum kisses me on the head tenderly, barely acknowledging them. 'I'll call you later, sweetheart.' He lays it on thick for our audience before walking out the door, pausing only to blow me a kiss. He's exceptionally convincing. No wonder he's so popular with the ladies. For a spilt second, I wonder why he hasn't kept any of them? What is it that he's looking for? He clearly hasn't found it yet.

'Holy mother of sweet divine.' Karen clamps her hand tightly over her mouth, while every Catholic curse she knows dances from her tongue.

'O M fucking G.' Emma perches on the unmade bed. 'Well?'

'A lady never kisses and tells.' I silently congratulate myself on behaving in a very ladylike fashion, for now at least, and help myself to a pain au chocolate, before flicking on the tiny kettle.

CHAPTER TWELVE

CALLUM

I crawl out of the car park in the Land Rover, cruising at ten kilometres an hour along the manicured driveway, exit Carton House and dial Marcus on the hands-free system. It rings six times before he answers.

'Missing me already, sweetheart? I'll tell Shelly she has competition.' His deafening voice booms down the phone and I turn the volume down a notch before I continue.

'You wish.' I indicate left onto the main road.

'Don't tell me you surrender already. A bet's a bet dude, I'm sorry if Ask Abby gave you the knockback. Did she hurt your feelings?' He pronounces feeelings in the babyish tone he normally reserves for his daughters.

'Ha, I'm only getting warmed up,' I brag.

'Course you are, with your right hand, you bloody bollocks.' He snorts with deep resounding laughter at his own joke.

'Guess who I woke up next to not even fifteen minutes ago,' I gloat.

'Fuck off, man.' Disbelief echoes around the Jeep, sweeter than any music my sound system has ever played. I'm enjoying his reaction so much that I'm tempted to raise the volume again.

'I swear to God.' I revel in his surprise.

'You must have drugged her. Never had you down as one of those Rohypnol wankers, but you must have slipped something into that champagne. She wasn't exactly flocking towards you when I left.'

'When you have it, you have it, man.' I pull out my Ray-Bans from the glove compartment and push them on to the bridge of my nose. This bet is shaping up to be much more fun than I initially anticipated.

'Whatever, dickhead. James's wedding is three months away. There's absolutely no way in the world she'll put up with your sorry ass until then.' Marcus's tone lightens considerably as he contemplates the time span.

'We'll see. It feels different this time.' I wind the noose tighter, basking in his disconcert.

'Ok, Romeo, let's increase the stakes. I'm one hundred per cent convinced you will not be able to follow through. Unless you count in your underwear, of course. So much so, that if you, can actually get her to attend James's wedding, I'll give you my car and fifty grand,' Marcus says.

'You have yourself a deal, man.' As if I need any more incentive to pursue the elusive Miss Queenan.

I don't need his money. I don't need his car, only for the fact that it'll give me untold pleasure to drive off with my two fingers hanging out the window triumphantly. And Shelly would likely kill him if he has to actually hand over fifty big ones. That'd be worth a look too.

Truly, I haven't got anywhere near Abby. Not in the way that I usually do with women. Worryingly, it's only increasing the appeal.

Some women throw themselves at athletes, not because they particularly like us, but because they like the idea of the status that goes with it. Abby Queenan is definitely not out to impress me. She doesn't give a flying fuck what I think of her. It's unbelievably refreshing.

It's a good thing she's immune to my usual tactics. One shag might not be enough. And then we'd be into a whole different ball game.

'Enjoy it while it lasts, Casanova. I give it three days, never mind three months. You might have scored the try, but there's no way you'll nail the conversion.'

'Enjoy the weekend with the girls. I just wanted to share my good news with you.' I practically sing down the phone.

'Drive home safely, dickhead.' He hangs up.

CHAPTER THIRTEEN

ABBY

With the sight and scent of Callum evaporating further from my mind by the hour, I convince myself it was merely the alcohol that lowered my inhibitions. No man could possibly have that effect on me in the real world, no matter how pretty the package.

A cup of chai tea sits on the coffee table in front of me. I close the book I'm reading for the night, tired after a ten-kilometre run this evening. A new message pings on my phone, I squint to read it.

Callum: Hi sexy. I'm emailing you a copy of my schedule, practice and game dates and times. Let me know what suits you. Callum.

I begin typing a response before remembering one of the first rules of advice that I frequently preach to the women of the nation: Do not make yourself too available.

Then again, if we're only pretending, is that even necessary? Erring on the side of caution, I leave it half an hour. Can't have him thinking he has me at his beck and call.

Abby: Call me Abby. Thanks for the schedule. We need to pick a date for you to come live on the show so I can promote it.

Callum: Do I really have to do this?

Abby: Do you want the Audi? Not to mention Marcus's pride?

Callum: Monday week. But one good turn deserves another – You owe me a dinner date. Somewhere public, I'd like to be seen with you.

Abby: After the show. We've formalities to negotiate, anyway.

Callum: How do I know you won't just use me for the interview and ditch me before the wedding?

Abby: You don't. You'll have to trust me.

A ripple of raw excitement assaults my abdomen. And it's not because of the show. It's been a long time since I've had dinner with a man, like a date. The beauty of it is, I can enjoy it for what it is, with the knowledge that it isn't really a date. It will be good practice, because, after four years, something is awaking in me. I have no intention of being the next notch on Callum's bedpost, but maybe, just maybe...it's time to think about dating again. And fake dating Mr Physical Perfection Personified provides the perfect practice run. As long as I don't do something stupid, like sleep with him.

'What have you come up with?' Candice cut straight to the chase. Today's T-shirt is black and emblazoned with the statement, Fragile Like A Bomb in silver diamantés.

'You won't believe it. I have the whole thing sorted.' My words trip over each other in excitement. I take a breath and tame several escaping strands of hair back into my trademark work bun.

'Spill.' She cocks her head to one side intently.

'I've found a man. He's only bloody perfect.' It's all I can do not to shout it from the rooftops.

'I have to agree.' Aoife nods, I updated her with my progress on our morning walk and talk.

'Well, come on, girls, the suspense is killing me.' Candice's knee bounces impatiently in front of her.

'Callum Connolly.' His name rolls from my lips like a delicious dessert.

'You mean, Callum Connolly, the Irish rugby player, associated with a string of beautiful and successful women, yet never spotted with the same one twice?' Candice checks, covering her mouth in shock.

'The very same,' I confirm with a tight smile. Though her statement is true, it grates my nerves.

'Genius. I knew there was a reason I hired you.' Candice fist pumps the air, jumping up from her seat in delight. The three of us do a short victory dance around the studio for thirty seconds, before she pauses mid-hip drop.

'How on earth did you get him to agree? He's one of the hottest, most masculine guys in the country. He did agree to talk about sex and relationships?' She's in awe.

'Tell her,' Aoife insists.

'I bumped into him at Carton House at the weekend...' I eyeball Aoife, a silent warning but she ploughs on regardless.

'Tell her the rest.' Thankfully, I hadn't mentioned our mutually beneficial deal.

'He asked me out for a drink. I said no. Then when I thought about it, I agreed to go out with him if he'd come on the show. For some bizarre reason, he took a shine to me in the hotel spa.' I summarise it as quickly as possible, shrugging it off, though it's meaningless. They're going to find out, anyway. If we're doing the fake dating thing, it's bound to be in the paper at some point. I make a mental note to myself to keep a little distance from him in front of the press. It's one thing being romantically associated with him, and an entirely different thing to be slobbering over him like a rabid dog.

'Did you shag him? Because if you didn't, you definitely should. About time you got back on the horse.' Candice is one of the few people in this building who would dare to say that to my face.

'I did not. Why is everyone so obsessed with him?' I roll my eyes, hoping they'll buy my I Totally Don't Get His Appeal act.

'Have you seen him with his top off? Scrap that, have you seen him with his top on? In fact, did you even look at him properly at all?' Aoife's clearly another member of Callum's apparently extensive female fan club. I can't contain myself any longer under their scrutiny.

'Ok, ok, I'll admit it. He's ridiculously hot. But I'm not going there.' I raise my hands to my face, signalling the end of the conversation.

'Why the hell not? You're mad in the head. If I was straight, I'd ride him like a wild horse,' Candice announces. Thankfully, she's not straight, so I don't experience the same stabbing jealously that assaulted me on Friday night.

'You know what I really like about him?' Aoife pipes up wistfully, as though she's known Callum for her entire life. She scrolls through her phone, searching the internet for something. I tap my Converse impatiently.

She hands her mobile over. A picture of Callum posing at training, with his arm around the shoulders of a boy of about ten years old lights up the screen. The boy's overweight, shy looking and in obvious awe of his apparent idol. The caption of the photo reads 'Training with my mate Martin.' It has 300,000 comments, 800,000 likes, and 40,000 shares on Facebook. My icy heart thaws marginally. Callum probably saved this kid from a lifetime of school bullies.

'Huh. A PR stunt. The man's an animal. Trust me.' I huff.

Even the photo of Callum sets my blood pressure soaring.

'He doesn't need any PR stunts. He's already made Player of the Year and he's listed as one of Ireland's most eligible bachelors.'

For reasons that I don't dare to dwell on, thoughts of Callum Connolly's sexual conquests send my pulse racing. Probably because I can't stop wondering what he's like on the job. Would he be as good in the sack as he clearly thinks he is? All that practice might have paid off...

'Anyway, the women of Ireland are going to go absolutely batshit crazy for the chance to talk to Callum Connolly about love. Great job, Queenan. Keep him happy until he's done the show, for God's sake. If that means shagging him, by all means, shag him,' Candice says.

I ignore her last comment and concentrate on the task at hand.

'Let's get marketing. I need the whole country to be counting down the seconds, setting reminders in their calendars, desperate to tune in.'

'When are you thinking?' Candice taps her pencil lightly on the desk.

'Next Monday.' I want him on ASAP, before he changes his mind. There's a mountain of work to be done in preparation. I need to capture his advert on a dictaphone for the jingle.

'For the show or the date?' Candice winks at Aoife as she turns to go out the door.

'Both,' I admit, hiding my face behind my monitor to disguise my embarrassing excitement.

CHAPTER FOURTEEN

CALLUM

'How'd you do it, man?' Eddie poses next to me, his chest puffed like a pigeon for the benefit of the camera. We'd been summoned for an annual photoshoot for promotional purposes and next year's official merchandise.

'I just talked to her.' I play it down with a shrug. They're all keen to discuss Abby. Unsurprising, given the circumstances.

Standing around in front of the camera is so boring. No wonder most of the models I've slept with were too. It wasn't their fault they had nothing to talk about – literally nothing happened all day.

'Turn to the left, Callum. Cross your arms, Edward,' the photographer orders. His patience is wearing thin, probably accustomed to taking pictures of attractive, obliging women in various states of undress. The quicker we escape, the better, for all of our sakes.

'I googled her, she's eternally single, hasn't been seen with a man in years, not since her childhood sweetheart,' James adds from the row behind us.

The photographer positioned the biggest at the back, so James stands shoulder to shoulder with Marcus, Ollie, Nathan and John – our two locks, and Gareth our eighthman.

'Stop talking, keep your mouths still,' the photographer shouts in frustration. He's one of those artistic types, with ratty facial hair that begs to be shaved and the temper of a teething toddler.

It didn't occur to me to google her, though I'd been preoccupied with Dad's condition. As the only one of my brothers remaining in Dublin, it's down to me to sort out his care. His sister, Linda, does a lot for him, but she needs help. The consultant warned us he'd deteriorate. I just didn't anticipate it happening so rapidly.

I find it tough visiting the house where I grew up, that's probably why I don't do it nearly as much as I should. It's been soulless since Mam left. Though it's been over twenty years, I'm unable to escape her absence. Neither is Dad for that matter. There's an unspoken hollowness emanating from the walls that no amount of Colourtrend paint will mask. Each time I pass the stairs, the same appalling image haunts me.

'That's a wrap.' The photographer places his camera on the floor in relief. Sweat drips from his shiny balding head. He'd be no good to us on the pitch if that's the height of his stamina.

'Sneaky beer?' Eddie suggests as we head out into the twilight.

'Why not?' I've nothing to rush back to the apartment for.

As we bid the rest of the team goodbye, Marcus reminds me about Friday afternoon. As if I could forget. The whole team's involved in a fundraiser for Pieta House, a charity providing therapeutic help to those with mental health issues, a charity close to my heart.

'Ask Abby. Excuse the pun,' Marcus bellows, chuckling at his own wit. 'Shelly would love to meet her. So would I for that matter. I need to check she's recovered from the roofie you slipped into her drink the other night.'

'Bet that's not the only thing he slipped into the other night, hey?' James teases.

If only.

'Guys, guys, have a little respect for my girlfriend will you?' I emphasise the word slowly to make my point. 'This could be the future Mrs Connolly your talking about.'

Even I have to laugh at that remark.

'Girlfriend – fuck off, you've only met her once.' Marcus says.

'How do you know?' I lie through my teeth.

'Ring her now and put her on speakerphone,' Marcus insists, towering over me.

'He probably doesn't even have her number,' James says with a snigger. The remaining members of the team laugh with him, reminding me precisely how I got dragged into this situation in the first place. Who needs enemies when you're stuck with these fuckers for the best part of each year?

Hesitantly, I pull the phone out of my pocket in the car park outside the studio on the outskirts of Ballsbridge, scroll through my contacts and send up a silent prayer that Abby's phone will either ring out or go straight to voicemail, preferably a voicemail that says 'This is Abby, leave a message.' That should be enough to get them off my back, for now at least.

The shrill dial tone pierces the otherwise silent car park. The boys circle like starving birds of prey. Things are bad when my love life's the height of their interest. Just as I'm about to hang up, the call connects.

'Callum?'

'Swit swooo,' Marcus catcalls. 'So she is real.'

'High five man.' Eddie, at least, is impressed.

Ollie claps me on the back and gives a silent thumbs-up before getting into his car to go home. I only wish the others would take the hint.

'Abby, hi. Excuse my teammates in the background, most of them were dragged up. The lot of them would benefit from a year in a Swiss finishing school.' I shoo them away with my middle finger, but they loiter, refusing to just get in their cars and fuck off home.

'How are things?' Her voice is filled with amusement.

'Grand. Apart from I've just spent the last three hours standing under a ridiculous amount of lighting wearing a stupid amount of concealer for our annual calendar. I don't know how those models do it.'

'You didn't ask any of the ones you encountered along the way?' There's a hint of knowing in her tone.

I groan. 'Please don't you start on me as well,' I beg. The guys overhear.

'Lover's tiff already?' Marcus says gleefully. 'Is it any wonder he can't keep a woman?'

Abby hears it all. Thank God I've been honest with her. However difficult the task they set me, it'd be ten times worse, had I not been truthful.

'Put Marcus on the phone,' Abby says to my amazement.

I hand it over to him and watch the smile fall from his face. He tries to push it back to me, but I walk away. Reluctantly, he holds it to his ear.

'Marcus? Give my fella a break, will you? I need him in tip-top condition for tonight. If he's wound up, he'll blow all over my bedsheets before I get near him.' Abby's confident authority resonates throughout the car park, a dirty laugh emphasises her point.

'Holy fuck, I'd recognise your voice from the radio

anywhere.' Marcus is momentarily starstruck, apparently forgetting he's equally famous in his own right.

'Lucky fucker,' Eddie mutters.

Abby's acting skills prevail once again.

'We're ringing to invite you to the Pieta House fundraiser Friday afternoon. Some of the wives are coming. It'd be great if you could make it.' Marcus adopts an eloquent telephone voice, unrecognisable as the balding baboon that instigated this entire farce.

'I wouldn't miss it,' Abby coos down the phone.

She's putting on one hell of a performance. I owe her big time.

'Now, put Callum back on. I'm wet and I need him.' She dissolves into pealing girlish laughter. Marcus hands back the phone in stunned silence.

'Abs,' I repeat the nickname her friends use on Saturday morning.

'Come to mine. I'll text you the coordinates. Come hungry,' she says before hanging up.

Is she for real, or is it me that's been slipped the roofie?

'I'll have to take a raincheck on that drink, bro.' I can't even pretend to be sorry.

'No wonder. Can I come with you? Abby might want the job done properly.' He winks at me saucily. I imagine physically removing the smirk from his pretty-boy face.

A text pings through with the Eircode. I set the sat nav in the Jeep and wave smugly at the boys as they lurk, stunned in the car park. Their shock is nothing in comparison to mine. I merely mask it better.

Twenty minutes later, I'm outside a detached house in a secluded, well-manicured estate in Tallaght. She opens the front door before I can knock. A sopping wet running top clings to her cleavage, damp wavy hair surrounds her glistening face and fresh droplets fall from her fingers.

Not exactly the scene I'd been hoping for.

'Know anything about plumbing?' She shrugs, completely unfazed. Another woman might have applied make-up at the expected arrival of one of Ireland's 'supposedly' most eligible bachelors. Not that I buy into that bullshit – those idiots know nothing about me. Abby hasn't even changed out of her running gear.

'Are we starring in some weird porno that I don't know about? Damsel in distress needs sex-starved man to examine her plumbing? Are you filming this?' I'm rewarded with uncontrollable hooting laughter.

'You're hilarious in addition to infuriatingly arrogant, I see. Should make the next couple of months a little more bearable.' She possesses an uncanny ability to inflate my ego, before instantaneously bursting it in the same sentence.

I roll up my shirt sleeves and follow her through to a traditional country style kitchen with cream woodwork and a huge Aga. I spot the problem immediately. It's hard to miss with the contents of the cupboard beneath the sink strewn across the cream tiled floor. I fight the urge to laugh and look pointedly at her as I turn off the tap. For a woman with two degrees, you'd assume it would have been the first port of call.

'I wanted to see where it was leaking from. I couldn't do that if it stopped,' she justifies.

'You know, if you'd mentioned this on the phone, I could have stopped at a hardware shop and picked up some tools.' I crouch closer to the source of the flooding.

'True, but where would the fun be in that?' Her cherry lips curl into a smile that extends all the way to expectant twinkling eyes. 'So, can you fix it?'

A crack in the U-bend jumps out at me. An easy opportunity to secure a few brownie points.

'Got any masking tape?' I'm drenched already, my nipples

poke through my Ralph Lauren polo. Life really isn't fair, why aren't hers?

'You're not going all Christian Grey on me? I'm not really into that kinky stuff.' She sniggers but searches the drawers and locates a roll.

'So what exactly are you into? I'd love to know.' I wrap the tape repeatedly around the crack. It's not meant to fix the problem, just control it until I get a replacement.

'You'll never find out,' she assures me.

The tape does the job for the short term at least. 'I'll fix it properly for you at the weekend.' Noting the make and size, I extract myself from the small space below the sink and glance down at my soaked shirt.

'I can put it in the tumble drier for you?' Abby offers, suddenly unable to meet my eye. The idea of me shirtless in her kitchen for half an hour is an interesting one, which I contemplate for a few seconds.

'It's ok. I've got a spare jersey in the car.' I jog out and fetch it from the boot, returning to her kitchen to change. I catch her eyes lingering on my torso. Busted. She turns her back to stir a pan of simmering gravy on the stove.

'I promise I can contain myself on your bedsheets, if you need me to scratch an itch for you or something...' I stare at her perfectly rounded bum secured with indecently tight black Lycra.

'Oh no.' She shakes her head with a little laugh. 'That was for Marcus's benefit. But if you really want to please me...' She produces a tiny recording device and realisation dawns on me.

'The advertising jingle?' I groan.

'You're not just a pretty face.' She beams at me, inserting her index finger into the pan and tasting her creation in an outrageously seductive fashion. She certainly knows how to turn it on when she wants something. It's killing me. If she'd only have sex with me, I'm almost certain I'd get over this inconvenient attraction.

A few minutes later she carries two plates of roast chicken, stuffing and sweet potato mash over to the kitchen table. Call it sexist, but there's something unicorn-like about a gorgeous woman, who's also a talented chef. The female form of the four-leaf clover. No woman has ever cooked for me, bar my mother or my aunt. Surprisingly, I like it.

'So what do I have to do to play the convincing WAG on Friday?'

'Judging by your performance earlier, you have nothing to learn. The boys were very impressed. Some more than others.' I grimace, remembering Eddie's offer to help me with Abby.

'Years of stage school as a child. Mammy had notions of me becoming an actress.'

'It'll be good to have you there.' I mean it. Not because of Marcus's stupid bet, but because the more time we spend together, the more I enjoy her company. This could be more dangerous than it's worth, but I'm weirdly compelled to find out.

'What do I have to do?' She swirls wine thoughtfully around her glass.

'It's a sports day in Phoenix Park for Pieta House Charity, an opportunity to give something back to the community.' I swallow hard, thinking of my own family.

Abby looks at me as though I have two heads.

'Callum Connolly, I don't believe it. Maybe there is a heart in that enormous chest of yours after all.' A tinkling laugh escapes her perfect mouth.

'You'd be surprised.'

It's there alright. But there's a reason no one's ever got near it.

As I tuck in, she pushes her food around her plate,

subdued all of a sudden; a fragile bird that could take flight at any second if I push too hard. Was it something I said?

The atmosphere's changed. It's charged, as though she's on the verge of saying something important. I refrain from breaking the weird silence with a one-liner. Something's bothering her. I surprise myself with the realisation that I care. A caveman urge awakens within – the urge to take care of her. I hope she's not changing her mind about the bet. Not because of any stupid Audi, but because things are just beginning to get interesting between us.

CHAPTER FIFTEEN

ABBY

I asked Callum here to record his advertisement, but also to lay some ground rules surrounding our agreement. I'm not sure how to word it without revealing too much about my past or without sounding like a controlling stalker. My flirtatious bravado's evaporated. I decide to simply cut to the chase. 'You know, I wasn't lying when I said I don't date.' I glance across at him almost awkwardly. I hate bringing up this shit, reminding myself of my previous failures.

'I heard.' He sits straighter in the chair, profoundly interested all of a sudden.

'I need to ask you to do one thing for me.' I cringe as the words leave my lips, I detest asking anything of anyone. Especially this. It sounds so desperate.

'Of course. What is it?' He leans forward, resting his elbows on the table.

The words tumble out bluntly and I can barely meet his eye. 'While we're doing this pretend dating thing, don't mess me around. I know we're only pretending, but please, don't get caught shagging another woman until this is over. It would be plastered all over the papers, and I can't be made a fool of. Not again.'

'Of course. It's only common courtesy. I don't need reminding. We made an agreement, one that will mutually benefit us. I'm not planning on messing it up. Player, though I might be, I've never deliberately hurt a woman in my life. I've been crystal-clear with every woman I've encountered.' His tone is almost wounded.

'When this is over, it needs to leave my reputation intact. My job is based on dishing out advice to women. I have to be seen to be practising what I preach. If you make a fool out of me, it'll jeopardise my career.' I pray I don't look as vulnerable as I suddenly feel.

'Abby, I won't let you down.' Sincerity rings through his words. He holds my gaze until I look away and pick up my fork again, relieved I'd finally voiced my concerns. He places a warm hand over mine and gives me a gentle squeeze, as if to reinforce the strength of his promise. I ask him what I should wear on Friday in an attempt to draw a line under that particular conversation.

Callum's exceptionally witty, when he isn't trying to get into my knickers, and even sometimes when he is. We wash the dishes side by side and he repeatedly attempts to infiltrate my personal space. From his fleeting touches and lingering looks, to outright offers of sexual gratification, all carried out in a hilarious, nevertheless seductive, manner.

If I slept with him, could he keep his mouth shut? Maybe we could discreetly let this thing run its course? Fizzle out naturally? No. There's nothing discreet about any of it. I've agreed to publicly date an A-list celebrity. I'm torn between W. I. Thomas's self-fulfilling prophecy – everyone thinks I'm shagging him anyway so I may as well – versus the necessity of keeping a clear head for our business arrangement.

Callum's the complete opposite to 'a one-woman man'. And I'm not supposed to care. But something shifted between us tonight. We reached a mutual understanding. I witnessed a tenderness to him that initially, I wouldn't have believed he possessed. An empathy, a mirrored vulnerability. In other circumstances, I'd almost even trust his sincerity. Isolated from his usual audience, I wonder if I've gotten a glimpse of the real Callum Connolly.

'Maybe I should just check your bedsheets before I go? You know, just in case anyone ever asks me what colour they are?' His cobalt eyes reflect my own lusty gaze as I walk him towards the front door.

'Nice try. But you've got absolutely no chance, big man.' He's six inches taller than me, and I tilt my head upwards to shoot him a softening smile as I reject his advances once again.

His head angles towards mine as he leans into the wooden doorframe, lingering long enough for me to inhale the scent surrounding his Adam's apple. I think he might be contemplating kissing me. It's safer if he doesn't. We both have too much to lose.

'Goodnight, Callum.' I nod at my next-door neighbour's window. 'Mrs. Boyle will be talking about me. The curtains are twitching already.'

'Goodnight, Abby.' He loiters in the dark a couple of seconds longer, leaning slowly in, his breath warm on my face. I offer him a curt peck on the cheek and practically slam the door in his face, sinking to my bum in the hallway.

I practically threw him out. I walked him to the door. Encouraged him to leave. I should be pleased, relieved even. So why do I feel suddenly empty? Like I've lost something. I need a cold shower. Or a ten-kilometre run. Or both. Though I've got a feeling neither will help. Callum Connolly's beginning to inch his way, slowly but surely, underneath my skin.

He took my requests way better than I could have anticipated. As though it were a given, like I didn't even need to ask. I lowered my mask, flashed the face that I rarely expose to anyone, and he empathetically embraced it. The rugby player has become less infuriating and increasingly inviting. Oh, he's a womaniser, I'm under no illusion about that. But my resistance is strong, as long as he doesn't touch me. Because if he starts, I don't think I'd be able to tell him to stop.

CHAPTER SIXTEEN

CALLUM

'Well? Was she any good?' Eddie shouts across the pitch as I arrive for another round of torturous training.

This is the type of dumb shit he usually spouts. Only until he started speaking about Abby, I hadn't realised it was dumb. I feel oddly protective of her, after seeing a different side to her last night. What happened to her? Someone must have really done a number on her.

'You will never find out,' I assure him.

'I thought we were on the same team, man?' Eddie whines.

'I'm starting a new team. And you and your crude remarks are not on it.'

'Coming from 'Touchdown Connolly' that's quite a statement.' James approaches and digs me in the ribs.

Coach blows the whistle. 'Enough small talk for one day, bitches. Give me ten laps of the field, last one back does a hundred burpees.'

We take off, James flanking my right and Marcus on my left.

'Seriously, give us some details,' James says.

As we begin our run, my heart rate increases, blood pounds through every part of me, damp drizzle stings my face and I feel more alive than I've felt in years.

'There's something about Abby,' I confess. Though I'm not willing to share the details, ha, not that there's much to share, but something is undoubtedly occurring. We've progressed from her borderline despising me, to forging some kind of mutual respect.

Surprisingly, I actually like her. Really like her. Four laps in and the Spanish Inquisition continues. 'Did you stay over?'

'How does she like her eggs in the morning?'

Their comments irritate me, but not as much as the increasing pain that's currently searing through my chest. I slow to a jog and eventually halt, kneeling on the damp grass.

'Were you drinking last night?' James mistakes my chest pain for nausea.

Coach jogs over to us. 'Connolly, what's going on?'

'Bit of a pain in my chest. Nothing serious.' I clutch the material of my T-shirt, squeeze it tightly and try and regulate my breathing.

'Do you need the doctor?' Concern etches in.

'No, I just need a minute. Sorry, Coach.' I wonder if it was the glass of wine I had with dinner. Or if it is the stress of the impending end of my career that's affecting me. This is the second time this has happened to me in a matter of weeks. At some point, I'll get it checked.

'I'm sound now.' I stand and begin to jog gently.

'Coach, tell him you'll let him off the burpees if he dishes on Abby,' Eddie helpfully suggests.

'I'll do the burpees.' I shoot Eddie a warning look.

The entire training session is torturous. Coach keeps

looking at me like I'm on the way out. A least my cruciate is behaving, for now. Finally, we finish up for the day.

'Coming to the bar later? United are playing.' Marcus flings his kitbag over his shoulder and lingers in the doorway.

'Not me. I have a few phone calls to make,' I tell them.

'You can't be serious? To who?' James looks incredulous. 'I'm all for you settling down, man. But there's such a thing as too keen. Women don't like it any more than we do, trust me.'

'Nah. I need to sort a few bits for Dad. And I need an early night. I'm wrecked after last night's activities.' I hope my sordid implications are enough to get me off the hook. If the truth be told I'm uneasy about that second bout of chest pain in as many weeks. What I need is room service and a rest. Sadly it doesn't work out as I hope.

After a quiet evening watching re-runs of *Love/Hate*, I fall helplessly into one of those awful recurring dreams. I know I'm dreaming, yet I have no control of what the dream version of me does. The same as watching a horror movie and shouting at the screen, 'don't go in there, the house is haunted, or the bad guy is in there waiting' yet the character waltzes heedlessly into the danger zone anyway.

This time, it's me walking into the danger; the front door of my childhood home. The door is unlocked. The dream version of me, merely a child, strolls ignorantly in, blissfully unaware of the horror show seven-year-old Callum is about to witness. I follow, silently screaming at this young innocent boy not to go any further, not to look. For I know too well, he'll never be able to unsee the image he's about to witness.

I've been here countless times before. It's always the same. We go into the gloomy hall. The sun has set. It's neither day or night, somewhere in between. Ironically, that's how I've felt my whole life, since this point, somewhere in between, unable to move on, yet unable to stay.

The body of a woman lies at the foot of the stairs, broken and crumpled. Her neck's bent in such an unnatural position that even the child understands the finality of. He lets out a long cold, curdling scream, rising each individual nerve ending on my back, penetrating my soul. He doesn't stop until his aunty finds him cradling the woman's head on his muddy knees.

Clammy sweat soaks my chest and drenches the cotton bedsheets. I'm stuck, a prisoner of my mind, forced to witness this horrific scene for the hundredth time.

Though there's something different this time. A sickening hollowing wrench in my gut compels me to watch as the boy strokes the face of the woman he desperately clings to, even though she has long since departed. My hot salty tears mirror his, streaming from my closed eyes, trapped in this state of torturous slumber. And there I see it, the difference. The woman no longer has the same bereft face.

This time it's Abby.

I finally drag myself from the awfulness to a state of semi-consciousness, waking petrified and alone in a Carton House hotel bedroom.

It's a good job Abby continuously refuses my advances. How can I even contemplate starting something with her, when I'm already consumed with the fear of losing her?

CHAPTER SEVENTEEN

ABBY

The temperatures in Dublin increase dramatically during the week. The June sunshine penetrates the clouds, casting an optimistic glow on even the dullest of buildings in the city. The weather's lightened everyone's spirits, superfood for the soul.

Today's Ask Abby was a good one; The Almost Affair. The amount of people in this country who embark on 'textual relationships' (full cyber relationships with emotional attachments or dependence) outside of their marriage or partnership is outstanding. The show caused an uproar.

My ratings are up already. I'm marginally ahead of Sally's Soul Show, and that's before I bring out the big guns.

Today we broadcast the first teaser of Callum's advertising jingle. For thirty seconds his voice echoed huskily around the studio, loaded with promise. I hate to admit that the rich depth and tone of it resulted in even me swooning. The women of the country will be clawing each other's eyes out in desperation to speak to him when the day comes. Callum's seductive confidence will provide the perfect entertainment for radio.

Thoughts of him have consumed me since Monday. The irrational part of my brain begs me to submit to his advances. It's only sex. Possibly the best sex I might have in my entire life, if the escalating chemistry is anything to go by. The rational part of me reminds me that if I were to really get involved, my humiliation would be on a whole new scale, a very public one.

I arranged to meet Karen for a late lunch in St. Stephen's Green, the first time I've seen her since Carton House, though she only works around the corner from me in a hotel on Merrion Square. We laze on a fold-up picnic blanket from a nearby souvenir shop, sitting companionably on the manicured grass, soaking up the first real warmth of the year. Couples stroll by us, arm in arm, and groups of teenagers gather in clusters between exams. This is my favourite time of year.

'How are the wedding plans going?' I ask between mouthfuls of a chicken tikka roll.

'Oh, Abby, I honestly don't know.' Karen waves her hand dismissively.

'What is it?' A sliver of worry tears through my stomach.

An image of Dan leaving her at the aisle flashes through my head. It's my first assumption, and I need to rein it in. Not all men are the same as Sean Fitzpatrick.

'I don't know...I just...' She struggles to find the right words as she runs her fingers over her thick fringe and pats it firmly back into place.

'Is something up with Dan?' I ask outright.

'It's me,' she admits shame-faced.

'What do you mean it's you?' I'm dumbfounded that she might let the daft notions of that old witch from Wicklow influence her decisions.

'I just don't know if it's right,' she says.

'Is this because of what Esmerelda predicted?'

Karen's impressionable at the best of times, giving way too much airtime to what other people think. But I didn't expect this.

'I'm not that daft, but it got me thinking to be honest.' She twists the corner of her navy pencil skirt around her finger distractedly.

'Well, what then?' A desperation to get to the crux of the matter niggles me, which probably has more to do with my past situation than her current one. I still fail to understand how a person could go from agreeing to get married, plan a wedding and yet not follow through with it at the very end.

'I'm having doubts.' She signals me to stay quiet with one finger, before I can interrupt with my protest.

I close my mouth and sit on my hands. People stroll by without a care in the world while my best friend rattles my insides with her unexpected revelation.

'Dan and I are so different. When I think about it, we kind of fell into a routine with each other. It's probably more a marriage of convenience than anything. After ten years, our family and friends expect us to get married, the questions keep coming. It's not as if either of us are desperate to tie ourselves to each other in that way otherwise.' She sheepishly glances over my shoulder, refusing to make eye contact, aware that this is a little close to home for me.

'What does Dan say about this?' I close my low-hanging jaw to mask my shock.

'I asked him why he wanted to marry me.' Hysteria tinges her voice as she remembers.

'And?'

'He said that's what people do.' Her eyes fall to the ground and she lets out a long-winded sigh.

'Ah.' He could have given her any other reason than that one.

'So what are you going to do? Maybe if you explain your feelings clearly to him, you could discuss it properly. Dan's a good man.' I can't just let her walk away. What if he's just being a typical guy about the whole thing? They find it hard to articulate the right words sometimes.

'He's a good man. I think that might be the problem... Sorry, I wasn't sure whether to tell you or not. I know it might hit a nerve with you.'

'Look at these.' I flash the waistband of the Calvin Klein underwear I have on. 'These here are my big girl pants. You're my best friend. You can tell me anything.' My sentiment's true, but that doesn't prevent my surprise.

'Don't go getting all mushy on me, Queenan,' Karen says.

Talk of calling off a wedding might have been awkward for me, once upon a time, but I've gotten over it. Clearly not enough to trust another man yet, but even pretend dating Callum's a step in the right direction. Our new public union's bound to raise a few eyebrows.

I'm beginning to accept that I can't avoid men forever. With the physical desires stirred by a certain hot rugby player of late, I'm not sure I want to. Though my heart wouldn't survive another shattering, neither would my pride. The shame and hurt of having to cancel my own wedding, twelve hours beforehand, had been one of the worst experiences of my life.

'I'm not going to do anything rash. But it's better that we talk about it now than afterwards.' Karen's says.

'Make sure you're both on the same page, that you want the same things out of life.' I wish I'd had the same opportunity with Sean.

'Want to meet for lunch on Friday?' Karen gathers her belongings and stands, ready to make tracks.

'I can't. I have this thing with Callum.' I brush some crumbs from my lap and avoid Karen's disbelieving stare.

'What thing might that be? Are you seriously seeing him?' She scrutinises my face for unspoken clues.

'It's a charity fundraiser. All the WAGs are going.'

She almost chokes on the final mouthful of her wrap. I pat her gently on the back and offer her my bottle of Ballygowan.

'So you're a WAG now?'

'Apparently.' I don't want to give too much away, even to her.

'Holy fuck. May I remind you that that man has never slept with the same woman twice?' She stares at me wide-eyed, as though I've lost my mind. Maybe I have.

'Firstly – how do you know that?' I challenge her, before adding, 'and secondly, I haven't slept with him. Maybe that's the attraction.'

'Sorry, he's never been photographed with the same woman twice,' she corrects herself, rolling her eyes dramatically. 'Same difference though... Don't go falling in love with him for goodness sake,' she begs. 'Whatever Sean did to you, Callum Connolly's in an entirely different league. I don't want to see you get hurt.' Her tone's gentle, but the warning is clear.

And she's right to offer caution. Because the more time I spend with him, the more I want him. It's the most unhealthy obsession I've ever experienced. And it is growing by the hour. But it's the one line I won't cross.

CHAPTER EIGHTEEN

CALLUM

The day of the fundraiser's warm and bright. We attract big numbers, it's not every day the public gets to witness the Irish rugby team competing in an egg and spoon race. I scan the crowds for any sign of Abby. She's late. I hope she hasn't changed her mind.

There's only one more event left before we're free to gather in the refreshment tents: the tug of war. Coach divides the team into two. James is behind me, along with Eddie and eight of our other teammates and subs. Marcus is opposite, fronting up his side, with Ollie directly behind him. Marcus is his usual cocky self. Shelly cheers from the sideline dressed like a pineapple in a luminous yellow floor-length dress and a bright green fascinator.

'Careful you don't break a nail princess,' I goad him as I crouch into position.

'Whatever. Get accustomed to losing, Connolly. This is only the start of it, man.' He huffs, sweating before we've even begun.

'Save your energy, big guy. You're going to need every ounce of it in a minute.' I talk the big talk, all that's left is to deliver.

Coach blows the whistle. Whooping ensues from the crowd. Shelly's screams are ten octaves higher than anyone else's. She and Marcus are a match made in heaven.

My forearms bulge as my fingers grip the wiry rope and drag. I grunt like an animal. With no idea which side of the line we stand, I give it everything, thighs aching from the persistent crouch position. Brilliant sunshine blinds me. I focus on the reflection from Marcus's sweating skinhead, blood pulsating rapidly through my veins.

Then I catch a glimpse of her pushing her way through the throng of people to get a better look. Wearing a slim-fitting white dress and gold sandals, Abby blossoms from the crowd, a rose amongst the thorns. Her long blonde hair falls freely, secured only by a pair of oversized sunglasses on her head.

Taking advantage of my distraction, Marcus and his gang pull into the lead. I force myself back into the competition. Raucous chanting reaches a deafening pitch as the event approaches a definitive end. Hauling the rope with every ounce of energy in my reserve tank, my fingers burn. Sweat clouds my eyes, but it's worth every second of discomfort as we narrowly secure our victory. I collapse back on top of James in exertion, and he whoops in delight.

'A taste of what's to come,' I pant across at Marcus with a grin.

'Whatever, dickhead. One battle doesn't win the war.' Marcus is a sore loser. If he's sore now, he will be a hell of a lot worse when I take his Audi. Then he'll experience the true meaning of defeat. Though the Audi's only the icing on the cake at the stage. The real prize would be Abby herself.

I'd be a fucking fool not to acknowledge it. Not that she'll let me anywhere near her. Maybe it's for the best.

Since our impromptu dinner date, I want to bed her more than ever. But another thought torments me, haunting me each time I close my eyes, when I take a shower, every time I pause to breathe, and I'm not referring to the monstrous thoughts that lurk in my subconscious and haunt my dreams. My waking thoughts urge me to really date her, to take her out for dinner properly, not this pretend bullshit. The thought refuses to go away. I can't even distract myself with another woman because of our agreement. And in truth, I don't want to.

Using my hand to shield my eyes from the sun, I turn to where she'd been watching in the crowd, unable to distinguish her shape anywhere.

A light touch on my arm tells me she's jumped the makeshift fence to reach me. I leap up and pull her into a bear hug instinctively, buzzing euphorically from our victory.

If Abby's surprised by my welcome, it doesn't show. She flashes a row of beautiful white teeth which reflect gloriously in the afternoon sunlight. I fight the urge to push my lips onto hers as the scent of her familiar perfume erotically assaults my senses.

Marcus appears immediately, a circling shark pursuing the scent of fresh blood. He rubs a sweaty hand on the front of his shorts before extending it to shake Abby's.

'Abby. It's a pleasure to meet you.' His charming tone is alien to anything I've previously heard fall from his traditionally foul mouth. Shelly jumps the fence and joins the party.

'Abby, I love your show.' She throws her arms around Abby, welcoming her as though they had been friends for years.

'Thank you. It's great to meet you both.' She leans closer

towards me, subconsciously seeking protection. I'm more than happy to offer her shelter.

James flocks in with Nadine, Eddie and Ollie tail closely behind, all of them desperate to get a look at my woman.

Ok, so technically she isn't my woman, not really. But with that flimsy cotton dress taunting me, lifting in the breeze, I'm even more determined to make her mine. Even if just for a night. Though at this stage I'm beginning to realise that one night won't be nearly enough with this woman, but the need to find out is killing me.

I usher Abby toward the refreshments tent, placing my hand possessively on the small of her back. Onlookers notice us, nudging each other and whispering as we pass.

'Have you got any underwear on under that dress?' I can't help myself. My mind is in the gutter. She has that effect on me.

Abby takes my hand in a deliberate show of affection for the benefit of my teammates and whispers firmly in my ear, 'You are never going to find out, Connolly.' She beams up at me.

To anyone else, it looks promising. To me, it's yet another knockback. She's driving me fucking crazy. Now and again, I convince myself the feeling's mutual, especially when her hand lingers on my arm longer than necessary. And she called me sexy, at least twice. But it's possible my ego's running away with itself. Each time she knocks me back, my determination to have her strengthens. It's not just the way she looks. It's her. She's the perfect balance of feminine and ferocious. She's everything I hadn't realised I wanted. I've never known frustration like it. On the plus side, it's good for my game, I've been acing practice lately. When I'm not keeled over in a heap, that is.

'Glass of prosecco?' I offer.

She hesitates for a millisecond. 'It's Friday I suppose.'

Shelly and Nadine beat us to the bar, slugging alcohol like it's juice. A familiar figure approaches in the distance, the shock knocks the breath clean out of my chest.

I didn't expect to see him here, especially today of all days.

'Dad.' Surprise colours my tone. I pray he's having one of his good days.

'Well done, son. A great turn out. Another great event.' He wistfully drapes an arm around me and glances intently at Abby and me.

'Dad. This is Abby. Abby, this is my father, Jimmy.' I mentally will him not to say something that I can't take back.

'It's a pleasure to meet you, Mr Connolly.' Abby extends her hand to his to shake his, but the old charmer takes hers and kisses it instead. She doesn't waver under my father's curious gaze. He's unused to seeing any of my women, and it couldn't be more obvious.

Linda hovers closely nearby. She obviously drove him here. I motion her over and introduce her, praying neither of them discloses anything too private to Abby. She does not require a full family history this afternoon. I can't even sell myself to her. I'm damn sure the whole sorry package won't do a lot for my cause.

CHAPTER NINETEEN

ABBY

I sip on the prosecco, soaking up the atmosphere. Callum's dad is a dote, if a little confused. His sister watches him like a hawk. I wonder where Callum's mother is. Perhaps she stayed at home, or maybe they're divorced. Either way, if I'm assuming the role of girlfriend for the foreseeable future, I'll need to know these things.

Callum looks ridiculously good in his team colours. White shorts display strong toned thighs. Thighs I long to touch. I manage to control myself, but the smell of his raw masculine sweat drives my hormones wild. Mother Nature's ability to incite the desire to reproduce has taken hold of me. Callum is physically the perfect mate. He's exactly what I need for my show, and exactly what I don't need entwined in my daily life.

The dynamics have subtly shifted between us. He stares at me as though we have a newfound, deeper connection after Monday night. I feel it too, but it doesn't change the logistics. The sensible side of my brain reminds me of the cold, hard facts. My rapidly pulsating heart reminds me of something else entirely. A booming voice resounds over thoughtfully positioned speakers in each corner of the drinks tent, summoning us outside once again for the afternoon's results. I wave goodbye to Callum's dad and aunt and follow him outside. Close to a thousand spectators gather in the park, in addition to the team and their families.

I strain my neck to the point of pain, scrutinising the crowd, a fleeting image of Sean Fitzpatrick in a red baseball cap sparks my attention. My mind has an awful habit of conjuring him up in the oddest of places over the years, probably because he left so abruptly. Subconsciously, I'm constantly looking for closure.

I used to openly fantasise that I'd bump into him somewhere and give him a piece of my mind, some cleverly worded, cutting retaliation for the way he just abandoned me. The opportunity has never arisen, and now I doubt I want it.

'You all know why we're here today,' Callum's Coach booms into the megaphone from a makeshift stage at the front of the crowd. A long round of applause follows.

'This is an annual event close to all of our hearts. I'd like to extend a special thank you to Callum Connolly, who is, of course, ambassador for Pieta House Charity. He organised everything once again this year. Callum looks like a brute, but there's a heart of gold in that hollow chest somewhere.' The crowd offers a thunderous round of applause.

I drop my sunglasses to cover my eyes and mask my shock. Callum organised this. I wouldn't have believed he had it in him. Double brownie points for not using it to impress me earlier in the week. The remainder of the speech escapes me, stunned with the revelation that Callum was an ambassador for any charity, let alone this specific one – the one that I had turned to myself for counselling almost four years ago.

'Now time for the results.' I'm lured back into the

moment by the noisy whooping of Shelly and Nadine as they wait to see whose man achieved the overall highest score. I've got a distinct feeling it'll be my man in the first place. I'll pretend he's mine, anyway, seeing as that's our agreement.

'Third place goes to James O'Malley. Coming first in the sack might work with Nadine, but it wasn't enough this afternoon, buddy.' Coach calls James forward with a laugh and places a makeshift bronze medal over his head. The crowd dissolves into laughter and a steady flow of clapping ensues.

Nadine throws her arms around her fiancé proudly. James squeezes her toward him.

Marcus and Callum realise they're head to head, jostling elbows playfully.

'Second place goes to Marcus Williams. It's not easy for a man of his size to transport an egg on a spoon a hundred metres.'

Marcus takes to the front but isn't overly impressed with the fake silver medal hanging round his veiny bulging neckline.

I hold my breath even though I've got a fair idea of what's coming. Callum takes my hand. I squeeze it tightly in anticipation, unwittingly drawn into the excitement of the whole event.

'In first place, with the highest score overall, is the one and only, Callum Connolly,' Coach shouts, raising his hands in the air. Callum's obviously his first choice, as well as mine. The crowd goes wild.

Callum struts confidently to the front, hops effortlessly up on to the stage and accepts his makeshift gold medal with a modest grin.

'Speech, speech, speech, speech,' the spectators chant. Callum raises a hand to quiet them, a natural at working the crowd.

'Save it for the Oscars; we aren't interested,' Marcus

shouts rudely. A ripple of annoyance flashes through me. I can see the appeal of taking his Audi.

Callum ignores him and clears his throat. 'Thank you all so much for coming here today and supporting this event, because without the spectators, there'd be no fundraiser. Hopefully, we've raised a large amount today for Pieta House and I'm fairly sure the loser, oops, I mean second place is going to donate another fifty thousand to the cause in a few short weeks.'

Marcus raises an eyebrow but says nothing. He hasn't accepted defeat yet.

'I'd also like to say a special thank you to a new friend of mine for joining us today...' Callum trails off, staring directly at me.

Oh shit. I will the ground to swallow me up whole. He edges forwards, extending a strong hand out to mine and pulls me unceremoniously on to the stage with him, forcing me into the limelight despite my obvious reluctance.

'This is Abby Queenan. You'll all recognise her voice, but you mightn't be familiar with her beautiful face. Her show, Ask Abby, airs daily at 11 a.m. on Ireland Today. I want to take this opportunity to remind everyone here, that it's ok not to be ok. There are people here to help you. Ring Pieta House if you are in bother. Ring a friend, ring a family member. If all else fails, you can Ask Abby, who I'm proud to say is my date today.'

This wasn't part of our deal.

Catcalls and whistling ensue. My cheeks flame in response. Blushing is becoming an awful recurring habit. Callum's doing a great job of marketing my show. Candice will be over the moon, but I'm mortified, preferring the anonymity of the radio studio to the bright lights of the stage. I never would have cut it as an actress, no matter how many stage school camps my mother paid for.

'Kiss, kiss, kiss, kiss,' an increasingly restless crowd demands.

The chanting grows louder and more consistent.

Horribly vulnerable, my heart pounds erratically, and my tongue traces my tingling lips uncertainly. I haven't kissed a man in years. I've forgotten how to. Saliva floods my mouth in anticipation. This is a terrible idea on so many levels. And it couldn't possibly be any more public.

Frozen to the spot, unable to even swallow, uncontrollable desire floods every cell within me. I yearn to give the crowd what they want, not for their sake, but for mine. Callum faces into me, resting his arms lightly on my waist. He removes my sunglasses and sparkling eyes search mine for permission. I'm exposed and protected simultaneously. My head warns me I'm hovering at the entrance of the lion's den, but my body craves him like a drug. I'll never get a better excuse. Swept up in the moment, I offer the subtlest nod, submitting to the man that I swore wholeheartedly I wouldn't.

His full, firm lips meet mine. His tender tongue pushes into my mouth, tasting, probing, dancing with mine. Sparks ignite my body, a match to the flame. I press my chest closer to his, enthralled by his warmth, dragging him towards me, wrapping my hands tightly around the nape of his neck, desperately hungry for more. The crowd melts. In this moment, there is only us. My rusty floodgates are thrust open. It can only mean a rapid downhill spiral from here on in.

'Easy!' Marcus interrupts from an all too close proximity.

'Get a room,' James yells.

'Lucky son of a...' Eddie breaks us up physically, resting his hand between the two of us on Callum's chest. As he pulls away, the aching intensity of his glassy eyes mirror mine. That was the most sensual kiss of my life. I can't meet his eye.

The crowd erupts, clapping wildly and wolf-whistling. The

distinct clicking of cameras and flashing lights illuminate the stage intrusively. Coach tries to settle everyone once again with the megaphone, but the damage is done.

CHAPTER TWENTY

CALLUM

In all the times that I imagined kissing Abby, I hadn't dared to dream it would be so explosive, so fuelled with promise. I spend the remainder of the afternoon walking around Phoenix Park with a loaded gun. My body hums with a longing so intense, I can't escape it. I only pray that she will now at least stop fighting the inevitable.

Whatever reason she'd chosen to avoid men, I just ripped the plaster from her old wound. Victory's fleeting, as I risk exposing myself here too. If this is what I think it is, then she isn't the only one in danger of getting hurt. But it's a risk I'm compelled to take. I refuse to consider the alternative option, not knowing. I've never experienced a want like it. It's too powerful not to pursue. I have to make her mine, really mine, not this pretend bullshit. That kiss just confirmed it.

The fact that I don't do relationships isn't an accident. I deliberately don't spend any time with my conquests, because I don't want anything to develop. I didn't want to like or love any of them before. It's safer that way. Abby doesn't realise it, but she has the potential to hurt me. Not in the physical sense, like on the pitch. That pain's insignificant in comparison to losing someone you love.

Every fibre in my being wills this to be the start of something serious, every ounce of sense in my brain wills it not to be. Intuition warns this could be so much more than anything either of us had experienced before. I'm willing to chance it if she is. It's progressed way beyond a simple want. That kiss soldered deep, etched onto both of us like a badge of lust-filled honour. She can no longer deny her interest in me, I felt the force of it first-hand. No amount of childhood stage school could have equipped her to fake the kind of sexual energy that charged through both of us this afternoon. There's nothing pretend about any of this.

With all the mandatory 'thank yous' and handshakes I'm obliged to extend, I don't get anywhere near Abby since that kiss. It doesn't stop me obsessing about her, mentally replaying her mouth on mine. I'm desperate to pick up where we left off.

Eventually, the crowd clears, the boys round up their families, ready to hit the road. I can't find Abby anywhere. I search the vicinity eagerly before a sinking realisation dawns on me. I'm not going to find her. Because she's not here.

I'd come on too strong, terrified her. One step forward, two steps back. Disappointment surges through me, crashing back to reality from the euphoric highs of the day. I return to my empty apartment, alone.

It might be safer for both of our fragile hearts. But I'm done with playing it safe.

CHAPTER TWENTY-ONE

ABBY

I flee the crime scene as discreetly as possible. The only crime I'd committed was one against myself and everything I claim to be.

People everywhere smirk knowingly at me. My secret is out. I tell Shelly and Nadine I'm going to find a toilet, but I'm actually heading home. They're on their fifth glass of prosecco. They wouldn't notice if the tent was on fire, let alone if I return or not. Callum's tied up doing the rounds, thankfully. I need to reinstate the distance between us. He crossed the line. I crossed the line. The line's so blurred at this stage, I don't even know where it is.

I can no longer deny it to him. I'm attracted to Callum Connolly. Ok, I'd appreciated his aesthetic appeal from the second I'd laid eyes on him. But at that point, he'd been aesthetically appealing, arrogant and infuriating. Now, after today's developments, he's also the kind of man that represents a charity organisation that counsels people with mental health issues. I can relate more than he'll ever know. He's a much better man than I'd initially given him credit for, even if he does have a reputation with the ladies.

This changes everything between us. I actually like him. Like really like him. As I finally admit it to myself, I realise I still don't want to be another notch on his bedpost. No, I want to be the last notch on his bedpost. Which is so much worse, because we all know that will never happen.

After the devastation that Sean left, I swore never to let a man that close to me again. I should run for the hills and never look back, but I still need him to come on my show next week. The jingle of his voice has been playing all day, every day. It's all anyone at the station can talk about. Candice will kill me if don't deliver the goods now. And I did promise Callum I'd go to James O'Malley's wedding with him, and worryingly, after today, I want to go with him now, as his date. Things are complicated. I'm a mess. I can't believe I fell at the first hurdle. I've let myself down not only spectacularly, but publicly.

When I get home I open a bottle of white wine and drown my sorrows in my back garden. My phone beeps with an incoming message.

Callum: We have unfinished business.

I throw the phone down on the rattan furniture and exhale a frustrated sigh. You might have got to first base, Callum Connolly, but there's no way you're nailing the home run. No matter how charming and believable you are.

After a restless sleep, I throw my runners on. The park run is never going to be enough for me today. I venture out into the early morning sun and don't stop until I have fifteen kilometres on my Garmin. Karen calls as I get back to my house.

'You have a hell of a lot of explaining to do, young lady,' she scolds.

'What have I done now?' I head straight to the fridge for water.

'I presume you've seen yourself in *The Sun* today? With your tongue stuck so far down Callum Connolly's neck you could eat his lunch from his stomach.'

I groan. Now it's public news before the show on Monday. All the callers will want to know if we're a couple. This is bad, really bad.

'I got carried away in the moment.' My excuse sounds feeble, even to me.

'I can see that alright. You look enamoured with each other. It's blazingly obvious for the entire country to see what you two get up to in the moment.'

Cringing, I open my laptop to search the news for the incriminating evidence. There's going to be a lot of questions come Monday. I'm relieved that Callum will be there to take half the rap for it. Then I reconsider as I remember I can't trust myself not to dry hump him.

The first picture that pops up shows me pulling Callum in closer, with my hand round his neck. It is pornography to my sexually starved vagina. I shut the laptop quickly again, in danger of developing a stupid idea, like inviting him over here right now. I even have the perfect excuse. My sink is still awaiting a part, and I've barely turned that particular tap on since.

'You haven't so much as looked at a man in four years, then all of a sudden you're plastered all over the newspaper chewing the face off one of the most high-profile womanisers around.'

The landline interrupts us; it's my mother. God help me. She must have seen it too. Candice is currently on call waiting on my mobile phone.

'Karen, I gotta go. I'll call you back later.' I take a deep breath and accept Candice's incoming call.

'Abby, you are an absolute marketing genius,' she screams down the phone at me.

'The entire country will be tuned in on Monday morning after this little stunt. I couldn't have staged it better myself. The fact that you've never been linked to a man since you started on the show, just makes the whole thing sooo much more intriguing. Not to mention that Callum Connolly is so freaking, knicker-drenching hot. You've got it in the bag, girl. I hope your passport is in date – you're going to the Big Apple.'

'Ummm... Thanks.'

'Holy shit, Abby...was it for real?' she says in astonishment.

'Ummm...kind of.' It was for me, anyway. I can't guarantee that Callum doesn't kiss every girl that way.

'This is even better. I for one, cannot wait for Monday morning.' A gentle click informs me she's hung up.

I put my head in my hands, wishing I could bury it in the sand until this blows over. How can one man have such an impact on my normally controlled life?

And who would listen to a word of advice from me, when Callum smashes my heart to pieces all over the media?

A message from Callum pings through, he's obviously reviewed the evidence of our exceptionally public kiss. It's fine for him. He's used to people commenting on his love life. I'm used to commenting on everyone else's.

Callum: I have the proof in black and white now, you CANNOT deny it. Give us a chance, Abs.

PS Looks like we're going to New York.

Give us a chance? He can't be serious. Men like him are all about the challenge. The scandal will do wonders for my ratings, shame I'm right in the epicentre of it. New York has shot to the back of my brain. At the minute, I have more pressing problems.

The most pressing one, currently, being my mother. She's probably horrified that her unmarried daughter is plastered all over the papers, sucking the face off one of Ireland's most famous sports stars.

I only pray she'll buy the story of the publicity stunt for the show. My running gear sticks to me. I need a shower, but better to get all my sweating over and done with in one go.

'Hello?' I brace myself for the onslaught.

'Abby Magdelena Queenan, have you seen yourself in the paper today?' Mammy says loudly.

'Sorry, Mammy. I—' I don't get the chance explain before she cuts over me.

'Fair play to you, girl.'

My mouth drops in shock, and I wonder if aliens have landed and disguised themselves as the human form of my devoutly Catholic mother.

'Your father and I never thought we'd see the day that you got over what that slimy bollocks Sean Fitzpatrick did to you. And snagging such a handsome rugby player as well. I only hope Sean reads the Irish newspapers from whatever hole he's hiding in.'

'Thank you?' Might be the right thing to say, although this is new territory for me and Mammy. Normally I get a curt nod and a pat on the back whenever we refer to anything remotely sensitive. We aren't an outwardly emotional family.

'When are you bringing him to meet us?' Mammy demands. 'Did you tell him about my fruit cake?' Her fruit cake has won awards all over the county, and she's very secretive of her recipe, unwilling to even share it with Alicia, or me.

I roll my eyes in despair. Mammy has an awful habit of inserting herself in the centre of everything. It's a familiar trait, but it grates on me. Like the time she had to tell all of our family that Sean had jilted me practically at the altar. Irrelevant that I'd just been humiliatingly and heartbreakingly dumped the night before my wedding.

'He's busy with training, Mam, but we'll get down soon, okay?' I cross my fingers and hope I won't go to hell for lying. There's no way I'd ever bring Callum to Carrick, and there's no way he'd want to go either.

'Bring him home for the weekend. We'd love to see ye. Tell him about my cake. Abby, I hate nagging, but you don't come home anywhere near enough'

She's right, but I have my reasons.

'Say hi to Daddy for me. Bye, Mam.' I exhale a sigh of relief. It could have been worse.

Two further texts from Callum insist we at least talk. I don't want to talk. I want to kiss every single solid inch of him, throw myself at his mercy and break every rule in my personal handbook. Instead, I force myself to do the complete opposite and don't even acknowledge his messages. Longing eats me alive as I imagine what he might be doing for the rest of the weekend. Will he refer to his little black book and seek company elsewhere? I try not to go there. There would be no going back.

CHAPTER TWENTY-TWO

CALLUM

I know why she's hiding from me. I feel the same; scared fucking shitless that we might actually have something here. But if she won't take my calls or reply to my messages, how can I even attempt to tell her how I feel. She's stirs something unnervingly deep in me. If she'd only give me the opportunity to prove it. I'm willing to put myself out there for her. All she has to do is meet me at the halfway line.

My phone vibrates in my pocket. I pull it out expectantly, I've checked it five thousand times since last night. I've turned into one of those desperate, love-sick men. I've never felt so helpless in all of my adult life.

It's my brother Brian. I'm fairly sure he's not texting to congratulate me on another successful fundraiser for a cause that should mean as much to him as it does to me.

Brian: Abby Queenan? Great photo. You must be so proud.

I scowl in response, firstly because it isn't Abby, secondly because Brian never misses an opportunity to stick the knife in.

Callum: She's different.

I seem to have to justify myself to Brian, more than anyone else, even my father. Dad's never been right after Mam, only ever half present, and that was before he got Alzheimer's. Brian assumed the head of the household role at the mere age of thirteen. And he's never seemed impressed with my achievements, sporting or otherwise.

I have an inexplicable streak that longs to make my older brother proud. I'm foolish to even think it a remote possibility. But he is happily married. Maybe he can offer me some advice. It's not like I've got anyone else I can go to.

Brian: Why? Because she has a brain?

Callum: I actually like her.

My phone rings instantly.

'I'm just checking it's actually you typing, and that your phone hasn't been stolen.' Brian's familiar voice does nothing to appease my jittering insides.

'It's me.' I sigh in helpless frustration. If he's ringing to torment me, he can piss off.

'So Abby Queenan, hey? Ireland Today's inhouse agony aunt and the nation's sweetheart.' A slightly more solemn tone indicates that he's taking me seriously for once.

'The very one,' I confirm.

'So what's the problem? Worried she'll break your heart?' he teases.

The sound of my niece and nephew fighting in the background distracts him for a second.

'Sorry. Melissa's gone shopping. I'm supposed to be parenting here. Apparently, you can't call it babysitting when it's your own kids.' Brian laughs at his joke.

'No worries. How are the rugrats?' I ask out of politeness

rather than interest. The only thing I'm interested in at this point is his help on the Abby situation. Which highlights exactly how desperate I am.

'So, what's up?'

'She's not into me,' I admit.

'She looks pretty into you on page two of *The Irish Sun*.'

'That woman has knocked me back more times than knocks I've taken on the field. Someone really did a number on her before. And with my past record...I suppose I can't blame her for being wary.' Another heavy sigh escapes my lips. It isn't hard to see why she's avoiding me.

'Well, well, I never thought I'd see the day. If you are serious, Callum – and I mean serious, you need to make some sort of grand gesture to show her. Preferably something public. So if all this blows up, the entire country will know it was you that pursued her. Abby Queenan makes her living dishing out advice to the women of this country. She can't be seen to have you make her a fool of her.' Brian unknowingly echoes Abby's words from the other night.

Man, my big brother is better than I gave him credit for.

'Like what, though?' I'm struggling to think of something.

'I don't know. But if you want her to know that she's different to the women before her, you have to treat her differently – show her.'

High-pitched squeals escalate again. There's a war starting over a volleyball.

'I gotta go, Callum. I hope it works out for you. It's about time you found someone nice.' What his tone actually conveys is, it's about time you grow up. But no harm. Brian was helpful for once.

'Take care, bro.' Could this be the start of a change in our relationship?

'One more thing,' Brian calls over the background noise.

'Don't break her heart after this. That would be the pits. Even for you.'

Thanks for the vote of confidence, Brian. He's right, though. Can I trust myself not to break her heart?

I head to the hardware store to pick up the perfect excuse to arrive on her doorstep. I have no shame. The part is basic, easy enough to locate. I contemplate stopping at the florist along the way but opt for a bottle of wine instead. I've always associated flowers with a poor excuse for an apology. I'm certainly not apologising for what happened yesterday.

As I enter her estate, a ripple of nerves whip through. What if she doesn't want to see me? What if that kiss repulsed her? No. I flick up the photo from the paper that I saved on my phone. She definitely isn't repulsed by me. Maybe by my reputation, but not by me.

I let the engine idle for longer than necessary, announcing my arrival. For an awful second, I consider the possibility that she might have company. Oh God, what if it's another man?

I'm being ridiculous now. She doesn't date. She's not likely to have started since yesterday afternoon. I straighten my T-shirt, hop out of the Jeep and rap the door with my knuckles. This shit is so much harder when you actually care. I'm not used to feeling vulnerable, and I don't like it.

It's the longest thirty seconds of my life before she opens the door in a pair of yoga pants and a slim-fitting black vest. Neat stylish glasses frame her make-up free face. She looked sensational in that red dress, but this natural look is a million times sexier.

'Callum.' She's not entirely surprised, though a little wary.

I brandish the plastic part for her sink. The modern-day equivalent of 'I carried a watermelon'.

She steps back, an unspoken invitation inside, and the door clicks promisingly behind me, alone at last. I intend to make the most of it.

She flicks on the kettle. I hand her the bottle of wine and head straight for the leaky sink.

'Opening this would be a bad idea,' she states aloud, as though she's trying to blame the drink for yesterday.

'Don't trust yourself, huh?' I don't mean to sound like such a smug twat. The words roll off my tongue.

'Get over yourself, big head. I've got yoga this evening, probably best if I do it sober.'

'I'll give you a workout instead if you like?' There I go again. I can't help it. If I want her to start taking me seriously, I'm going to have to start behaving a little more seriously.

'In your dreams, man-whore.' There it is, like a punch to the gut. I can't blame her.

'Ouch. Sorry. I get nervous when I'm around you. Stupid corny stuff comes out.' I'm so accustomed to deliberately keeping things light, I don't know how to be serious with a woman.

'Nervous? You?' she scoffs.

'Stranger things have happened.' I work quietly for a few minutes, trying to think of a way to convey my sincerity. She places a mug of tea on the worktop next to the sink alongside a Crunchie.

'How did you know Crunchies are my favourite?'

'Coincidence. Don't think by liking the same chocolate, we have anything in common. Cut the bullshit, Callum, please. We both know what we signed up for.' She leans against the kitchen counter next to where I kneel, her shapely legs extend forever. No matter how enticing the outer package is, it's the inside that's the real draw. That 'don't fuck with me attitude' is something I've never encountered from a woman. It's sublimely sexy.

'I know what I signed up for, and I want to renegotiate.' I glance up at her.

'Callum, it's never going to happen—'

'Let me finish.' I stand to meet her eyeline, but she sidesteps away from me. 'You're a beautiful woman, Abby. I had hoped for some extracurricular activities in the beginning, but now that I've got to know you better, I want something different, something more.'

'Ha. You are absolutely hilarious, Callum. If I was foolish enough to succumb to you, I'd never hear from you again.'

I sidestep in front of her, an inch away from her face. Her arousal emanates from her in waves. She swallows hard, intense eyes burning with desire. I begin to close the distance, gently not to startle her. My lips are millimetres away from hers. I can smell the sweetness of the chocolate on her breath. She doesn't push me away. I make the final movement forward and close the gap.

'Hellloooo...' a voice calls from the hallway.

Abby pushes me forcefully away, breaking the spell, just as an older woman strolls into the kitchen carrying an enormous package.

'I took these in for you yesterday, Abby. There are another two at the front door,' the woman announces, looking back and forth between the two of us in open curiosity.

'Thank you so much, Mrs Boyle. Callum will carry the rest in. He was just leaving anyway. Weren't you, Callum?' She eyeballs me pointedly. Without even taking a mouthful of my tea, I've already outstayed my welcome. Before I can protest, Abby pulls out a fresh cup for her neighbour and instigates small talk about the weather.

I release a frustrated sigh as I carry Abby's parcels from the door into the hallway.

'Thanks, Callum, for fixing my sink.' Her thanks are sincere, yet she still refuses to meet my eye, ushering me out the door.

'I'll see you Monday,' I tell her meaningfully.

She leaves me no choice. If she won't listen to me, I'll make her hear me one way or another. Even if it means telling the entire country. My mind is made up. I have to have her. I have a feeling that kiss was just the start of us, and I'm going to make her see it.

CHAPTER TWENTY-THREE

ABBY

Aoife nudges Candice wide-eyed when I arrive at the studio in a fitted denim dress with my hair professionally blow-dried and contacts instead of glasses.

'Someone's got it bad,' Candice announces to the entire building. Today's cerise pink T-shirt reads, Becoming a DJ Saved Me From Becoming A Pornstar.

'Alright, girls, don't broadcast it to the whole of Dublin. I'm not prepared to jump headfirst into the rabbit hole, but I can still take a bit of pride in my appearance.'

'The papers showed us exactly how deep you're prepared to venture into the rabbit hole. He's here, by the way,' Aoife says.

'Already? He's an hour early.'

'He's been here since nine o'clock, said he had to talk to you.' We approach the recording studio, whispering though he might hear us through the soundproofed walls.

'Tell him I'm running late. I'll talk to him after the show. I need to get my head straight before I go in.' I pace the corridor impatiently.

What I need is to prepare myself for the effect he has on me. The last thing I need is for him to get me all riled up before the show. Anything he has to say can wait. Thank God Mrs Boyle arrived when she did because when Callum is in the vicinity, all rationale goes out the window.

I lurk in the filing cupboard along with a million old reels of recordings and a couple of friendly mice. Following the events of the weekend, the thought of being in such close proximity to him panics me more than I care to admit. I try to hum a M.O.D.E.R.N. song and remind myself why I am doing all of this.

At ten fifty-five, I can hide no longer. Waltzing into the studio as bold as brass, I take my seat opposite him, meeting his eye with as much confidence as I can muster. Thankfully, there's a desk between us, because it would be too easy to sit my ass onto his lap instead of my chair.

'Hello, Abby.' Callum's husky tone infers he's been waiting his entire life for me, instead of a couple of hours.

'Callum.' I acknowledge him curtly and busy myself with the pretence of checking my headphones, adjusting the volume unnecessarily. One of a hundred methods of distracting myself from staring at his infallible appearance.

He's wearing the same shirt he wore the night that he arrived at my hotel door.

'Abby, you can't avoid talking to me forever. Either we do it now, or we are going to have this conversation on national radio,' he warns.

My head snaps up in alarm. 'You wouldn't dare.'

'You have no idea what I would do for you, Abby, and it has nothing to do with a ridiculous bet. I'm going to make you mine. Properly mine.' His quiet confidence demands my attention, yet I can't trust the words that leave his lips.

'Is this another one of your well-rehearsed lines from your extensive manual?' My reply is sharper than I intend.

Before he can answer, Candice appears at the window and begins the countdown. 'And you're on in one, two, three...' Aoife hovers in the background, anxious to see how this will play out.

'Good morning. Thank you for joining us this morning on Ireland Today. I'm Abby Queenan, your inhouse agony aunt. I hope you are all well on this beautiful Monday morning. Today I have a special guest with me. Someone I know you've all been dying to welcome on the show; it's Ireland's one and only rugby legend, Callum Connolly.'

I sit back and gesture for him to speak into the microphone the way I'd asked Aoife to demonstrate. There's no way I could have risked leaning over him like that and inhaling those intoxicating pheromones he emits.

'Thanks for having me, Abby. It's a first for me I have to admit.' Is he talking about the show or us?

'Well, the listeners of the country are hoping you'll shed a bit of light on their romantic questions today. We're excited to be privy to the deepest darkest secrets of the world of The Single Man's Perspective.' Candice came up with the title for the show. Not particularly original, but it cuts to the chase.

'Well, I'm not sure how much light I can shed, especially given my newfound status...'

I kick him swiftly underneath the desk.

'But I'll certainly give it a go.' He winks flirtatiously, displaying dimples which have the potential to make me forget my name.

'Great, well, as you know, Callum, we've been advertising your appearance here and asking listeners what exactly that they want to ask you. There's been an overwhelming response. Your popularity knows no bounds. The same few questions keep flooding in...'

It gives me a great deal of pleasure to watch Callum's face drop. He recovers quickly and resumes his usual infuriating arrogance. At least Arrogant Callum is easier to deal with than Compassionate Callum.

'Great.' He even manages to sound enthusiastic. Oh, he's good.

'We'll have some music now, but don't go away. You are listening to Ask Abby on Ireland Today 97.5 FM with special guest Callum Connolly, who is about to reveal, The Single Man's Perspective.'

Aoife hands me a prompt, the main points for us to discuss during the first half of the show. There's an opportunity for listeners to call in on the second half. We'll see if he's able for the pressure when things heat up live.

Jon Secada's 'Just Another Day' plays loudly through the studio. The song is four minutes and thirty-four seconds long. I hope it might deter Callum from trying to talk to me. It does precisely the opposite.

'Are you trying to tell me something?' He nods to the speaker with a devilish smirk.

'Not likely. The playlist's mostly compromised of Friday's requests from the desperate housewives of Ireland.' I'm being hard, cold even. I'm angry at myself for feeling the way I do about him, and he's bearing the brunt of it now. It's the only way I can handle being near him.

'Ahh, Friday, there it is. The massive elephant in the room that you've been avoiding. And Saturday's near-miss for that matter.' He claps his hands sarcastically.

'It was a kiss, Callum. We both know that you've had plenty of them. Let's not pretend it meant anything.' I stare at the clock intently, three minutes and fifty seconds remaining on the track. The last thing I want is our conversation to go out on air for the entire country to witness.

'Ah hah.' He practically leaps out of his chair. 'That's the point though, isn't it? We were meant to be pretending. Well, you were. I made my desire for you painfully obvious from the very first time I bumped into you, half-naked at Carton House.'

Aoife and Candice gawk open-mouthed. 'That's enough, Callum.'

'That's the problem, Abby. It's not enough. Not for me anyway.' Sincere though he sounds, I don't trust him, or myself for that matter.

'Please, Callum. Can we talk about this after the show?' I assume a different tactic. Two minutes left on the clock, and I need to scan the bullet points in front of me.

'On one condition,' he insists.

'What?' I sigh.

'You owe me a date. I'm cashing in on it immediately after the show. Not later, now.' He crosses his arms over his powerful chest. It's pointless attempting to negotiate. And now he's here in front of me, I don't think I want to.

'Fine.' I shrug noncommittedly.

'You guys are so going to have sex! The chemistry is astronomical. The ratings will be through the roof.' Candice raps on the window in delight. I turn a horrible shade of cerise.

'If only...' Callum doesn't even bother to deny his intentions.

CHAPTER TWENTY-FOUR

CALLUM

Abby puts her headphones back on and motions for me to do the same.

'That was Jon Secada there, a classic from 1992. Thank you for joining us today. Callum Connolly's about to the reveal The Single Man's Perspective.'

It's uncomfortably cramped in the studio with both Aoife and Abby in the room, not to mention Candice watching intently through the window. All she's missing is a big bucket of salted popcorn. At least someone's enjoying the show, and I haven't even started yet.

'So, Callum, what the listeners want to know first is what men look for when they are looking for a life partner?' Abby crosses her long and inviting legs, not three feet away from me.

It's hard to focus when she's within reach. Oh, what I wouldn't reach, given the chance. I arrived intending to make her pay for throwing me out on Saturday. But she came armed herself, with that dress revealing just enough cleavage to ensure I can barely think of anything other than what lies beneath.

'Ha. I might not be the best person to answer that one, I clearly haven't secured my life partner yet.' I shoot her a flirtatious wink. 'Though I'm pretty sure she's not a million miles away from me.'

She flashes me another distinct warning, which I have zero intention of heeding.

'Answer the question please, Callum. The women of Ireland are dying to find out.' She imitates an air of boredom, but anyone with half a brain could read between the lines. I'm going to make sure they don't have to.

'Okay, well, first of all, I think honesty is of the utmost importance from a partner. You need someone that's going to be straight with you, right? Nothing worse than living a life of pretence...'

'Valid point.' She acknowledges reluctantly. 'Anything else?' She's desperate to move on, but I'm only beginning to find my feet.

'And then there's the big one, of course...' I say, conspicuously tapping the side of my nose, though I'm letting her in on a well-kept secret. 'You need chemistry. A burning, passionate, overwhelming urge to rip the clothes clean off that person.' I pause for effect, allowing my words to sink in. She shifts uncomfortably in her chair, the plastic pen that she's gripping between her fingers snaps under increased pressure.

I take her silence as an opportunity to continue. Candice nods vigorously from the window.

'Let's face it, if you don't have that overpowering, all-consuming attraction in the beginning, you won't find it in the bottom of your laundry basket ten years later,' I continue.

Abby's turned on at the prospect of clothes ripping. Fire

dances in her enormous eyes. She clears her throat, keen to move on.

'Interesting perspective, Callum.' She attempts to sound blasé, though I'd bet my life she's imagining the same scene as me right now.

She needs to understand that I want more than just sex from her. 'Another thing that's equally important as the physical aspect, is to find someone you're comfortable introducing to your family and friends. Or in my case, my teammates. Someone that fits into your circle. That's the clincher for me. When you find that person, you'll know. Even if you're not looking for them, that's my experience, anyway.'

Abby's face clouds over. She's troubled.

'Thank you, Callum, for sharing your vast experience with us. We'll take some more music now, but stay tuned. Callum will be answering your questions live on air shortly.' Abby hits play and Bonnie Tyler's, 'Holding Out for a Hero' blasts round the tiny room. She rises from her chair and bolts from the room without looking back.

I spring to my feet and follow, three seconds behind her. Candice places a hand lightly in front of me, but wild horses won't stop me now. I hear her shout to Aoife to run an ad break. My eyes remain on the prize, which dives into a door four metres further along the corridor on the left. I fly through it before she can close it in my face.

Her breathing is ragged. She's visibly flustered. Confusion mists in her chocolate eyes. On closer inspection, she looks tired.

'Callum, what are you doing to me?' She presses her back against the closed door of a four-foot cupboard.

'This.' I lunge forward, placing a hand either side of her tiny frame on the solid wooden door so she can't wriggle away from me this time. I bring my face to hers and inhale the scent of her perfumed skin. Never have I wanted a woman so much in my life. She makes me want to be a better a version of myself, someone who people could turn to for advice, someone solid, who has it together, supported by a good woman beside him. I want her to be that woman. I'm done fucking around.

'Tell me you don't want this, and I swear, I'll never pester you again,' I whisper, gently pressing my body against hers, tempting her with every inch I have.

'I don't want to be another notch on your bedpost,' she confesses.

'I don't want you to be either. Go out with me, for real. I've never wanted anything as much in my life. You have to believe me.'

A hesitant upward glance from beneath those extensive charcoal eyelashes offers the response I crave. My lips crash onto hers, the heat of her mouth scorches my tongue. She yanks me closer, her breasts pressing promisingly against my chest. Hungry mouths explore, loaded with long harboured anticipation. I run my hands over the front of her dress, fingertips skimming her chest before tracing the curve of her waist.

Abby responds with the force of a gathering hurricane. Her lips are made for mine and mine alone. A sharp gasp permeates her desire. She wants this. And I can't wait to give it to her.

A loud knock from behind the door reminds me that now is not the time or place.

'Coming.' Abby frees herself from my grip.

'That's what worries me,' Candice declares.

'You have a date later. But I am warning you now, if you mess me around, I swear to God I'll break your legs. You'll never play another day of rugby in your life.' Her tone may be jovial, but the warning's clear. I'd be a fool not to acknowledge the weight behind every single word. She's been hurt by somebody. I want to make sure it never happens again.

We return to the studio together. Abby can't look either Candice or Aoife in the eye. We discuss where to take someone you want to impress on a first date and when's appropriate to introduce a partner to your family, blah blah blah. All I can think about is getting Abby Queenan into my bed and making her mine.

As the questions end, when I can see the sweet finishing line, the live calls begin, just to really test me.

The first caller asks my opinion on which style of vaginal waxing men prefer. It's possibly the first time in my entire life that I'm stuck for a one-liner. As I 'umm' and 'ahh' my way through it, Abby comes to my rescue with the number of a Dublin based salon who caters for all 'styles' apparently. I realise afterwards that it's her friend's salon, the brunette from Carton House.

The second live caller is a man wanting to know what I think of 'sexual experimentation' by which he blatantly asks if I have, or would ever consider, playing for the other team. And I'm not talking about Scotland. My answer is an instant resounding no. Abby put her hands over her microphone to stifle her laughter.

'Now, we have time for just one more caller before we finish up for today. Who do we have on the line?' Abby pulls herself expertly back into presenter mode.

'It's Sean,' a voice states aggressively across the line.

Abby pales and struggles for a response. Horror creeps onto every single one of her perfect facial features. Her lips freeze, forming a small o shape before opening and closing twice. Nothing comes out.

She saved me more than once today; I step in and return the favour.

'Hi, Sean, thanks for calling. What can we help you with

today?' I clear my throat and summon the most professional radio voice I can muster.

'I'm glad you asked me that, Callum,' he practically spits. 'What I really want to know is, how exactly long have you been sleeping with my fiancée?'

Abby acts out drastic cutthroat motions with her hands to Aoife, to cut off our caller on line one. The first few bars of Take That resound over the speakers with 'Back For Good'. Abby mutes it instantly.

'What the fuck was that about?'

'That, Callum, is the reason I don't date.' She takes a shaky sip from a bottle of still water on the desk in front of her and stands.

'Aoife, can you finish up here for me? Thank Callum once again on air and remind them to tune in at the same time tomorrow.' Abby leaves the room quietly, and for the first time since the day I met her, I'm unsure if I should follow her.

CHAPTER TWENTY-FIVE

ABBY

The very minute of the precise day that I make a conscious effort to move on, Sean Fitzpatrick waltzes back into my life with the audacity to call me his fiancée. On national radio, no less. Once the initial shock subsides, I'm spitting pure rage. How dare he?

Callum sits opposite me in a cocktail bar just off Grafton Street. It's thinning out after the lunchtime rush. We attract a few stares, but nobody approaches. My thunderous mood must be palpable. It isn't exactly how I imagined the afternoon developing after our encounter in the cupboard not two hours earlier.

'I can't believe that bollocks would do that to me.'

Callum leans across the table and takes my hand. I don't brush him away. 'What happened? You don't have to tell me if it's private, but I'll happily listen.'

Funnily enough, after his confession in the cupboard, I'd love to talk to him about it. I brought him on so the women of the country could benefit from the male perspective, yet here I am cashing in on it.

I take a deep breath and begin. 'Sean was my childhood sweetheart, my only sweetheart, actually. We were engaged.' I glance up to see if he understands what I'm telling him, that there's only ever been one man in my life. 'Mammy, my sister Alicia and three of my closest school friends gathered in our house in Carrick the day before our wedding. Neighbours popped in and out throughout the day with cards and well wishes. Relations from Canada and the States were settling into the hotel where the reception was booked. I strutted confidently around the house in a white personalised dressing gown emblazoned with 'Mrs Fitzpatrick' with no idea of the shitstorm that was headed my way.'

Callum listens intently, lavishing his undivided attention on me, while I divulge the woeful humiliating story of my life.

'Daddy pretended having a house full of hyperactive women was unbearable, but he'd been secretly thrilled to be a part of it, refilling our glasses and making a fuss. Then, around midnight, I received a text message from Sean. He said he couldn't go through with it. At first, I thought it was some kind of sick joke, the best man's idea of a stupid prank. His phone went straight to voicemail, and when I rang his parents' house, his mother confirmed Sean left almost two hours earlier with a rucksack.

I couldn't even cry. The humiliation was unbearable. One hundred and fifty-four invitations had been issued. The photographer was due to arrive in nine hours. Everything was booked and paid for. All he had to do was turn up, but it had been too much to ask.

Daddy drove almost two hours to Dublin Airport. Of course, by then, Sean was long gone. Weeks afterwards, I heard he'd booked a one-way ticket to Australia. I haven't seen or heard from him since.'

Callum's exhales a slow thoughtful breath. 'Wow. Who does that to someone they love? And in a text message? The guy is obviously a complete dick.'

My sorry little secret's out. Callum knows everything. This agony aunt to the nation is the biggest fraud going. Clearly, no one should take my advice – I can't even sort my own life out, let alone anyone else's. It had been devastating at the time, but the worst part about the entire episode, I Hadn't Seen It Coming.

It's barely a dull ache now, rather than the soldering gaping wound that once consumed me. Shame and humiliation still ring through me, one of the reasons why I don't go home as much as I should. My sister barely speaks to me. When I left Carrick, I left behind everything that reminded me of Sean. For my own sanity, that included my family and friends. By the time I'd healed enough to reach out again, Alicia had moved on in her own life. I'd done what I had to, at the time, to survive. I hadn't meant to hurt anyone, I simply hadn't known what else to do. To this day, I can't even drive by The Landmark Hotel without feeling nauseous.

The psychotherapy degree helped me to process my thoughts differently, allowing me to feel them and deal with them, rather than harbour them while they silently fester away at my soul. But no matter how hard I try to convince myself that the problem lay with him and not me, I've never fully shaken the feeling I must have done something to drive him away for him to leave me like that.

Callum moves across the table to sit next to me, slipping an arm around my shoulder. I wonder if I should brush it away, then I realise that ship has long since sailed following our second explosive and unavoidable kiss.

'I'm so sorry,' I tell him.

'Why on earth are you apologising to me? I'm sorry he did

that to you. I'm sorry I can't drop-kick his sorry ass for you right now.'

I smile, picturing it.

'Seriously, Abby, you are one of the most amazing people I know. The guy's a fool. You're the entire package. Brains, beauty, heart and soul. I'm not just saying that because I'm trying to get into your knickers, by the way. Although I am actually hoping that's still a runner...' He winks at me.

Something in me begins to stir. I struggle to place an unfamiliar feeling descending. It comes to me then, like a flash of lightning – the possibility of hope. Callum's easy acceptance of my past offers a different perspective. He doesn't think it was my fault, and he's a guy. A gorgeous, successful, intelligent one at that.

'I'm not sorry that you aren't married, by the way.' Callum's intensity scorches me from the inside out.

'Me too.' I love how he brings it back to us.

He gazes at me with a newfound tenderness that I'm still adjusting to.

It's time I got my life back on track, my new life, the one in which I'm about to have filthy sex with Callum Connolly. I take out some lip gloss, generously reapply it, and fluff up my hair.

Sean's reappearance earlier forced me to admit the truth of my past to Callum, and because of this, our understanding has reached a whole new level. Sean had been my childhood sweetheart; we were getting married, our future was set in stone, yet it wasn't. Callum, on the other hand, has had more women than I've had hot dinners. Yet here he is, claiming to want something more for the first time. For some crazy reason, I'm inclined to trust him. There's an earnest vulnerability that he fails to fully conceal, no matter how arrogantly he acts.

I'm finally ready to move on, and Callum Connolly's the

man I'm going to move on with. My secret's out, I'm damaged goods, yet he still wants me. I refuse to fight my feelings any longer, though I can't promise I won't send him running for the hills or the nearest plane.

Callum finishes his drink and pulls me to my feet, enveloping me in a protective embrace. He leads me into the street outside and hails the next passing cab.

'My place or yours?' This time it's for real.

CHAPTER TWENTY-SIX

CALLUM

A nervous energy thrums through my veins as I insert the key into the lock of my penthouse apartment. As a rule, I never bring women here. It's violating another level of privacy. But Abby's not any woman.

She scans the place, wide-eyed, heading straight toward the open plan sitting room. Six enormous floor-to-ceiling panels of glass boast an exceptional view of the Liffey; the middle panel slides sideways onto a grey paved terrace. She unlocks the door and steps out into the rare Irish sun. 'This place is unreal.'

I creep up behind her and place my hands around her waist, revelling in the fact that I can. Resting my chin on her shoulder, I absorb the view with her. It's easy to take for granted. Seeing her unfiltered appreciation reminds me just how fabulous it is.

Are we really doing this? After everything, I have to pinch myself to check she's actually here. And now she is, I have to pray to fuck I don't get performance anxiety. It would be a first, but everything else has too when it comes to Abby.

'I didn't bring you through my front door for you to run straight out the back one,' I murmur into her ear. I wanted this woman since I first set eyes on her. Now that she's here, it's almost too good to be true.

She turns, pressing herself promisingly against me. Scratch that, I'm definitely not going to have a problem performing.

'I can feel your excitement.' She stares hotly into my eyes.

'The pounding of my heart, is it?' I'm certain that's not what she's referring to. I won't apologise for the effect she creates.

'Want to feel mine?' she offers, her fingers slowly trace her dress, where a zip runs lengthways down the middle of it. Outwardly she's confident, but earnest eyes hold a slight vulnerability.

'I think you already know the answer to that.' I lead her back through the glass doors by the hand. She lets out a squeal of surprise as I swoop her into my arms and carry her down the corridor to my bedroom.

I place her gently onto her back, enveloping her in the folds of the navy cotton bedspread. Balancing on my elbows, I pinch the zip of her denim dress between my fingers, searching the delicate features of her face for permission. She nods her consent. The subtle sound of metal releasing and the sight of her increasingly exposed cleavage is more stimulating than any aphrodisiac. I unzip her to the belly button, revealing a white lace bra, a tanned, toned tummy, and white panties that I can't wait to remove. She has me almost ready to blow, and she hasn't laid a finger on me.

Abby tugs me closer, silently pleading me with frantic kisses. Our tongues thrust relentlessly in and out, loaded with the promise of what's to come. I pull off my shirt and her hungry eyes linger on my half-exposed body.

'That dress would look better on my floor.' I barely recognise my voice, husky with desire.

She rises from the bed and discards her dress. Purposefully slowly, she unhooks her bra, allowing the straps to fall one by one, dropping it to the floor, baring what I've been longing to see. My greedy eyes drink her in. She is without a doubt the sexiest woman I've ever laid eyes on. She's driving me crazy, deliberately standing just out of my reach, running her hands lightly over herself teasingly, enjoying my obvious approval as I perch, shirtless and aroused in wait. I wet my lips in anticipation as she places one finger in the side of her waistband.

'Lose them.' I'm teetering on the edge, impatient for more.

I want to kiss every single bit of her body.

Abby drops her last stitch onto the floor, taking a step towards me, offering herself to me. My hands reach for her exposed breasts and I simultaneously dip my face to the most intimate parts of her. She arches her pelvis up to meet my tongue. It takes less than three minutes for her to come undone, pulling my hair with her trembling fingers. She falls to her knees in front of me and reaches purposefully for my buckle.

'Do you have any idea what you're doing to me?' I already know she's going to be the best I've ever had. The most intimate encounters are the ones that have been exchanged in the eyes a hundred times before.

'I haven't even started yet.' Abby lowers her head and takes me into her mouth. I groan with pleasure. Within a minute, I hoist her up onto my lap, into a sitting position and pull her legs around my waist.

'I need to feel you on me.' My voice is guttural, overflowing with need.

She allows the tip of me to rest at her entrance, as she stares into my eyes with a burning intensity.

'Do we need something?' she asks as she pushes forward enough for me to penetrate her a single inch. My eyes roll back into my head.

'I always have done before,' I tell her truthfully.

'In that case, we don't. I'm on the pill.' Another demonstration of our newfound trust.

She inches herself further on top, allowing me complete access to the deepest parts of her. My hands grip her backside firmly, fingers gently digging into her skin, guiding her to a slow, grinding rhythm.

'I won't last long,' I warn her.

'Neither will I,' she whispers into my ear. I kiss the lust sheened skin of her neck and move my hand to her nipple to tease. The pace increases, along with the pressure and we both explode in an inevitable climax within a matter of minutes.

CHAPTER TWENTY-SEVEN

ABBY

We spend the rest of the afternoon in bed, getting to know each other intimately several times. Callum collapses back onto the pillows and pulls me gently down to rest on his chest, enveloping me in the security of his strong arms. My lips taste the sweat from his dewy supple skin, and I listen to the comforting pounding of his heart. Planting a tender kiss on my forehead, he exhales a low whistle.

'Abby Queenan, you might be the death of me yet.' I hear his smile, though I can't see his face.

A brief flash of Esmeralda's words about losing someone close to me flits nauseatingly through my mind, followed closely by a reminder that this fabulous man also isn't called Patrick. It's a good job I don't believe in her ridiculous notions. It doesn't sit well that she had been right on the work opportunity prediction, but it was a fluke. It had to be.

'You okay?' Callum mistakes my prolonged silence as regret.

'Never been better,' I assure him.

'You hungry?

'Actually, I am. Shall we order take out?'

'I'll get some menus from the kitchen.'

We order sushi and sit on the couch with it, half watching *The Snapper* on RTE. It was an eventful day, in more ways than one. I contemplate hitting the road. The walk of shame to the radio station in the morning's not an option I'm prepared to consider.

'You're not going already, are you?' Callum asks in surprise, from his position next to me.

'I've been here all afternoon. I should give you a bit of space. Or do you normally keep a woman around the place for your pleasure any time you feel like a bit?' I ask curiously.

'Do you want to know the truth?' Those beguiling blue eyes pull shamelessly at my fragile heartstrings.

I don't relish the thought of the skinny models before me, but there's no point avoiding the issue either. All I'd have to do is type his name into Google and see multicoloured images that would be forever imprinted on my mind.

'Go on then.' I readjust my bra strap.

'There have been a lot of women. You wouldn't have to do a lot of digging to see for yourself.' He's not proud. 'But I didn't have any real feelings for them.' An earnest intensity transfers in his stare.

'None of them came to my home. I never let anyone in before.' He's no longer merely talking about his apartment.

'Why not?' I'm desperate to glimpse behind the carefully construed wall.

'I didn't trust them not to use me.' He shrugs.

'So you used them instead?' I'm missing something here, but what, I have no idea.

'Yes and no. I never lied to anyone. I never led anyone on.'

I'm flattered that he considers me different. But where do his trust issues originate? Why wouldn't he let anyone in? He trusted them with his body, but not with his heart. With my background in psychotherapy, I can't sit with it until I understand his trigger. Especially because now I've crossed the threshold, I'm conscious of doing something, even by chance, that might drive him away.

'Did you never want to settle down?' I probe carefully.

'Honestly? It didn't occur to me, not until lately anyway,' he admits.

I will him to expand. I laid myself bare to him today, both emotionally and physically. I need him to do the same for me. It's a big ask, but if he does, it could be the start of something meaningful between us.

He takes a sip from a glass of water positioned on the coffee table next to him, trying to summon the right words.

'When I was seven, my mum left us,' he begins quietly.

Immediately the pieces fall into place. It makes perfect sense. He experienced his own version of a broken heart, delivered by the only woman in the world that he didn't expect it from. Not only did he lose his mother, but presumably, he would have been raised with only his father's masculine role. A role which mightn't have been the most objective when it came to women, if his wife walked out and left him.

'I'm so sorry, Callum. I had no idea.' I stroke the back of his hand sympathetically.

'How could you have? We deliberately kept it out of the papers.' He sighs, as he remembers.

'Have you heard from her since?' I wonder aloud. He laughs bitterly in response.

'When I say she left us, I mean she left this world.' Pain inches onto his face, even years later. 'She took her own life. My younger brother, Mark, was two. Maybe it was a breed of postnatal depression. People didn't talk about that stuff back then.'

The final piece of the jigsaw slips into place; that he's an

Ambassador for Pieta House. Is it any wonder he's nervous of becoming emotionally involved with a woman?

I curl up into his lap, rest my knees against his chest and run my fingers through his hair.

'I'm so sorry. I can't even imagine what you went through. It makes my past woes seem laughable in comparison.' I trace the tiny scars on his face with the knowledge that the deepest cuts are on the inside.

'We all have our crosses to bear.' He kisses me on the mouth, signalling the end of this particular conversation.

Suddenly doing the walk of shame doesn't seem like the worst thing in the world. I can't leave him after this revelation.

'Do you want me to stay the night?' I offer.

'Yes.'

'I can't go to work in the morning in these clothes or I'll never live it down.'

'I'll drop you home first thing. I'm training at ten o'clock,' he offers.

'Perfect. Don't go chatting up any blondes in the spa,' I warn him.

'I wouldn't dream of it. I've got enough work cut out for me here.' He winks suggestively.

'Coach won't be happy when you have no energy left for the pitch.'

'He'll get over it.' Callum lifts me off the couch and carries me through to his bedroom for the second time today.

My body doesn't know what hit it. Nothing for years, then four times in one day. My muscles ache from trembling under Callum's touch.

Afterwards, I lie in his arms, my newly established safe haven and current favourite place in the entire universe. 'Do you mind if I take a bath?'

'Help yourself.' He nods towards his en suite. 'Want me to run it for you?' he offers, glancing down sleepily.

'No. You stay there.' His heavy eyes fight to stay open.

I creep into the bathroom, turn on the taps and smear a pea-sized helping of Sensodyne on to his toothbrush to clean my teeth. We'd exchanged a hell of a lot more than saliva today.

CHAPTER TWENTY-EIGHT

CALLUM

I watch Abby walk safely through her front door before reversing out of her driveway. She's infiltrated all of my carefully assembled defence mechanisms, and I invited her to do so, willingly.

I drive to Carton House consumed only with thoughts of her. The last twenty-four hours were eventful. I wouldn't change a second of it, apart from her dickhead ex phoning into the station. But perhaps if he hadn't called, she mightn't have confided in me about her past. And neither would I.

The outside temperatures are cooler than yesterday, but intermittent blue skies make for pleasant training conditions. The lads are on the track, already warming up with some laps.

'If it isn't Ireland's one and only agony uncle,' Marcus bellows loudly, and the others offer a mock round of applause.

I'd completely forgotten about the show, consumed only with thoughts of all that occurred afterwards. I'm about to get slaughtered, but it was worth every second.

'Testing out my radio voice in case this fucking cruciate

goes again,' I joke, but the truth of the situation occurs to me as the words escape my mouth.

'You've got it bad, man,' James says in a knowing tone. He approaches me from behind as I pull my kit out of my bag. 'Remind us how it went again... When you find the right one, you'll bring her to meet your teammates...'

'You nailed her, bro, didn't you? No woman could have resisted that,' Eddie says, frothing at the mouth, like a stray dog begging for the scraps. 'She is one serious piece of ass. I'm dying to hear how that went.'

'You will die before you get any details from me,' I warn him with a not so light thump on the arm. Abby's mine. I will not be sharing any private info with him or anyone else today, or any other day.

'He's got it bad,' James repeats, confirming what I already know. 'Marcus, I think your Audi is gone for good.'

'I couldn't give a fuck about your Audi, Marcus. In fact, I want you to keep it. Abby means so much more than a stupid bet. I think I've proved enough at this stage, don't you?' I tell him in all seriousness. 'You guys were right,' I admit, as I remove my hoody. 'I think I've finally found the perfect combination of ingredients.' I grin sheepishly as the words tumble out.

'Fucking hell, we never thought we'd see the day.' Marcus's shoulders visibly relax in open relief, no longer concerned about parting with his precious Q7. His family orientated streak also approves of my new relationship status. In his eyes, having a good woman made you more of a man. He might be right. Abby seems to bring out the best in me. She brings out the caveman in me. I want to protect her, cherish her and make sure nobody else gets near her. I want her all for myself.

'It's early days, but if last night's anything to go by, its fucking promising,' I admit.

These guys have seen me at my best, at my worst, and everything in between, over the trials and triumphs of our careers. My feelings for Abby are not something I could hide from them.

Coach blows the whistle and yells at us to break up the party. I'm dying to ask their opinions on the ex, but it'll have to wait.

CHAPTER TWENTY-NINE

ABBY

Candice and Aoife are desperate for details. I remind Candice that she's a lesbian and not remotely interested in the specifics of Callum Connolly's anatomy. Suffice to say, I can't wait to see it again. Her black T-shirt today reads Dyknamite in pink tiny sequins.

'I bear gifts,' Candice squeals, popping a bottle of Bollinger. 'Yesterday's show received the highest ratings of the decade. Pack your bags, girls, you're going to New York.'

'The competition doesn't end for another six weeks.' Aoife voices my exact thoughts.

'Pah.' Candice swats a hand in front of her face. 'No one will be able to come close to that, trust me.' She fills three paper coffee cups with a generous helping of bubbles. Aoife raises her eyebrows and puts hers to one side. I sink mine in three mouthfuls, celebrating my own personal achievement yesterday, wildly different to the one that Candice's celebrating.

The tech team screen my calls carefully today. The last

thing I need is another blast from the past. Now that I'm away from Callum's reassuring side, my thoughts return to Sean. His phone call doesn't mean he's home, but it shook me, nonetheless. Why now? What does he want?

Today's topic is Dating Apps & Social Media, specifically the way that social media and online dating sites influence how we approach the opposite sex nowadays.

Candice pops her head into the studio just as I'm winding up for the day. 'Abby, come to my office before you go.'

'Sure.' Normally anything she had to say would have been shared in front of Aoife. After the champagne first thing, it's hard to imagine bad news, yet a wiggling worm of worry warns it's not good. I wonder if she's pissed about Sean ringing? Maybe unwittingly I said something inappropriate today? I rack my brain unsuccessfully for an answer, but I can't think of a single thing I've done that might have annoyed her.

I pat my hair into place and knock on her office door. Candice's on the phone. She rolls her eyes in exasperation but motions for me to sit.

'Abby.' She places the receiver down.

'Is everything ok? The plan worked yesterday. We blew Sally No Soul out of the water.' I'm justifying myself pre-emptively.

'It worked exceptionally well,' she muses, kicking her feet up onto the desk. Her black biker boots rest on a pile of messy paperwork in front of her. 'I want to offer Callum a permanent position on the show.'

'You want him to replace me?' Of all the possibilities, I hadn't considered that one.

'I want him to co-host with you. You two have the most fantastic chemistry on air. And off the air, apparently.' She chews the tip of her biro, gauging my reaction.

Over the past eighteen months, we've discussed the potential for a co-host. Aoife's turned the official role down twice. Until now, I assumed we were looking for another woman. But Callum changed everything yesterday. He's a natural. And the frisson between us is palpable. But would it work long term? What if things don't work out between us, and I'm forced to look at him every day of the week? It's a brilliant idea, but I'm not sure I'm ready for him to permanently infiltrate my workspace as well as my heart and body.

'Do I get a say in the matter?' Shock vibrates through my shaky fingers. This is not how I envisioned things progressing.

'Of course. It's your show. But after yesterday, you'd be mad not to consider it.' Her head angles to the left as she weighs up my reaction.

'He couldn't commit, not with the rugby.' I'm not trying to put her off. It's a fact.

'Ask him how his cruciate is, and if he has any plans for his retirement.'

'Retirement? He's thirty-three.'

'Take it from a rugby fan, he's fast approaching the end of his career. Ireland Today's offering another option, one with generous benefits. Think about it,' she says.

I open the door to leave.

'Abby, be careful. You know his reputation with the ladies. I'd hate to see you get hurt.' She's only voicing what I already know, so why does it make me so anxious?

CHAPTER THIRTY

CALLUM

The three nights training at Carton House feels like a life sentence away from Abby.

I trawl the internet for agencies providing qualified carers that might be helpful in the search for increased help for Dad. So far, I have whittled down a list of four potential candidates to run by Brian.

'If it isn't Romeo the rugby player,' he answers my call cockily.

'Funny fucker, aren't you? All everyone wants is for me to settle down, then when I try, the piss-taking starts.'

'I honestly never thought I'd see the day. I loved the grand gesture live on the radio. Melissa nearly died when she heard it. After all the hearts you broke along the way, she finally thinks you might have found your own.' A low chuckle rumbles from the phone.

'Do me a favour, when you meet Abby, get Melissa to keep that small piece of information to herself.'

'When we meet her... Now that sounds promising.'

'It's inevitable at some stage.' I hope he won't do his big brother act and shame me.

I relay the information I gathered from the potential carers, and we agree to sleep on it. Both of us would prefer live-in care for Dad, but there's no way he'll agree to it at this stage.

In the last week, Brian and I seem to have forged some sort of common ground. After years of resentment and awkwardness, things appear to be evening out. It's as if he's taking me seriously these days.

Is his lukewarm approval because I turned to him with my feelings for Abby?

Or do I simply seek less approval now that I have Abby? Either way, I don't feel the negativity he usually emanates.

She's rubbing off on me. I'm even starting to think like a shrink. I'm changing, evolving. Is this what growing up feels like? At the age of thirty-three – maybe Brian had a point, it's time.

A new email pings as I'm about to shut my iMac. It's from a guy called Declan that James introduced me to a couple of years earlier. We call him our fixer, he researches things for us; products, services, people. He's sourced some information on a property investment that James and I are considering in Spain and attached a list of everyone involved in the deal and

everything about them, including what they had for breakfast yesterday. He's good.

As I skim through his message, an idea occurs to me. I run a hand over yesterday's stubble as I contemplate it.

The reappearance of Abby's ex isn't sitting well with me. After four years of nothing, why has he re-emerged the second there's a photo of her in the paper with me? Does he simply want her back? Or is he looking for something more? Why did he leave in the first place? Who jumps the country the night before their wedding? Was he running from something? Or someone? I can't let it go until I know. It feels like a loose cannon waiting to blow.

Before I can overthink it, I compose an email asking Declan to investigate where the mysterious Mr Fitzpatrick has been for the previous four years and why he's returned now. I hope Abby won't mind. It's for her benefit as well as mine. What she doesn't know won't hurt her.

I close the laptop and wait.

CHAPTER THIRTY-ONE

ABBY

Twice this week, I arranged to meet Karen for a late lunch, to check up on her after her revelation. Twice, she cancelled on me at the last minute. I get the distinct impression she's avoiding me. It's not like her.

In contrast, I've spoken to Callum every day, both of us desperate to hang on to the bridge that we forged, fearing the other might slip back to the familiarity of the masks that are easier to shelter behind.

It took a lot to admit our truths. For me, it was a relief to voice them. By hiding behind my fear, I've been holding on to it. I'm lighter than I've been in years. The last person in the world that I would have expected to attribute that to is Callum Connolly. Yet his vulnerability mirrored my own. In sharing it, we're united by more than just lust. This has promising potential for the other L-word...though it's far too early to speculate yet.

A bouquet of a hundred roses arrives at the studio with

my name on the label. The only thing missing is an accompanying note.

'Not exactly original,' Sally sneers as I pass her in the corridor on my way out.

Regardless of my escalating feelings for Callum, I'm unconvinced about his role on my show, on a permanent basis. Candice reckons Sally No Soul is pulling out all the stops to up her ratings, to win the competition for the trip to New York. Amazingly, only a short time ago, it seemed like the most important thing in the world. Now, since the start of my new unpredicted relationship with Callum, I've barely given it another thought.

Sally's enticing listeners with daily competitions, gig tickets, prize money and a live slot to meet the team and co-host her show. I admire her determination. The other presenters have more or less given up after Callum stole the show on Monday. He received the highest ratings of any show to date. It's going to be almost impossible to beat.

I text Karen checking if she's ok before heading out for a long run. The afternoon's balmy in Dublin. The good weather promises to hold for the next few days at least. It'll break soon though. It always does in Ireland.

The commuter rush has begun. Traffic's backed up around the city; hurrying feet pound the pavements. I opt for a familiar route around Phoenix Park. It's only been a week since the Pieta House fundraiser, yet everything has changed.

Images of Callum's perfectly toned physique invade my mind as I loop back on myself past a yoga-in-the-park session. I'm desperate to feel his arms around me again. Mentally, I scan my wardrobe for an outfit for our date tonight. It helps pass the time while my legs do the hard work. I finish back where I parked at the entrance to Dublin Zoo, and stretch my hamstring, leaning on my red Mini for support.

Tiny hairs prickle abruptly on the back of my neck. Despite the pleasant weather, a cold shudder rips through my core. I have a weird, uncomfortable sensation someone's watching me. I glance around the vicinity. Several cars down from mine, a figure rests casually against the bonnet of a black Golf.

It looks suspiciously like someone I used to know. The lean frame distinctly familiar, but the full identity protected by a baseball cap and retro-looking sunglasses. Rugged stubble disguises the lower half of his face. He turns away as I notice him. I fumble, inserting the key onto the dash and nudge the car into the swarm of Friday afternoon traffic, sweaty legs sticking distastefully to the leather interior. I don't look back until I'm safely out of the car park. I don't want to confirm what I already know. Sean Fitzpatrick's back in Ireland. In Dublin, no less. And he's watching me.

Only when I reach the security of my own front door does my hammering heart slow. What does he want after all this time? And why does the thought of seeing him terrify the living daylights out of me?

I busy myself with a shower and attempt to push all thoughts of him out of my mind.

An hour later, Callum arrives in his grey Jeep. I fling open the front door before he has the chance to even step out of his vehicle. The mere sight of him sets unruly butterflies wild within me once again.

Callum is visual Viagra for women. A slow smile spreads across my face as his long, powerful legs swing out from the driver's seat. He pushes his Ray-Bans onto his head to get a closer look at me.

'Do you want to leave the house at all tonight?' He eyes my black low-cut dress appreciatively and strolls confidently up the tiny narrow path to where I'm barefoot on the top step.

The curtains next door twitch again. I'm fairly sure Mrs Boyle is copping an eyeful of absolutely every exchange between us. Nosy neighbours are something I'd hoped to leave in Carrick, though God love her, she always takes my parcels for me.

Callum presses his full lips against mine, searing me with dizzying intensity. We back into the hallway and slam the door without breaking our kiss. Considering I'd only recently allowed him into my life, it's been a long few days without him.

He lifts me into his muscular arms, effortlessly wrapping my legs around his waist. Supporting the nape of my neck with a reassuring hand, he leans me gently against the wall, moulding my figure to his, our tongues dancing an explicit tango.

My strawberry lip gloss sticks sweetly over his mouth. I imagine covering the rest of him in it, but he breaks away, gazing wistfully into my eyes. Raw, unfiltered desire ebbs at me and the reflection in his prolonged stare reassures me it's mutual. Earnest eyes bare his soul. How had I failed to realise the heart-swelling depth to this man until only a week ago? He can hide behind his reputation and those Ray-Bans no more.

'We're late,' he groans.

'Where exactly are we going?' I smooth down my dress and attempt to regulate my erratic heart.

'Marcus's house,' he says.

'Marcus the Barbarian?' I check.

'The very same.' He chuckles and kisses the back of my hand, interlocking his fingers with mine. 'He's actually a great guy, if a little brash. They host a party every summer before the league starts again.'

He looks at me like I should know what he's talking about.

'You know most of us play provincial rugby as well?' he checks.

'Of course.' I had a vague idea.

'The friendlies start again at the end of August. We'll be travelling a lot.' He runs a finger over my bare shoulder, eyeing my cleavage like he might eat it.

'Right.'

Is he telling me that he won't be around? Letting me down gently already? The niggle of doubt is always the first to rise. I push it forcefully away, reminding myself that Callum is not Sean.

'I'll be expecting you to be screaming for me with the other WAGs. You can rub my injuries better after each game.' His suggestive tone soothes my insecurities, a tidal wave of sweet relief.

I made an agreement with myself to move on, to trust Callum. Yet my thoughts revert to him leaving me already.

Callum glances at the roses on the hall table and tilts his head.

'Someone has an admirer. Should I be concerned?' he jokes, but there's an underlying question in his tone.

'Very funny, Callum. I meant to thank you. It slipped my mind when you slipped your tongue in my mouth.' I swoon outwardly again, melting at the thought of his hot mouth.

'As much as I probably should have sent you flowers this week, they're not from me.' A frown forms on his tanned face.

'Did you pack a bag?' he changes the subject. We have an unspoken agreement: to be entwined in every way possible for the next forty-eight hours.

'Did you want me to?' I tease, wanting to hear it from his lust-driven lips now that he stands merely a foot in front of me.

'Well, you're coming home with me tonight. I don't care if

you have nothing to wear tomorrow. In fact, I might even prefer it that way.' His eyes glint mischievously as he traces a finger from my cheek, along my neck and cups my breasts seductively.

'If you want to leave this house any time soon, I suggest you stop that immediately. Because I don't care if I never make it to Marcus's,' I warn him throatily.

Callum carries my weekend bag to the boot of his car and opens the passenger door for me.

'Such a gentleman,' I observe.

'What can I say? You bring out the best in me.' He slips into the driver's seat and places a hand firmly on my exposed thigh as he exits my driveway.

CHAPTER THIRTY-TWO

CALLUM

Waitresses slip discreetly round the garden, topping up champagne glasses and distributing canapes. Someone has gone to great effort decorating the garden with glass lanterns and white fairy lights. It must have been Shelly, Marcus doesn't give a shite about the frills and flowers. She has an interior design business that's doing very well by all accounts.

Twilight hovers closely around. It's very *Midsummer Night's Dream*. George Ezra resonates from an iPod on the decking area, as the smell of burning logs rises from a glowing fire pit. It's a serious house. Classy, but homey.

Abby's at the makeshift bar with the other WAGs. I admire her slender figure from behind in that indecent, yet casual, dress. Nadine and Shelly erupt with laughter as she says something apparently hilarious.

I've cracked her outer shell, witnessing her secret softness within. Her newly exposed, trusting vulnerability is like nothing I've experienced before. She's given me so much more than her body this week and I'm determined to prove worthy of it.

She leans promisingly in to me as I approach, her face flushed with lust or the free-flowing champagne. An overwhelming urge to break her out of here overcomes me, a primal need to have her all to myself. But if we leave before the dancing starts, I'll never hear the end of it. Mind you, if we don't leave now, I'm likely to punch Eddie in the face. He's not even trying to keep his beady eyes from her. The sooner he gets his own woman, the better.

A quick flashback to those roses sitting on her table momentarily pisses me off again, and I force all thoughts of them from my mind.

'You having a good time?' I whisper into her ear.

'Yes. They're a great gang.'

Abby angles her face towards mine, willing me to kiss her. I don't need an excuse to put my lips on hers again, enthralled at another public opportunity to claim her as my own. I tug her light frame closer to me and drop a kiss onto her luscious mouth, marking my territory to Eddie in the process.

'Get a fucking room, will you?' Eddie unknowingly voices my thoughts with disgust, which likely stems from the fact that he's lost his last wingman, rather than him witnessing a minor PDA.

She disentangles herself from me and asks. 'Which way is the bathroom?'

'I'll show you.' A sense of an impending opportunity stirs within. I accompany her through the garden toward the main house. Curious eyes follow us. I don't care.

I lead her through the patio door into the downstairs bathroom. It's the size of a bedroom, with a free-standing bath in the centre of the cream marble floor. I flick on the low lamp over the mirror, close the heavy walnut door and lock it firmly behind us.

'Can I help you?'

'Maybe I can help you.' I lick my lips, contemplating where to begin. I want to be the only one who can unlock every part of her, the only man with that specific key. 'I couldn't kick the ball straight all week for thinking about you.'

I kiss the side of her neck and run my tongue the length of her chest and lick her bare skin, reaching inside her bra. Her muffled moans are lost against my shoulder.

I trace a finger up the inside of her thigh and locate a flimsy scrap of material, barely concealing the very part of her that I long to touch. Pushing the fabric to the side, I find her desire parallels my own. She gasps as I stroke the most sensitive parts of her. I love how she gives herself so openly to me, how her legs weaken in response to my touch.

'You like that?' I whisper in her ear.

'You know I do.' Hot eyes plead with mine, her black pupils dilating as she reaches for my jeans.

'Not here.' She deserves so much better than a quick fuck in Marcus's bathroom. And she's going to get it, once we get home. I kiss her firmly on the mouth, basking in the lusty way she stares at me.

'You're driving me crazy. I need to feel you,' she pleads.

It's so much more than sex. It's the newly unlocked intimacy that we'd both been missing that we crave. And we won't satisfy that in here.

I plant another kiss on her full lips. My feelings are off-the-scale intense. Instead of feeling alarmed, it's as sexy as hell. We bid good night to the gang, fighting protests that it's too early to go. The real party is in my apartment, it's obvious to all.

'Careful, Callum. You're like a man in love,' James says lowly, as he fist pumps me goodnight.

I grin back at him. I'd never understood my best friend as

much as I do now. The way he put Nadine before our friendship used to irritate the fuck out of me. But now, I'm beginning to get it.

'Let's renegotiate the bet.' Marcus rubs his hands together thoughtfully. He's clearly learnt nothing from the last bet he tried to make with me. 'If you marry her, I'll give you the Audi as a wedding present.'

I already told him I don't give a flying fuck about his car, or any of his worldly possessions for that matter.

'Keep your fucking Audi. The only thing I'm interested in driving, is that woman over there,' I tell him quietly, nodding at Abby as she bids goodnight to the women.

'But I fully expect you to donate that 50k to Pieta House,' I remind him.

Half an hour later, Abby perches on my granite worktop a couple of feet away from me. I open the bottle I bought her, an image of licking champagne from her belly button at the forefront of my mind. She smiles at me as the loud popping of the cork breaks the loaded silence.

'I missed you this week.' I clink my crystal flute against hers.

'Are you getting soft on me, Callum?' Her eyes twinkle with mischief.

'Not everywhere.' I place my hands on her smooth tanned thighs. She pulls me between them. I grip her waist and stare at her soft red lips, any trace of lipstick long since kissed off. Chocolate brown eyes sparkle suggestively at me. She has me eating out of the palm of her hand. Only a couple of weeks ago, I would have refused to believe that any woman could have this effect on me.

Abby places her drink on the counter beside us. Slow hands deliberately tease my jeans open. I stand before her, allowing her to take the lead. She frees me and a low moan escapes my lips. She's beginning to realise the power she wields over me. Surprisingly, I trust her with it, somehow knowing she's not the kind of woman to use it against me. She's way too classy for that. And she has a heart the size of the country.

She shimmies forward, inching closer to me, offering a full view of everything I spent the week fantasising about touching. She senses my hands about to home in and places them back either side of me, it's sexy as hell.

'You like that?' She takes me in her hands, mimicking the exact words I used on her earlier. It's payback time, apparently. I'll explode if she isn't careful.

'I need you.' It's blinding. I can't see straight for lust.

I can't take it. My hands slide under her dress pulling her towards me, closing the distance between us. With her back pressed against the granite, she slides on to me, slick with excitement. A tenderness in her eyes touches my soul. She doesn't kiss me, it's far more intimate than that. With our eyes locked together, bound by our united hunger, we examine one another's pleasure, sharing every tender fleeting emotion that passes between us.

It's a whole new level of intimacy. There's nothing I won't do for this woman.

CHAPTER THIRTY-THREE

ABBY

However good it feels going to bed with Callum Connolly, waking up in his arms is equally fulfilling. Today's papers headlined, Does Callum Connolly Have Another 'Injury'? One More Limiting Than His Cruciate? My headshot from the radio website stares back at me from the second page .

He reads the article over my left shoulder. The delicious aroma of pancakes and sickly sweet syrup lingers in the air. I perch on a leather stool at the breakfast bar with a strong black coffee in front of me. Callum chuckles into my ear.

'I wouldn't exactly call you an 'injury',' he muses.

Though we're both aware there's the potential for casualties along the way, we can only trust one another not to inflict them.

'What are your plans for today?' I glance casually at him, not making any assumptions.

'You mean, what are *our plans* for the day?' he corrects me with a raised eyebrow.

'Do you think I've nothing better to be doing than

hanging round here having sex with you, Callum Connolly?' I smirk.

We're both fully aware that neither of us has anything else to do that could remotely compete.

'I know you don't.' The arrogance which initially infuriated me has even become sexy.

'I need to call in on my dad at some point. Do you want to come?'

I take a sip of my coffee to mask my surprise. Bringing me home to his family takes our relationship to a whole new level. Though technically I've already met his dad at the fundraiser, so maybe it isn't such a big deal. The prospect of unravelling another dimension of him is an offer I can't turn down.

'I'd love to.' I mean it.

Callum drives us through the city in the direction of Dun Laoghaire. The temperature on the dashboard reads nineteen degrees, though it's currently cloudy. The weather report on iRadio promises sunshine by the afternoon. Automatically I change the radio station, re-tuning Callum's Jeep to Ireland Today with a meaningful glare. He laughs and shrugs.

'That's like me coming to your game and cheering for the other team,' I huff in jest.

'Don't even think about it.' It's an effective analogy. I'm pretty sure I'll never have to change his radio station again.

'I didn't realise you grew up in Dun Laoghaire.'

'I try not to spend too much time here.' He reaches for my hand, kissing it lightly as he concentrates on the traffic.

It never ceases to amaze me how the psyche of men and women differs so much. If it were me, I'd probably never leave, desperate to relive the memories of my mother. Then again, I shouldn't judge. I barely visit my own since I left.

We park on the main street outside a row of three-story Victorian terraced houses directly overlooking the sea. His usual humour is absent. Taking my hand, he leads me to the last house in the row. A white recycled-plastic picket fence surrounds the overgrown garden and a stone-paved path leads the way to a red front door.

'This garden needs attention,' he says.

Callum knocks on the door lightly and his Aunty Linda opens it with a smile. Her red curly hair is pinned up on her head, and she wears a rainbow printed pinafore, dusted in flour.

Knocking on his own family's front door is clearly for my benefit. He's afraid of what we might walk in on.

'Callum. We weren't sure if you'd make it over this week.' A surprised smile crinkles on Linda's face, instantly giving her a more youthful appearance.

'How is he today?' Callum asks conspicuously.

'He's the right side of the soil, anyway.' She laughs at her own joke and leads us through a dark corridor. The walls are painted a similar shade of grey to Callum's place. White skirting boards contrast dark wooden floors. The place is beautifully restored and very well kept, especially considering it's the home of a single elderly man. Callum lingers for a second at the bottom of the staircase, and Linda tugs his arm as if to hurry him on.

'How are you, Abby? You're still suffering him, I see,' she says with a knowing smile.

'Someone has to.' The only suffering I have is if an hour passes by without me getting my hands on Callum's body. But the poor woman doesn't require the details.

I absorb my surroundings as the pieces of Callum's childhood slot into place. The absence of any childhood photos speaks volumes. Callum's father sits in the kitchen at a mahogany table, today's papers open alongside a cup of milky tea.

'Callum.' Jimmy stands shakily to greet him, his delight

obvious. He throws his arms around Callum, who stands somewhat stiffly in front of him. For a man that demonstrates such tenderness toward me, his reaction to his father surprises me. Does he blame him for the death of his mother? Or does he keep him at arm's length in case he leaves too? There goes my natural psychoanalysis again. The ins and outs of their relationship are none of my business.

'And you remember Abby?' Linda prompts him with a reassuring nod.

'Sit down.' Linda pulls out a chair next to Callum's father, and I sit without hesitation.

'You'll have tea.' It isn't a question.

Linda takes down another two cups from the cupboard and pours tea for everyone from a steaming hot pot on the Aga. The traditional kitchen has high ceilings and sash windows, but it's dark, even gloomy in places.

Callum's father enquires about the rugby. I slip in and out of the conversation, noticing that Callum can't relax. There's a tension in this house that I can't fathom. Like we are all waiting for something, but I'm not sure what.

An hour later, following three refills of Barry's tea, Callum asks if I mind if he does an hour's work in the garden.

'Belt away. I'm absolutely fine,' I assure him.

'You can come out with me if you like? Or you could walk the East Pier if you prefer?' he suggests.

'She's perfectly fine where she is. And you're right, that garden does need a bit of TLC.' Linda refills the teapot again and touches my arm affectionately. It occurs to me that if he didn't let a woman into his apartment, he probably never brought one home before, either. They're as curious about me as I am about them.

'I won't be long.' He shoots Linda a warning look and opens the back door in search of gardening tools. The door bangs hard behind him as the wind from an open window flies through the house, rattling the panes of glass.

'Do you bake?' Linda asks me.

'I try.' I love baking, but usually avoid it, I have a tendency to eat the entire batch of whatever I make.

Linda pulls out flour, raisins and butter and begins kneading dough for scones. I stand to help her. She offers me a sideways smile and some ingredients, and we work side by side. Callum's father watches with a wistful smile. He's present but displays minimal signs of presence.

'She always wanted a daughter,' Jimmy says. I'm unsure if he's referring to Linda or to his late wife. He doesn't elaborate.

Linda looks at least fifteen years younger than her brother. I ask about other siblings and listen quietly as the two of them regale stories of their brothers and sisters and a childhood home a stone's throw away from here. Callum's father bounces off his younger sister, who has what can only be described as a very Irish sense of humour. The insults roll from her tongue in a hilarious yet endearing manner. I'm left under no illusion that these two are not only siblings, but great friends as well. She has a super knack of bringing him back to the present with humour.

'Our Jimmy here used to be a swimwear model, Abby. Bet Callum didn't tell you that, did he?' Linda nudges me and winks at Jimmy who rolls his eyes to the ceiling.

'It was entirely by accident.' He recalls the memory instantaneously. 'I was on the beach and they happened to be taking photos of some rare passing naval ship. It was just by chance they caught me in the image in my Speedos. There was no such thing as swimming shorts in those days. Of course, it was all over the front page of *The Irish Times*. No such thing as Photoshop then.' He chuckles deeply, crinkled eyelids creasing at the memory.

Callum returns from the garden an hour later, as promised, hot and sweaty. His nostrils flare in appreciation of Linda's baking, and he helps himself to a pint glass and some water.

'Hope you're all having a nice relaxing time in here while I'm breaking my balls out there' he says with a smile.

He's testing me, whether he knows it or not is another thing. He deliberately left me with his family to see how I'd manage. He should know me better than that. I'd talk to the wall. I'm used to mostly talking to thin air – though the entire country may actually be listening, they don't ever immediately reply.

An hour runs into two as we sit once again around the table, buttering the scones and drinking fresh cups of tea. I'm worlds away from my usual Saturday park run, but I wouldn't be anywhere else. Callum eventually relaxes, apparently reassured that his family are no more embarrassing than anyone else's. Wait until I throw him into the deep in with my mad lot, then he'll know about embarrassing.

'We better head back.' Callum pushes his chair back to leave, clutching his empty mug in his right hand.

'Don't go yet,' Jimmy urges.

Callum winces in apprehension of what his father is about to say, but he doesn't try and stop him.

'Your mammy will be home any second and she'd love to see you,' Jimmy announces with such certainty that it breaks my own heart, never mind Callum's. Another piece of the puzzle slips into place.

Callum crosses the room to reach him. 'Mam's gone, Dad, remember?' Callum speaks slowly and softly. Confusion flickers, deepening the creases of Jimmy's face for a few short seconds before he begins to sob, huge heartfelt tears.

I look away, an intruder violating such a private moment. Linda puts an arm around both of them, and I wash and dry our plates, the silence broken only by the muffled sobs of Callum's father as he's reminded of the cruel world we live in.

As they bid us goodbye from the doorway, Callum promises to visit one evening during the week. Linda sends us home with a bag full of scones and urges me to call again anytime.

Callum negotiates the Jeep out on to the road, his knuckles white as he clenches the leather steering wheel and sighs heavily.

'I'm sorry about that.' He rests a hand lightly on my knee as we stop at a red light.

'Don't be. I'm so sorry for all of you. It must be so hard when you have to keep reminding him.'

'It doesn't get any easier,' he acknowledges.

The afternoon sun emerges from behind the clouds.

'Are you in a rush back?' I look longingly out at the East Pier, the seagulls soaring overhead.

'No.' He slows the car.

He parks outside the library and we set off hand in hand, strolling the entire length of Scotsman's Bay, pausing only to look in the amusements before heading on towards People's Park. The hazy sunshine toasts our skin and the familiar scent of sun cream lingers in the air around us.

'My older brother mostly raised us,' Callum opens up as we walk.

'I didn't realise.'

'Brian's the polar opposite of me. He settled with his college girlfriend, became a teacher, got married, had a family. Brian's life is so clean-cut, so straight forward. He has a knack of making everything look so simple. I'm sure all he had to do was hang his trousers on the end of his bed and Melissa was instantly impregnated. He doesn't approve of me, no matter what I do.' Callum's pace slows as he stares thoughtfully at the powerful crashing waves of the Irish Sea.

'Did you ever consider that maybe it's himself he doesn't approve of? It must be hard being the brother of a professional athlete. Even the best-natured people might find it hard to measure up. Often traits that we don't like in a person are actually a reflection of something we see in ourselves.'

'Ha. No. I think he resents me and Mark. Because Brian's the oldest, we looked to him when Mam died. He was only thirteen himself.' Callum seems to be having a moment, some sort of an epiphany.

'So how are things between you both now?' We take a seat on a nearby bench.

'Funny you should mention it, but he always annoyed me about settling down. As you know, until recently, I had no intention. But I sought his advice after our kiss at the fundraiser. I didn't know who else to ask. Since then we've developed a weird sort of understanding of each other.'

'Well, I'm delighted I played a small part in it. When can I meet him?' A fuzzy warmth tingles inside of me.

'He's dying to meet you. If all else fails, you'll meet him at James's wedding. Melissa, Brian's wife, is actually Nadine's second cousin.'

'Only in Ireland.' It was the truth of it.

'What are we doing?' His gaze exudes a warm intensity, one that hints at more than lust.

'We're having a walk on a sunny afternoon...' I deliberately keep it light.

'You know that's not what I mean...' He continues to stare at the ocean, as if the answers will be washed up in the tide.

'Will I let you in on a little secret, Callum?' I pause conspicuously. 'Nobody in this world knows what they're doing. And if they say they do, they're lying.'

He takes his phone out of his pocket, opens the camera and wraps an arm territorially around me. He snaps a few different angles and opens his Instagram app.

His fingers hover over the 'post now' button. 'Do you mind?'

'Is this the modern-day equivalent of asking me to be your girlfriend? Or what do the Americans call it?' I muse, knowing well they called it going exclusive.

'As far as the rest of the world is concerned, you're already my girlfriend. I'm just making it official. Is that ok?'

'I suppose I can put up with it.' My heart's doing a hundred beats per minute. It's only been a couple of weeks, yet he's taking our relationship to the next level, a very public next level. His commitment is unexpected and exhilarating. I hope he continues to see in me whatever it was he didn't find elsewhere before. I'm free-falling into an addictive relationship with this spirited, sensitive man, who I can now officially say is no longer one of Ireland's most eligible bachelors.

He posts the picture on his social media and entitles it 'The Mrs' before switching his phone off and returning it to his back pocket.

'I suggest you do the same,' he advises. 'Three hundred and twenty thousand followers can cause a lot of vibrations.'

On days like these, it's easy to forget that Callum is one of the most famous sports heroes in the country. On days like these, he's just human, vulnerable, lovable, and by some mad, unpredictable twist of fate, officially mine.

CHAPTER THIRTY-FOUR

CALLUM

I'm waiting for my dinner in the bar at Carton House when Declan's number flashes up on my phone.

'I need to take this.' I give Marcus and James a curt nod as I push past them and head out into the lobby.

A hundred scenarios have infiltrated my thoughts since last week, each one more damning than the one before. Sean Fitzpatrick is the lowest of the low in my book, regardless of what Declan finds out, simply because he didn't even have the balls to break up with Abby in person. Spineless little shite.

'Declan?' I pace the immaculate tiled floor in anticipation.

'Callum. How are things? I did a bit of digging for you.' Declan's smooth, authoritative British accent travels all too slowly into my ear.

'And?' I should thank him before he elaborates, but curiosity is killing me.

'I didn't exactly acquire the information legitimately, if you know what I mean, so what I'm about to tell you, you should probably keep to yourself.'

I push the phone tightly to my ear and glance around to make sure no one is in the vicinity. A couple are checking in across the room, but they pay me no attention as they listen to the receptionist's directions to their suite.

'Go on.' I hold my breath, concerned even the sound of my own exhalation might prevent me from accurately processing the information that I need.

'It turns out Mr Fitzpatrick flew directly into Sydney on the night of the thirteenth of July 2014. He booked on the same flight as a Miss Zoe Wilson, with whom he then resided for the next three years. Zoe had been in Ireland on a working holiday visa, employed by a boat tour company in Carrick, coincidently the same tour company that Sean booked for a work party in April 2014.'

'The cheating little bollocks.' That explains a lot. Whatever I've done in my life, I've never ever cheated on anyone. Possibly because I've never had a proper girlfriend as such, but still, I'd never stoop that low.

'That's only the beginning,' Declan informs me. 'In December of 2014, Zoe gave birth to a baby boy named Taylor.'

'So he has a child with her? Why would he leave them now?' I scratch my head in wonder. Maybe Sean is just a commitment-phobe. Maybe he can't follow through on anything.

'Well, that's the thing that's not strictly legit, you see. Zoe named Sean on the birth certificate, but when I hacked the medical records, I discovered that Sean took Taylor for a DNA test two months ago. It turns out that the child isn't actually his.'

'Fuck.' A low whistle escapes me. The receptionist shoots an enquiring look, I smile reassuringly and turn my back to her.

'There's more,' Declan says.

'Go on.' So the plot thickens. A tiny sliver of sympathy for Sean slithers in, before I remember that he'd obviously been shagging Zoe behind Abby's back if he thought the child was his in the first place.

'There was some sort of showdown. Zoe called the police to report a violent disturbance at the house, but by the time the authorities got there, Sean was long gone and records state that Zoe did not wish to follow up with an official complaint. According to British Airways flight log, Sean took a flight to Heathrow two days later, then boarded a connecting one to Dublin.'

'What date did he arrive back in Ireland?' I don't know why it matters if it was before I met Abby or after, but I want all the facts.

'He's back four weeks tomorrow.'

It was before. At least Abby's relationship with me wasn't the driving force of his return. But the idea of him being aggressive to the ex, doesn't bode well. I'll need to keep him on a short leash if he attempts to get near Abby.

'Thanks, Declan. You've been very helpful, as usual. I'll transfer the funds for your time now.'

'No. This one's on the house. I know who he is to you, to Abby. I hope he's not looking for a reunion.'

'Me too. For his sake.' My jaw tightens at the prospect. 'Take care, Callum.'

'Thanks a million, Dec, I'll be in touch.' I disconnect the call and head back into the bar area. My lamb cutlet is getting cold on the table while the boys are heartily tucking into their own grub.

'Everything ok?' James asks with a raised eyebrow. He must have seen the caller ID.

'Grand. Thanks.' I sit down and take a forkful of my luke-warm lamb.

I can't shake the conversation from my thoughts. Are

things grand? Or should I still be concerned about Sean's reappearance in relation to my new relationship? He obviously didn't come home especially for Abby. But clearly, now he's returned, he hasn't ruled out the prospect of winning her back. Surely she wouldn't even contemplate it at this stage? She definitely wouldn't if she got wind of Zoe and Taylor, but should I even tell her? Would you rather know that that you had been cheated on by your childhood sweetheart and the man you agreed to marry. Or is ignorance truly bliss as they say?

CHAPTER THIRTY-FIVE

ABBY

'Did you speak to Callum yet?' Candice's jaw is tightly set, and she uses the haughty tone she specifically reserves for people who don't respect her boundaries. Today's T-shirt is rainbow coloured for gay pride and the slogan reads, Stroke It, Don't Poke It.

A full week has passed. Despite my escalating feelings for Callum, I've reached the conclusion I don't want him on my show on a permanent basis. I'm not afraid of him taking over, of living in his shadow. I'm more afraid that this won't last, that I'll drive him away somehow. If he breaks my heart, I'll have to share a six-foot studio with him every day. If we were co-hosts on top of everything else, it would be unbearable.

'I'll ask him tonight.' Only because Candice isn't really giving me any other choice. But I certainly won't be encouraging it.

I sigh dramatically, unable to conjure an answer to my problems. Aoife scans the incoming messages as U2 vibrates around the studio. 'I have news.' A knowing smile plays on her lips.

'You're not leaving me?' I shoot a look at Candice, who we both adore, but jointly acknowledge is madder than a box of frogs.

'For a short while.' She places her hands on her tummy in a protective gesture.

'Oh, Aoife. Congratulations.' I throw my arms around her across the desk, and she weeps soft tears of joyous relief.

If I hadn't been so self-absorbed, I might have guessed. I kick myself for not being more intuitive, only last year I'd cried with her as she confided a second miscarriage. I hadn't realised her struggles, and the topic on the show that day centred around accidental pregnancies and the abortion rules in Ireland.

'How far gone are you?' I squeeze her hand gently with encouragement.

'Sixteen weeks.' Please God this time, she'd get to hold her baby in her arms and watch it grow into a healthy boy or girl.

'Congratulations darhlingggg...' Candice air kisses Aoife, but as usual, her face barely twitches.

'While we're on the subject of announcements...' Candice rubs her hands together in excitement. I couldn't envisage her pregnant as well, but stranger things have happened.

'There's more good news confirmed.'

'Go on.' What else have I missed while consumed in my Abby/Callum bubble?

'The final figures are in. The producers closed the competition early. You won, as I knew you would. No one could come close to you and they wanted to secure a date for the interview with M.O.D.E.R.N. ASAP.' She pats my back and Aoife's bump simultaneously.

'This is fantastic news.' I leap up from the chair and

throw my arms around Aoife for the second time in the space of a minute. The three of us do our victory jig around the tiny studio.

'When are we going?' I turn to Aoife, who is already shaking her head.

'Sorry, Abs, I'm not going anywhere.' She places her hand over her tiny bump again. 'Bring Callum. He deserves it, being his appearance that caused the frenzy.'

'What date is it?' I ask.

'Fifteenth of August.' Candice waves the itinerary in front of my face.

Fuck. Fuck. Fuck. My face drops.

'Trouble in paradise?' Candice asks intuitively.

'Not exactly.' The fifteenth of August is James and Nadine's wedding. The exact reason Callum and I started 'dating' each other is now back to bite us in the backside.

James is his best friend. I know how badly he wants me to go with him. And it has nothing to do with an Audi at this stage. Yet this trip to interview M.O.D.E.R.N. is a once in a lifetime opportunity; it could do wonders for my career. My name will be in every newspaper on both sides of the Atlantic. There's no way I can turn it down. The song ends, saving me from further questioning.

I leave work troubled, but force it to the back of my mind for now.

Karen is waiting for me in Temple Bar, one of our usual spots in the city.

'You have the glow of a woman in love,' Karen warns me over glass of wine.

'I have the glow of a woman who is having lots of sex. It's wildly different.' Even as I viciously deny it, I recognise the truth of the matter.

I'm falling further in love with Callum than I ever was

with Sean. That dizzying, lust fuelled, all-consuming passion, is plastered all over my face.

'At least someone is...' Karen confides.

'Things not great with Dan?' I sympathise.

'It's over.' She doesn't flinch, seemingly indifferent to what should have been one of the most upsetting events of her life: calling off her wedding.

'Is there someone else?' I ask. To me, it came out of nowhere.

'No.' She responds defensively with a hand over her chest.

The funny thing is, I meant had he met someone else, not her. But her guilty reaction leaves me wondering if there's more to it than she's actually letting on.

'What will you do, Karen?' I was sure she had wanted to marry Dan. Their easy, laid back relationship had given me hope when I felt nothing lasted in this modern world. Above anything else, the two of them were the best of friends. Where did it go so wrong?

'I don't know, but I'm excited about not knowing. I'm relieved.' She sips her merlot, and I marvel at how she's escaped the devastation that had consumed me for years. Part of me respects her strength, the other part wants to delve into her psyche and ask how.

I long to ask her all the questions that I wish I could have asked Sean at the time. I don't, of course, it's a different situation entirely and none of my business. I thought she'd elaborate. We've always been close, yet we barely discussed one of the biggest decisions of her life. I try not to analyse it obsessively.

With hindsight, and my new relationship with Callum, I'm beginning to appreciate the humiliation and rejection were the real problems for me. Of course I missed Sean after he left, but I missed being part of a couple more than I actually missed him.

If Callum were to leave me now, it had the potential to be so much more humiliating. Yet, that isn't the thought that troubles me. The devastation of a life without him is a much worse fate than what any relative, or even the national newspaper, might say about me.

The world works in mysterious ways. As Karen's relationship ends, mine's beginning to flourish. Last weekend, I nearly let slip the very three words I'm determined not to say first. They were there, though, hovering in the background, the most natural thing in the world.

I'm glad Karen is happy, truly. Neither of us mentions it's exactly as Esmerelda predicted, or the fact that I'm apparently destined to marry a man called Patrick. Something I've consciously chosen to forget.

If it weren't for Esmerelda's silly predictions, would there still be a niggling part of me that worried about allowing Callum to infiltrate every single part of my life?

And then there is the tiny issue of deciding what's more important: the trip to New York and my career, or my new relationship and my boyfriend's best friend's wedding.

Technically, I have to go to the wedding. It was our deal, and Callum held up his end of the bargain. Which is the single reason I'm getting the opportunity in the first place, but surely now we're a real couple, he won't actually hold me to it?

CHAPTER THIRTY-SIX

CALLUM

I bring Abby to Marco Pierre White, my favourite steakhouse, but she's barely swallowed a morsel. Normally she clears my plate as well as her own. The girl has a fantastic appetite. It's one of many things I love about her. I wonder if she's stumbled across some unflattering newspaper clippings on my past, a fear I've been harbouring for a while. She's so wholesome, and I'm so tainted. Does she know what she's getting herself into with me? Or maybe she's realised my family is crazy and I'm no better. Either way, her off-kilter behaviour's making me uncomfortable.

'What's up, Abs?'

She stares at her plate. I use two fingers to gently lift her chin, raising her face to meet my eye.

Two rugby fans approach to ask for an autograph. I convey a look that they're interrupting something important, and they leave us in peace.

'If you won't talk to me, I can't help you.' I'm terrified of her closing me off again. We've come too far now. Maybe it's that dickhead Sean. Maybe he's resurfaced in the flesh to beg for forgiveness. No, she'd have told me.

'Candice wants me to offer you a permanent job on the radio,' she blurts out.

'What? No way.'

Abby's cocks her head to the side. 'You're not interested?'

'Absolutely not. The only reason I agreed to talk about love and stuff was to win you over. I'm not doing it again. We made a deal. I wouldn't let you down.' She flinches at the mention of the deal, but relief washes over her face. 'Candice pretty much forced me to ask you. Don't get me wrong, the thought of you hanging around the studio's pretty appealing in a lot of ways, but to be honest, it's my thing.'

'There is no way I'm signing up for regular questions on *where to get waxed in the city* or that other girly guff...sorry...' I do not want or need another job. Not yet, anyway.

'Is that all that's bothering you?' I can't believe she had her knickers in a twist about something so insignificant in the real world. I suppose it is her real world. It's her employment after all.

'Yep.' She looks away.

'Abby?' She's holding out on me... I know every line of her face, have memorised each and every one of her expressions, and right now she has one of guilt.

'It's James and Nadine's wedding...' She looks at her plate, anywhere but at me.

'What about it?'

'I can't make it.'

'What do you mean you can't make it? He's my best friend, you're my girlfriend, we had a deal.'

'I'm sorry.'

'I don't understand.' Hurt gnaws at my gut. Have I been used? Now she's succeeded in winning the trip am I getting the boot? It would be karma for all the using I've unintentionally done in the past.

'I won the trip to New York. Thanks to you. It's the same weekend. I'm so sorry, Callum. It's the opportunity of a lifetime. I can't turn it down.' Dark apologetic pools gaze tentatively at me.

'We had a deal.' It's not about Marcus's stupid Audi. She's my girlfriend, and I want her there with me to enjoy the day and show her off.

'I'm sorry.'

'What about us?' It's barely a whisper.

'It doesn't change the way I feel about you.' She takes my hand.

Does it change the way I feel about her? No. But if the roles were reversed would she be equally as forgiving? Disappointment reverberates through me.

CHAPTER THIRTY-SEVEN

ABBY

Callum plants a lingering kiss on my mouth with no regard for the frustrated commuters beeping at the hold up in traffic outside the Ireland Today building. As I cross the road, a burning stare penetrates my shoulder blades. I turn to catch a flickering sight of the figure in the baseball cap again. The figure then merges into the throng of people on the pavement, leaving me to question if it's, once again, a figment of my imagination.

I enter the glass doors, distracted by the knowledge that Candice is going to blow a fuse when I tell her Callum declined her offer.

I'm relieved. The thought of our relationship developing so publicly...listeners forming opinions on us based on the way we interact on air. We're already in the spotlight. It would be nice to keep some part of us private.

The news of the trip and wedding clashing created a tiny rift in our, so far, perfect start. The underlying issue doesn't sit well with me: Do I value my career more than my relationship? In the past, I always put Sean's wants before my own. I vowed to do things differently this time, but it seems unfair somehow that Callum's already on the backfoot because of my previous experience with Sean.

I walk the length of the corridor, where Aoife greets me as usual with notes for the show and a black coffee.

'You're a lifesaver.' We'll soon have to advertise her maternity cover. Though I hate the thought of being without her, I don't begrudge it either.

'Sally's upstairs already,' Aoife warns me quietly.

'What's she doing here already?' I roll my eyes, desperate to avoid unnecessary confrontation.

'She's showing someone around. They arrived literally a minute before you. Remember she ran all those competitions over the last few weeks trying to increase her audience? One of the prizes was a tour of the building and the opportunity to co-host her show,' Aoife relays in hushed tones as we approach.

'Well, they'd want to be moving on with this part of the tour fairly soon, because I'm done with co-hosts for now, except for you of course,' I tell her wryly.

'He didn't go for it?' Aoife tuts, but I gather from her monotone that she's unsurprised.

'Is it wrong that I'm relieved?' I shrug. Candice's going to hit the roof. She was relying on our chemistry to attract interest. We round the corner, and I grin at the memory of Callum in my favourite cupboard.

The smile freezes on my face at the studio door. Sally's sitting in my usual seat, across from a man who looks dangerously like Sean Fitzpatrick, complete with a red baseball cap. Apparently, I didn't imagine him after all. It's the one time I would have liked to have been wrong. Light stubble lines his face and his hazel eyes glint in anticipation. At the sight of me, he springs to his feet, as though he'd been waiting especially.

Shock roots my sandals to the spot. Every single cell within screams at me to move. The repetitive thud of my hammering heart floods my brain, preventing all rational thought.

Does Sally know who he is? Did she do this deliberately? Why not just leave me alone?

He had no problem leaving me alone four years ago.

'Abs...' He places a hand tenderly on my shoulder. His touch sears my bare skin. I flinch and jerk away as he scrutinises my face for any sign of weakness.

'Don't call me that.' It's barely a whisper.

Aoife stands two feet away from me with no clue of the gaping wound that Sally slit open. The demon of my past thrust into my present.

'You look unreal, Abby.' His eyes scan the length of my casual maxi dress with an open appreciation.

If I do, it's because Callum reignited a spark in me. One that I assumed I'd lost forever when he left.

'Don't, Sean. Just don't.' I push him away from me, repulsed by his inappropriate familiarity and general sense of entitlement.

At the mention of his name, Aoife instantly reverts to high alert, remembering our caller who voiced the much-discussed question: 'How long have you been sleeping with my fiancée?'

'Will I call security?' She places a hand on her pager. 'He has a pass,' Sally says smugly.

'Keep him away from me.' Finding my feet at last, I shoo them out of my studio like unwelcome stray animals.

'We need to talk, Abby. We have unfinished business...you know it...' His voice trails off as I close the soundproofed door in his face.

The irritating fecker has aged well. A flood of memories engulf me, reminding me of everything I almost had. We would have been married almost four years. Would we have had children by now?

Aoife carries me through the show. I barely say two words for the entire three hours. I can't think straight, unable to process my emotions.

He was my first kiss, my first boyfriend, my first love, my best friend; my everything. It wasn't just me he abandoned. It was everything and everyone that we'd ever known. I hadn't just lost him. I lost myself and my life as I knew it. To this day, I can barely even bring myself to visit my own family. At home, everywhere I looked, everything I touched, I saw him.

With all the therapy in the world, I still can't understand how he could just up and leave. And a part of me will never be satisfied until I know why.

After the show, What's left When There's Nothing Left? I walk out into the July sunshine and pull my sunglasses from my leather satchel, unsurprised to see him leaning against the building waiting for me. Sean always was unusually determined, even when we were children. He catapults forward, blocking my path. I sidestep, and he falls in line beside me.

'You can't avoid me forever. We need to talk.' With his hands in his chino pockets, he keeps the pace with me.

I had hoped he might have at least gained a few pounds, maybe even a few grey hairs, or better again – gone bald. I try painfully hard not to look at him, unwilling to give him the satisfaction.

'You were perfectly happy to avoid me for the last four years, when I actually might have wanted to talk to you. Why the urgency now?' My fists clench white with years of built-up anger.

'Abby, I made the biggest mistake of my life. You and I are

meant for each other. You know we are.' He attempts to take my arm.

Esmerelda's words echo through me. 'He's called Patrick.' I push them away to a vault in the depth of my subconscious, along with his hand, which once again lingers on my shoulder.

'I'm warning you now, get your hands off me. You lost the right to touch me long ago.' His presence ignites a fury of buried memories, memories which I'd worked extremely hard to forget.

'Can we at least go somewhere to talk?' he pleads, running one hand over his stubbled jawline desperately.

'Why? What's to say after all this time? I've moved on. I'm with somebody else. It's like you felt the force of my happiness and crawled out of whatever cave you were rotting in to take it from me, again.' My words are heavy with emotion. He views it as an opportunity, pushing his lips forcefully on to mine. It takes a millisecond longer than it should to push him away as I'm frozen once again with shock. It's a millisecond long enough for a camera to click to the left of me. We've gained an audience, fan-fucking-tastic.

'If you touch me again, I will have a restraining order enforced against you. Get out of my life. For good.'

I make the journey home in a zombie-like state. Behind my front door, tears cascade over my face like a waterfall. All the memories, the possibilities, everything that could have been, but never were. I'd literally just got over him, only now finding the courage to seek a little bit of happiness for myself.

Sean Fitzpatrick broke my heart once. I won't let him do it again.

CHAPTER THIRTY-EIGHT

CALLUM

It's been barely eight weeks since I first laid eyes on Abby, yet I know without a doubt I'm falling hard and the weight of it consumes me from the inside out. She must feel it every time I touch her, with every stroke, with every kiss. She stirs emotions within me, that until recently, I hadn't believed I was capable of. I'd been missing this woman in my life for as long as I could remember, forever even. I should have been more understanding yesterday when she mentioned the trip. I want her to be happy, underlying tension doesn't sit well with me.

I arrive outside Abby's before seven and park in my usual spot on the tarmac drive next to her Mini Cooper. For once, she isn't at the front door to greet me. The curtains twitch from the window of her neighbour's house. I raise my hand in greeting, but the old woman drops the net quickly. I knock, check my watch and wonder if she's gone for a run.

The door inches open, an unrecognisable version of my

girlfriend appears before me. Crimson eyes, tear-streaked cheeks and scarlet blotches set alarm rippling through me.

'What is it?' I immediately embrace her. She buries herself into my chest, inhaling the scent of my shirt.

'Don't go mad,' she pleads, handing me her mobile phone from the table in the hallway.

A photo of a man with his hands placed meaningfully on my girlfriend's shoulders illuminates the screen. The man looks suspiciously like he's about to kiss her. And it's all over the evening gossip columns.

Searing, stabbing jealousy pierces my insides. The thought of anyone else placing their disgusting hands on her sickens me.

'Who the fuck is that?' I ask.

'Sean Fitzpatrick,' Abby says quietly, beckoning me into her sitting room and flopping onto the cream fabric couch.

Fevered anger consumes me. He couldn't just stay away. This man has a whole lot of history with my girlfriend. He'd meant more to her at one point. More than I do now. She'd agreed to marry him, for fuck's sake. He probably knew the curves of her body better than me. He met her family, went on holiday with her, shared a home with her – all of the things I was yet to do. His reappearance now could signify the end of us, a thought that has the potential to ruin me. I briefly consider telling her what I learnt about him, but then I'd have to admit I sent someone snooping.

I've never seen Abby looking so wretched.

Is she upset because she still cares about him? Or because he won't leave her alone? I pray it's the latter, but a sinking sense of hopelessness hovers. If she chooses to take him back now, I'd have no choice but to accept her decision. Even if it's the wrong one.

'Talk to me, Abby.' I take her hands in mine, itching to ask her a million questions. 'Do you still have feelings for him?' I prefer to face the situation head-on, have some idea what I'm up against.

Her prolonged silence is deafening and hurts more than any words she could have uttered.

I gently disentangle myself from her and stand to leave. 'Wait, Callum,' she begs. 'It's not what you think.'

My stomach balls into a hundred knots and nausea sweeps through me with a greater force than the strongest tackle.

'He launched himself at me; it's not what it looks like. He's been following me. I thought my mind was playing tricks on me, but it really was him. I don't have feelings for him, not like that. I just feel an overwhelming sense of sadness about the whole situation. He constituted my entire life since I was fourteen years of age. I didn't know who I was when he left me. I didn't really like the me that he left behind... until I met you.'

This is new territory for me. I struggle to relate to the pull of the first love, having nothing to compare it to myself until now.

'I still have no idea what exactly I did to him that drove him away, so how do I know I won't do the same thing to you? Seeing him today reminded me of the me I used to know. A simpler version of me. But I'll never be that me again. It's her I mourn, not him.'

I could tell her what drove him away, and it wasn't her. But is it my place to? I don't think it is. It might do more harm than good.

Abby pulls me towards her, her eyes searching mine for the connection that we have, the one that's between us and only us. Tears fall from her long, wet eyelashes as she unbuttons my shirt. I'm in no doubt of what she wants, but for the first time in my life, I hesitate. I want her more now than ever, desperate to stake my claim on her, remind her what we have, but a tiny lingering sliver of insecurity eats at me.

Is it really me she wants? Or is she just seeking comfort from me because I'm the one standing here? How can I compete with years of history?

I consider it rationally for a few seconds, battling the ugly green-eyed monster lurking within. If she wanted him, it looks pretty clear from the photo that she could have had him. He's her past. I'm determined to be her future. The concept of purchasing an enormous diamond is increasingly appealing. Some might consider it a little early, but I'd be a fucking fool to leave it too late.

There's only one way to deal with the situation – to remind her exactly what we have, what I would do for her. And trust her to make the right decision.

I lift her into my arms and carry her upstairs to the bed that I've spent the last few weeks with her in. Her eyes don't leave mine. She's hungry and wanting, enough to get me off by itself. She's like no woman I've ever had before, and with the threat of losing her, I reach an unwavering conclusion – nobody else will ever do.

Tiny prickling goosebumps ripple over her soft skin as I remove her dress. My tongue traces her stomach, kissing every part of her. Tense legs clench beneath me. Her body begs for more. I draw it out deliberately.

'Please, Callum,' she moans, pulling me up towards her.

Undoing my jeans, she grips my backside hard, pulling me into her with an urgency that matches my own.

She writhes against me. Sweat beads her skin, mixing with my own. She tugs my hair and cries out my name again as she reaches her release. I follow suit, placing my mouth over hers to muffle the words that I long to say.

I collapse onto her chest. Her heartbeat reverberates throughout my soul. Lifting my head to meet her eyes, I'm surprised to find silent tears falling freely from her eyes. I had hoped she was done crying.

'Sorry.' She wipes them away with the back of her hand, embarrassed at her emotional display.

'Don't be. You're beautiful.' I love her in every way, make-up or no make-up, fierce or emotional.

'Callum, don't look at me like that, or I'll have no choice but to tell you I love you,' she whispers. Cautious chocolate brown eyes lock into mine with a shy vulnerability.

A triumphant grin assumes centre position on my face. The resounding victory within superior to any win, any try, any game, league or championship.

'I needed to hear you say that,' I confess, stroking the tears away from her perfect face. 'I fell in love with you the very first time I kissed you in front of the entire country in Phoenix Park.'

'Good job you didn't say it then. I'd have run a mile. No offence. We made enough news that day.' She smiles at the memory.

'You took a bit more convincing than I did, but I knew you felt it. It was like nothing I experienced before.' I lie on the pillow next to her and lift her onto my chest, wrapping my arms tightly around her.

'I've been thinking...' She looks up at me with those puppy dog eyes. 'About New York. I'm not going.'

A gasp slips from my mouth. It's a big gesture, choosing James's wedding over the biggest opportunity of her career. Obviously, I want her to come with me, but will she resent me later when she sees someone else's name attached to the most exclusive interview of this decade?

She lies silent and thoughtful for a few minutes staring at the intricate coving of the ceiling.

'I want to go to James's wedding with you, as your date, way more than meeting some man band that will probably be so drunk that they won't even turn up,' she reasons.

'Are you sure?' It'd mean the world to have her with me on

such a big day, but I hate the thought of her missing out. I can bring her to New York before the year is over, but I can't offer her an exclusive interview with anyone but me.

'I'm sure.' She kisses my chest lovingly, suddenly sure. 'Aoife can't go, she's pregnant. Candice isn't allowed to go because she's a manager. I could give it to the boys downstairs that do the morning show...' she trails off thoughtfully. 'But I think I'm actually going to offer it to Sally No Soul.'

'What? After everything she's done?' I don't believe it.

'That's exactly why she needs it. Whatever happened to her along the way made her the way she is. Maybe what she needs is a little bit of kindness.'

'One more thing,' I add. 'And it's not up for negotiation. We are filing a restraining order against Sean Fitzpatrick. I don't want him anywhere near you.' He might not be violent, but after Declan's discovery, I won't take any chances.

She nods. We have to draw a line under him one way or another, and we can't do that while he continues to cross it.

'Thank you.' I kiss her button nose. 'I can't actually wait for the wedding. I might even pick up some tips for my speech, when the time comes,' I joke, but it's not as far from the truth as I once imagined.

CHAPTER THIRTY-NINE

ABBY

'Sally.' I find her in the large staff room on the second floor. A few technical staff lounge on the couches, but for most part, it's empty. I'm relieved. We don't need an audience.

She has the grace to look at the floor. Her red short-sleeved blouse is tucked roughly into high waisted trousers, which are half a size too small for her. I examine her properly, for what seems like the first time. Normally, I avoid being anywhere near her. On the odd occasion we crossed paths, I saw an enemy objectified, not a real-life breathing human, one who might need a little help. Sally's thrown together, dishevelled and forever rushing.

It is the first time I've laid eyes on her since last week's incident. The pictures of Sean trying to kiss me were removed as soon as Callum promised *The Irish Sun* an exclusive interview with the two of us in his apartment next month. It was a near-miss, and there was me thinking it would be Callum publicly humiliating me all over the papers.

I'd come very close to letting us both down, thanks to Sally here.

Candice begged me not to reward bad behaviour. But Sally must be hurting somewhere inside. Why else was she was so desperate to hurt me?

'I have something for you.' I hand her the itinerary for New York.

Her naturally protruding mandible drops in shock. She smooths her black hair behind her ears nervously, wondering if this is some sort of joke. She skims the paperwork and steps back in disbelief.

'You can't be serious.' She thrusts the itinerary back into my hands.

'I'm deadly serious. I have a wedding that weekend that means more to me than anything else. Aoife can't go. I want you to go instead.' I nod with unwavering certainty, forcing it back into her hands, closing her fingers tightly around it. 'It's yours. Enjoy it. Be happy.' I turn to go but she catches me by the wrist lightly. She throws her arms around me, water pooling in her black eyes.

Had anyone ever shown this woman any kindness at all?

There's clearly a reason why she behaves so aggressively. 'Can I buy you lunch next week? To say thanks?'

'Thank you.' I flash her a genuine smile. There's no reason we have to be rivals.

I finish up at Ireland Today and head to the Jervis Centre for my hair appointment with Emma. I haven't seen her since that weekend at Carton House, and I'm in desperate need of root colour again.

Callum's coming to Carrick this weekend to meet the outlaws, and I want to look fresh for it. It's my parents' thirtieth wedding anniversary. I generally try to ignore the fact that I'm turning thirty in five months. You do the maths. The party is at The Landmark, the very same hotel where my wedding reception was supposed to take place. I haven't stepped foot in the place in years. This presents an opportunity to separate the past from the present, make new memories, happy ones, which centre around my family and my fabulous new boyfriend.

'Are you still shagging Callum Connolly?' Emma is not backwards at coming forwards, pulling me into a crushing bear hug before placing a black plastic cloak around my cream chiffon shirt.

The salon's full as usual, but between the noise of the hairdryers and the women, nobody even glances in our direction.

'Actually, we've moved on since then.' I'm unable to resist playing with my inquisitive friend.

'What happened? Tell me everything. You know I need details.'

'We've moved on from just the shagging, although there is still plenty of that too, thankfully.' I wink knowingly at her.

'So it's serious?' Her emerald eyes light with excitement as she runs her fingers through my hair.

'He said the L-word,' I confirm, without elaborating that I said it first.

'Feckin' hell, Abby, has he got any friends?'

I can't help but laugh. Refreshingly, Emma doesn't pretend to be anything other than man mad.

'Actually, he has. What about Eddie Harrington?' The two of them are a match made in heaven, I wonder which of them would spend the longest in front of a mirror preparing for a night out.

'Hell yes. Have you seen that man's cheekbones? He has the whole pretty-boy thing going on, with a rugged twist. Set me up, please.'

From what I've heard about him, they'd actually be perfect for one another.

'I'll mention it to Callum tonight.'

'Do you seriously think he might be interested in me?' A rare glimpse of insecurity from my stunning friend strikes a chord that probably every woman can relate to. Emma is absolutely beautiful. When we go out, she has to beat men off with a stick. Yet here she is, wondering if Eddie would be interested in her.

'He'd be lucky to have you.' I grab the hand that holds the hairbrush and squeeze it to stress my sincerity.

'Thank you, Abby,' she squeals in excitement.

A junior brings me a coffee and a stack of magazines. It's pointless. I won't read one of them with Emma talking the ear off me, but I love it really. It's been too long since we had a good natter.

'Have you seen Karen?' Emma focusses on wrapping my hair in foil as she speaks.

'Not in about a week.' Callum consumes so much of my thoughts and attention, I haven't been the best of friends lately, considering all that she's going through. I'm still receiving the impression she's avoiding me, maybe because our lives are going in the complete opposite direction. Maybe Karen's finding things harder than she lets on, and maybe my new relationship status does rub salt in fresh wounds.

'Such a shock, her and Dan splitting,' I say.

'Really?' Surprise taints Emma's tone. 'We weren't shocked at all.' She refers to herself, Kerry and the rest of the girls they went to school with.

'They were together so long. I thought they were happy.' I take a sip of coffee and pull a packet of sweeteners out of my bag.

Emma stands back from what she's doing and looks at me like I have two heads.

'Did you never wonder if Karen was...?'

'What?' I have no idea what Emma's getting at. She stands

deathly still and stares at me incredulously. She doesn't normally beat around the bush. Whatever she's trying to say, I wish she'd just come out with it.

'Gay?' she hisses lowly.

'What? No way.' My mouth falls open in total shock. I'd have known.

Wouldn't I?

'At school, we were absolutely convinced. She had zero interest in the opposite sex at all.' Emma resumes her position wrapping foil, glancing round her salon occasionally to check on her employees and their clients.

'Nobody has the same level of interest in the opposite sex as you do,' I remind her. But I was re-evaluating every relevant conversation we'd ever had now the seed had been sown.

Karen's a girly girl, quirky and feminine in her appearance. She loves Tina Turner, floral headbands and skirts. I immediately chide myself for stereotyping people's sexuality by their appearance. It's so wrong. It's just, Candice for example, is so openly gay, literally wearing it on her T-shirts. Karen doesn't seem to fit the bill. Maybe she hadn't wanted to.

'She was the biggest tomboy of all. Then all of a sudden, she got the job at the hotel, met Dan and started wearing those crazy hairbands and skirts all of a sudden. It was like she'd had a personality transplant.'

Were the eccentric clothes a camouflage to disguise her underlying sexuality?

I honestly can't believe it. Karen's my best friend. I would never judge. In fact, it physically pains me to think that she couldn't be honest with me.

She did have a friend once though...

When she and Dan parted company for a couple of months, Karen had been very friendly with a girl called Eve, the one she travelled Europe with. She used to stay at our apartment a lot, then when Dan came back on the scene Eve just disappeared.

How could I have missed this?

Karen could've dropped a hundred hints and I wouldn't have picked up on it, because to me she'd always been 'Karen and Dan'. She's forever asking after Candice, with a previously unexplained sense of admiration.

Deep down, a part of me acknowledges Emma's right. It's the reason she couldn't marry Dan. Snippets of four years' worth of conversation flash through my mind, about fate, about identity. He's a good man. That's the problem.

Though a part of me is shocked, I know with a sudden certainty that it's true.

I wish Karen could have told me. It must be eating her alive. Esmerelda's parting words to her ring eerily through my ears. Admit your truth. I thought she was spouting mumbo jumbo, or at the very best, referring to her relationship with Dan. She was actually referring to Karen's relationship with herself. The first thing on my to-do list when I return from Carrick is to hunt Karen down and make sure she knows we're all here for her. I don't care if she's gay, straight or indifferent. She's my best friend. Everything else is irrelevant. She undoubtedly needs a friend right now, just not for the reason I imagined.

CHAPTER FORTY

CALLUM

Before I even contemplate heading to Carrick, I head to my childhood home, for peace of mind. The new carer has been calling every morning, and Dad actually seems to like her; a fifty-year-old woman with a maternal air about her. She rings with a daily report. It's win-win all round, a break for Linda, company for Dad and the easing of all our guilt. In the darkest hours of the night, my conscience torments me. I should spend more time with him. I should have more patience. But it's mentally exhausting recovering the same painful ground repeatedly.

'How are ye?' I call as I let myself in the front door.

As usual, I'm compelled to do a double-take at the bottom of staircase, as though I might see Mam still lying there, over twenty years later. It's an image that will never leave me. It was me that found her that day.

Dad told the neighbours she had a terrible fall. I was thirteen when I first found a note explaining otherwise, folded in a drawer with her wedding ring. It had been hard enough to accept that she was gone, but that she'd chosen to leave us is something I struggled to forgive, until recently. For years, I resented my father for not doing more, for not being able to stop her. Now, I mostly pity him.

'In here,' Linda calls from the kitchen.

Dad's perched in his usual chair, with *Sky News* blaring from the flat-screen television on the wall. He stares, mindlessly entranced, barely glancing up when I walk in.

'He's not having a great day,' Linda confides. 'Might be an idea to get Dr Tomson to have a look at him on Monday.'

'I'll phone the surgery and make arrangements.' I dial the all too familiar number and am issued an appointment for Monday afternoon, before spending a fruitless hour in the gloomy kitchen with Dad, who's apparently engrossed in the election campaign for the future president of America.

'Will ye be ok?' I ask Linda as I stand to leave.

'We'll be grand. Don't worry. Enjoy your weekend with Abby. Must be getting serious if she's bringing you home.' Linda raises her eyebrows knowingly at me.

'I can only hope so.'

CHAPTER FORTY-ONE

ABBY

Callum drives us to Carrick in the Jeep. It's far more practical than my Mini, and I love having my own personal chauffeur, especially one who smells so enticing. I glance at him intermittently as he concentrates on the road ahead, memorising every inch of his clean-shaven jawline and high-set cheekbones.

'Are you nervous?' I ask, as we reach Carrick and unload our weekend bags.

'Don't be silly,' he scoffs, but a hint of uncertainty forms in the crease of his features.

'I'm sure Mammy will have done up the spare room really nicely for you,' I tease.

'The spare room?' His oceanic eyes nearly pop out of his head.

'You didn't expect to sleep in with me? Have a little bit of respect, Mr Connolly.' His mouth opens and closes like a goldfish.

'Chill out.' I rub his arm affectionately. 'I doubt she'd do that to us... But if she does, you better lock your door, because it won't be me sneaking in the middle of the night for a kiss and a cuddle after a glass of wine...'

'Abby, how are you?' Mam rushes out and awkwardly hugs me. I wonder if she's started on the booze early. The only time she hugs anyone is following copious amounts of alcohol at a wedding or funeral. A simple pat is nearly always sufficient.

'Mam, this is Callum.'

She looks him up and down like he's a fresh cream cake in the bakery window.

'Mrs Queenan, it's a pleasure.' Callum kisses her on the cheek and for a second I think she might faint.

'It's a pleasure to meet you. Call me Cathy, please,' she coos, patting her short curled hair in a feminine fashion that I'm unaccustomed to witnessing.

I wouldn't have pegged Mam for a starstruck rugby fan, but she seems to be one of the millions of women ready to fall at Callum's feet. Nobody's ever allowed to call her Cathy, apart from Daddy.

Daddy intervenes, unsure whether to be amused or concerned at the flirtatious behaviour of his normally predictable wife.

Callum extends a hand, and after a millisecond hesitation, Daddy takes it firmly and grimaces, not even pretending he's pleased to meet Callum. An unspoken warning's delivered in that tiny exchange, 'do not dare hurt my daughter' emanates from my father's less than friendly stance.

'I'm Noel.' I'm torn between wishing he'd go easy on Callum and touched by his concern for me.

'Pleased to meet you.' Callum nods in response to Dad's silent exchange. The message is delivered.

Callum carries both our bags through the glass porch and into the hallway, where the familiar smell of home-baked bread summons a thousand long lost memories. This time, I don't feel that suffocating sense of sorrow upon my return. The prospect of introducing Callum as my boyfriend at the party tomorrow is one that excites me.

Mam and Dad have gone all out in anticipation of Callum's arrival. Short of only a welcome banner, the place's transformed. I'm under no illusion that they'd gone to such lengths for my benefit.

'Your sister's on her way over,' Mammy informs me with a raised eyebrow.

Alicia's the wild child in our house. She's tried approximately three hundred different college courses before abandoning all of them to be a wedding photographer, which would be fine if she actually bothered looking for work in that field.

Her nose must be bothering her if she's coming to Mam's for dinner on a Friday night instead of hitting Finnegan's, Carrick's liveliest pub.

Mammy bustles around the kitchen, and Daddy sets about reluctantly fetching Callum a drink. I shoot him a warning look, be nice to my new boyfriend, which he pointedly ignores.

Mammy has the finest silver cutlery on the table, the good crystal wine glasses and some of Daddy's 'cellar wine' as we call it, basically, it's the good stuff they get delivered in bulk, twice a year from some wino geriatric club they subscribe to and pay dearly for. Alicia and I are never normally allowed near it. Dad firmly believes we could drink bucks fizz and not be able to tell the difference. In fairness, he's probably right.

'You okay?' I whisper to Callum, squeezing his hand as both parents turn their backs to us.

'Yep...' He trails off as Dad fills two glasses of red wine and hands one to each of us.

The front door bangs loudly announcing the arrival of my little sister.

'You must have heard the cork pop.' I throw my arms around her tightly, and she squirms in true Queenan style at the PDA. I'm determined we'll be close again one of these days. Sooner rather than later, if I can help it.

Alicia looks fantastic; her honey-coloured hair's a few shades darker than my own. We have the same big brown eyes. She sports a pair of light faded skinnies and an oversized T-shirt which hangs loosely from her right shoulder. We have a similar sense of fashion, though tonight I'd opted for another maxi dress. Something about Callum's distinct masculinity seems to extract the femininity in me.

Alicia's eyes linger on Callum. She weighs him up as she awaits a formal introduction. I receive a glimpse of how he appears to the rest of the world reflected in her curious stare. Impressive.

'Any boyfriend we should know about?' I ask Alicia across the rectangular dinner table. I already know the answer, but I'd like her to open up. Callum pushes his prawn cocktail around his plate next to me.

'Now that you mention it...'

Daddy releases an exasperated sigh from the head of the table.

'Alicia changes her boyfriends more often than I change my feckin' socks. I only wish you girls would settle down for good, don't you, Cathy? All this "dating this one" and "shifting that one", it wasn't like that when we were young,' he reminisces nostalgically.

'Grandchildren...that's what we need at our age,' Mammy pipes up, tiny splatters of Marie Rose sauce decorate her chin. Both of them seem to have forgotten that at least one of us tried to settle. It hadn't exactly gone to plan.

Callum's wine lodges in his throat. He coughs and uses his fist to thump his chest a couple of times. I snigger, enjoying his discomfort. If he thinks these two are bad, wait until the extended relations corner him tomorrow.

'You do want children?' Dad asks Callum, sensing a weakness and exploiting it.

It isn't something we've discussed, preoccupied practising conceiving them. My cheeks colour slightly at the thought. I place a hand on his leg under the table in silent solidarity.

'It's not something I've given a lot of thought to. Realistically, I only have a year or two left in my career, and that's if I'm lucky. Maybe after that...hopefully.' Callum glances sideways at me, and I smile widely.

'You two make me want to vomit.' Alicia sticks her tongue out in disgust.

'Tell us about this man of yours.' I'm desperate to get her to confide in me again.

'Man? He is still a boy, trust me. He has no idea about the real world,' Dad scoffs, so cynical in his old age.

'He's only three years younger than me, Dad,' Alicia reminds him.

'He's still at bloody school,' Dad persists.

'He took a year out to work in Uganda, it's not like he's sitting his leaving cert.'

'What's he studying?' Callum attempts to defuse the situation, ignoring Dad's blatant glare across the table.

'Ecology,' Alicia replies. 'He graduates next month.'

'Wonderful. Perhaps then he'll join the rest of the taxpayers that support this lazy country.' Dad claps his hands sarcastically, and I snigger.

Dad's fronting a stern show for Callum's benefit,

cementing his position as head of this family. Mammy puts heed to it very quickly, eyeing Callum with a reassuring stare.

'Noel, will you kindly pull that poker out of your arse please, before it gets wedged up there permanently.'

Everyone, Daddy included, erupts with laughter, dissolving any remaining tension in the room. I clear the starter plates as Dad reluctantly asks Callum about upcoming rugby fixtures. If he'd only give him a chance, they'd get on like a house on fire.

'What do you think?' I whisper, stacking the starter plates in the dishwasher, falling into the familiar routine from years gone by.

'He is an absolute hunk,' Mam states the obvious. 'He's a good man,' I tell her sincerely.

'He better be, for his sake. If he breaks your heart, they'll find that boy's body in the Shannon, because your father will not tolerate seeing you hurt again.'

I nod, accepting the truth of it, and return to the dining room to check they're playing nicely. I hadn't expected Dad to be so cold towards Callum, though his caution's understandable.

Sean had been accepted as a part of this family for a long time before there was any mention of a wedding. He used to sit round this very table with his school books, drinking infinite cups of tea with the rest of us. It wasn't just me he rejected – it was all of us.

Mammy excels with roast beef and homemade Yorkshire puddings. Her final course is a rich pavlova. The atmosphere improves as the wine consumption increases. Callum helps me with the dishes while the other three retire to the lounge to watch *The Late Late Show*.

'You ok?' I place my arms around his toned stomach from behind.

'Yes.' He turns and places his sud-covered hands on my

waist. I lean on tiptoes to reach in for the kiss that I've been fantasising about throughout dinner, only to be interrupted by Alicia.

'Get a room will you,' she jibes.

'We thought we'd start with yours,' I tell her with a laugh.

'There'll be none of that under my roof,' Dad bellows from the sitting room.

That's what he thinks.

CHAPTER FORTY-TWO

CALLUM

The regular thrumming of light raindrops bounces lightly from the double-glazed window. Abby sleeps peacefully next to me, her blonde hair scattered over her bare shoulders, the covers bunched round her waist.

It's all too easy to picture her here, surrounded by her friends and family, the night before she was supposed to get married. It must have been horrific, but I can't bring myself to feel sorry, or I wouldn't be here now. I'm not sure if she ever did file that restraining order against Fitzpatrick, but I trust she did. There's been no word since. I'd love to believe that's the end of it, but I'm not holding my breath. If it were me, I wouldn't be giving her up so easily. Then again, I wouldn't have cheated on her, or abandoned her, in the first place.

The noisy hiss of a boiling kettle travels up the narrow stairs from the kitchen below. I decide to brave the prospective out-laws alone and creep out from under the floral duvet, gently kissing Abby on the head. I pull on a pair of jogging bottoms and one of thirty team jerseys that I own.

I automatically assume it's Cathy making the tea, not Abby's less than welcoming father, Noel.

'Good morning.' I make my presence known as he stands with his back to me, sporting a navy dressing gown and slippers that I'm not awfully comfortable meeting him in.

'It was.' Noel grimaces as he pours boiling water into a red teapot.

'Sorry.' I back away and raise my hands in retreat. I can't force the man to warm to me.

'No, I'm sorry.' Noel shakes his head, chastising himself. 'Sorry, son, it's not you. You, unfortunately, are just bearing the brunt of my anger. It's not right.' He nods a sheepish apology in my direction and gestures to a small circular kitchen table with only two chairs at it.

'I promise you, I'll treat her well.' I scrape back the chair and gratefully accept the huge chipped mug he hands over.

Noel nudges the kitchen door shut with his right foot and sits directly opposite me, placing the teapot between us, along with a carton of skimmed milk from the fridge.

'Cathy and I never thought she would get over what that last bollocks did to her.'

'She told me,' I admit.

'Did she? Because she refuses point-blank to talk to us about it, to even hear his name. We've barely seen her the past few years. I suppose this place reminds her of everything that happened.' He drops two heaped spoons of sugar into his tea and stirs thoughtfully.

'Hopefully this weekend we'll make new memories, get a bit of closure. I'm honoured to be here.' I'm not ass-kissing. It's the simple truth.

'You're the first that we know of, since Sean. She must like you a lot,' he concedes. 'I wasn't sure booking the party at

The Landmark was a good idea myself. But Cathy wanted to mark the occasion, and it's the finest spot in the area.'

'It'll be a great night. Abby's been looking forward to it.' I sip on the steaming tea, delighted Noel's addressing me as an equal. Not like one of Alicia's many conquests, by all accounts.

'Just don't break her heart. She might not get over it a second time.' His voice is low, the warning clear.

'I won't,' I assure him for the second time that morning. 'Did she mention if she got the restraining order for him?'

Noel's head wrenches back from where he'd been staring out the window.

'For who? Sean?' His voice drops dangerously.

I didn't mean to put my foot in it, Abby's going to kill me. 'I thought you knew.' I run my fingers through my hair hastily, unsure how to backtrack now.

'Is he definitely back? I heard the phone call, but he could have made that from anywhere. Last I heard he had a kid in Australia, not that we passed that piece of information onto Abby, mind. Clearly, that doesn't mean what it should to him.'

'He turned up at her work two weeks ago.' Noel obviously didn't see the pictures I had to trade my soul with the devil to get erased. And I'm relieved to know I'm not the only one that's keeping Sean's murky little secrets. No point hurting Abby with the knowledge of it now.

'Selfish son of a bitch, couldn't just let her move on. He had an unhealthy hold on her. Her entire life revolved around him; his wants, his needs. Now she's doing well for herself, she's finally moved on... I could wring his neck with my bare hands.' Noel slams his mug down on the table, spilling half the contents in the process. I reach for the kitchen roll and mop up the milky liquid while he fumes.

'We have more in common than you initially thought.' I nod firmly in agreement with him.

United in a loathing for a mutual enemy forms the groundwork for what I hope will be the start of a very open and firm friendship. I'm in this for the long game. It's important to have Abby's family onside. Today might not be the day I ask for his daughter's hand in marriage, but who knows, it could be on the cards somewhere down the line.

Before either of us can utter another word, Abby bursts in through the kitchen door in her cream sleep shorts and vest top, clutching my vibrating mobile in her hand. 'Sorry, Callum, it's the fourth time it's rang. I'm not prying, but it's Linda.' She hands the phone over with a concerned expression drawn on her sleepy face.

'Who's Linda?' There's no malice in Noel's question after our chat.

'My aunt, she minds my father. He has Alzheimer's.' I rise to take the call in the sitting room in relative privacy.

'Hello?' The reception isn't great.

'Callum, I'm sorry. I know you're away with Abby, but it's your dad.' Linda's voice cracks. She holds it together long enough to explain.

'Is he hurt?' I screw my eyes tightly shut and brace myself for the worst, realising it's a phone call I've been subconsciously waiting for.

'I don't know. That's the problem. I can't find him anywhere.' Linda blames herself, she always does.

'Did you ring the hospitals?' At least she doesn't say he's dead. It isn't the first time he's gone walkabout. It won't be the last, once we get him home in one piece that is.

'Yes. And the guards. Nobody's seen him.' A worried sob escapes her.

'I'm on my way. Keep calm, he'll turn up. He always does.' I end the call and sigh heavily.

Abby lingers in the doorway. 'Everything okay?' she asks tentatively, tucking her wavy hair behind her ears.

'Dad's gone walkabout. I have to go and look for him.' I cross the room and put my arms around her, inhaling the familiar scent of her exotic fruit shampoo.

'I'll come with you,' she offers.

I'd love her company, but she's needed her with her own family to organise tonight's party. Noel made it very clear that he didn't often get his daughter home. It wouldn't be fair to drag her back across the country with me. I'm ninety per cent sure Dad will turn up, he always does. Though there's a niggle of doubt in my stomach that I forcefully shove down.

'You stay and help Alicia decorate the venue. It'll be a good opportunity for you to bond. I'll be back as soon as I find him.' The last thing I want to do is leave her at The Landmark, waiting for a man for the second time in her life.

She visibly cheers at the prospect of my return.

All I have to do now is find him. I throw on a hoody and hop into the Jeep. Abby passes me a reusable cup containing a strong coffee and two croissants through the window.

'Let me know when you find him. Be careful.' She blows me a kiss and takes a step back.

Noel lurks at the front door and raises his hand awkwardly.

I break every speed limit ever implemented in my rush back to Dublin. Worry settles at the pit of my empty stomach. Dad's condition's deteriorated rapidly even in the last few weeks. There's no choice. He's going to have to accept a live-in carer. Relocating him into one of those homes, no matter how nicely they're decorated, is not an option. Neither is me moving back into that house, not unless Abby comes with me. Now there's a thought. The place has plenty of room for a generous extension. I file the romantic notion for a less stressful day.

The rain in Dublin is damp rather than drenching. I hunch my shoulders, scouring the streets of Dun Laoghaire for a silhouette resembling my father. The obvious spots are none runners. I jog the entire length of the pier for the third time with no success.

We'll be lucky if he hasn't caught pneumonia in these conditions. I ring Brian in Cork, but it rings out. I fight the rising panic, struggling to summon places of significance to him, or my mother, somewhere he might be reminiscing.

I make a quick trip back to his house to check he hadn't returned by himself. The way things are going, I'd never be that lucky. Clouds blacken overhead. At almost five o'clock, despair is edging into my soul, my return to Carrick's looking increasingly less likely. A depressing thought which I feel utterly shit about. To abandon Abby at The Landmark again is unthinkable. But unless I find Dad, there's no way I can leave. My stomach rumbles. The only thing I've eaten was the croissants this morning.

Cruising the streets in the Jeep, I scan the area. One thing's for certain, if and when I find him, he's not getting left alone for a single second ever again.

The fish and chip shop that Abby and I ordered take out from only a couple of weeks earlier looms ahead. I double park outside and stick my hazard lights on, weak with hunger. The smell of grease and vinegar wafts through the stifling air. A middle-aged woman in white overall and a chef's hat shovels chips into brown paper bags behind the counter. There are four people in front of me. My feet tap the laminate floor rhythmically, I try not to look as impatient as I feel.

After what feels like an eternity, I reach the front and ask for whatever is already cooked, desperate to make every second count before resuming my search. She hands me an open packet of battered cod and chips, which I drown in vinegar before leaving the shop. Traffic's quiet, I leave the

Jeep idling and cross the road to sit on a low stone wall overlooking the sea, my spirits soggier than my chips.

The outline of a figure hunched over a bench ten metres away catches my attention. I jump to my feet, unable to believe my luck. Dad clutches his head in his hands, sporadic jolting movements imply he's crying. Passers-by slow to look, but nobody stops to check if he's ok. I close the distance between us in three seconds, lunging for him as though it were the final chance of the game.

'Dad?' I put an arm round his shoulder, and he turns his head sadly towards me.

'I've looked everywhere, son.' His sorrow winds me. 'I can't find her anywhere. She's left me. None of her clothes are in the wardrobe.' He wipes a stray tear from his cheek. I pull him closer to me.

'She didn't leave you, Dad.' Though that's exactly what she did. 'She died, Dad, do you remember?'

His crinkled eyes screw tightly as he battles unsuccessfully to remember. His shoulders shudder again. I attempt to shelter him from his pain in an unnatural embrace. The rest of the world goes on around us, as his shatters yet again.

A while passes before he straightens up to apologise. 'I'm sorry, son.' He's unable to meet my eye.

'Don't be sorry, Dad. I need you to be safe. Linda's worried sick about you.' I pull my phone out and call her. She answers immediately, relief flooding her voice. Dad stares at the ground, ashamed at losing it again. He picks at the chips silently while I wonder what will become of us all.

'Do you want to go for a drive?'

'It's not like I'm doing much else.' A glimmer of his old self flickers through as he manages a sad smile.

I guide him towards the Jeep, formulating a plan.

'Where are we going?' He gazes out the window while I drive. At a nearby petrol station, I lock him in the car with the view that if he tries to open the door, at least the alarm will sound. The quality of flowers left so late in the day aren't great, but it's the thought that counts. They're an apology; for not being able to help her, for not being enough to keep her, for not taking better care of Dad.

'We're going to visit Mam.' I need closure, never mind him. Dad will forget again, it's inevitable. But I don't know what else to do. At the cemetery, I hand him the flowers.

We cross the overgrown pathway, past hundreds of headstones; some expensive marble, some moss-covered stone, a reminder that none of it really matters in the end. Eventually, we reach my mother's final place of rest. It's not a place I visit often. I've never truly felt that she's here.

Dad collapses onto the ground, sobs wracking through him again. It's heartbreaking. For the first time in my life, I can almost imagine what it was like for him, when he lost my mother. Only now that I've found love myself, does the horror of losing it so permanently resonate with me. I can't lose Abby. I'm suddenly certain that I need to spend the rest of my life with her.

CHAPTER FORTY-THREE

ABBY

Stepping through the front doors of The Landmark is like taking a step back in time. The large reception area's been redecorated, but the outstanding river views to the right remain precisely as I remember: the idyllic backdrop for the Pinterest-perfect wedding album with my not-so-perfect groom.

I swallow the golf ball forming in my dry throat and breeze past the informal dining area through to the back bar to begin decorating for the evening's event. It's paramount to my mental health that I do this now, that I face this place before tonight. I have to let go of any emotional attachment in private, not in full view of every extended relation I have.

Alicia accompanies me, silently glancing around. Her quiet thoughts mirror my own, contemplating the previously agonised over details of a wedding that didn't materialise. We brought a bag filled with pearlescent heart bunting to hang, lanterns with LED candles to add romance and hundreds of photos of Mam and Dad at various weddings and other family functions from the past thirty years.

We set to work carefully in the designated area that the manager pointed out to us. He's the same man that made our booking almost five years earlier. If he recognises me as the bride who got dumped the night before her wedding, he's polite enough not to mention it. Luminous chair covers now brighten up the previously dark room. The decor isn't to my taste, but it's a relief that it's at least different to how I pictured it.

Armed with a mountain of Blu Tack, we hang the various photos, pausing to smile or reminisce as the memories resurface. There are photos from the eighties – Mam sported a dreadful tight curly perm and Dad with some sort of mullet and a cigarette hanging from his lips. He'd stopped smoking the day Mam announced she was pregnant with Alicia, apparently. I tried not to take it personally that he hadn't done that on my behalf. By all accounts, I was 'a pleasant surprise'. I still can't believe that two people who have unprotected sex could still be surprised at a resulting baby, but hey ho.

Another image captured the four of us on holiday in Spain. I look about ten and Alicia looks six or seven. It was our first time abroad. The bubbling excitement we'd experienced rushes back to me, even twenty-odd years later.

The final photo I come across had been taken in Dublin last year. Mam and Dad arrived on the pretence of a trip to the theatre. They'd been checking up on me. I had literally just received word I'd landed the position on Ireland Today. It had been a wonderful opportunity to share my good news with them. Though that was the weekend it finally sank in that I was never moving home. No matter how many demons I put to bed this weekend, Dublin is my home now.

'This is thirsty work,' Alicia announces after a victorious battle with the final row of bunting. We survey our handiwork. It looks good. Mam'll pretend that she hates the fuss, of course. Though we all know she loves it really.

'I'm buying. What do you want?' I pull out two bar stools nearby and we perch companionably next to each other.

'I'll have a Bulmers. Better not start on the wine too early. Can you imagine Mam's face if we turn up shit faced to the party?'

'Better yet, if we just sit here like this, drinking until everyone else arrives.' I gesture down to my ripped skinny jeans and sweatshirt and snigger at the thought.

The barman fetches our drinks and disappears into the background again. Several tables are occupied with couples and families enjoying lunch. I'm glad to have braved it. All thoughts of Sean and that wedding scratched from my mind. It's only a hotel, after all. It shouldn't be personal. In my head, I'd built it up to be more significant than necessary. Mind you, it hadn't been particularly lucky for me in the past. I only hope

Callum finds his father safe and well. I pray he makes it back again in time, not relishing the thought of everyone assuming Poor Abby has once again been stood up. The situation is wildly different, but I'd prefer to avoid anyone's pity, and prefer even more to show off Callum Connolly as my boyfriend.

'Did you ever hear from him after that?' Alicia interrupts my thoughts of Callum.

'About an hour ago. Still no sign of him. I hope he's ok. I hope they're both ok.' I take a sip of my gin and tonic.

'Not Callum. I meant Sean.'

I hadn't laid eyes on him since the day he forced his lips on mine, resulting in that embarrassing picture in the evening gossip column.

Once the dust settled, I hadn't pursued the restraining order. Bar the occasional paranoia, I have nothing to file against. In the eyes of the law, Sean is a model citizen. And I know he would never physically harm me. His return into my life isn't exactly a welcome one, but once I adjusted to the initial shock, his presence doesn't bother me. Out of sight, out of mind.

'You saw the photo?' I shrug.

'The entire world saw the photo. Then it disappeared without a trace,' she reminds me with a small laugh. 'My big sister, the celebrity, with not one, but two handsome men chasing her. It's tough at the top.' Alicia's lips curl with a sliver of envy.

'I'm sorry, Lesh.' I use her childhood nickname for the first time in years.

'Me too. I wish things could have been different. Not because I particularly wanted you to marry Sean, but because when you didn't, you changed.'

Her remark stings, primarily because it's true.

'I couldn't stick it here. I'm sorry.' She's right. I literally cut off everyone that witnessed my humiliation. It was the only way I could reinvent myself. I refused to be near anything or anyone that reminded me of who I was when I was with him. The girl that almost had it all.

And now I really do have it all. Surrounded and enveloped by Callum's love, I expect the world, and my friends and family from before, to just jump back into line with me. Selfishly, it never occurred to me that they might have changed too. How it might have affected them when I shut them all out of my life. It was self-preservation, but that didn't excuse my coldness. Realisation floods me, and I place my arms around my little sister again. This time, instead of flinching, she cries.

'Don't ever think of leaving me again,' she warns, wrapping her arms around me and returning the hug.

'Oh, Alicia, I wasn't thinking straight. I didn't realise until now.' The words catch in my throat.

We break apart. 'Come home more, sis. We all miss you.'

'I will, I promise.'

By eight thirty, the bar area's overflowing with relatives, neighbours and family friends from years gone by. Over a hundred guests arrived, including Sean's parents, who I'd so far managed to avoid. Mammy's in her element, working the crowd, feebly proclaiming she didn't want a fuss. Daddy stands at the bar, buying drinks for everyone and anyone he meets.

Alicia's new man, Luke, the college boy, arrives. Dad's renamed him Alicia's 'jailbait' as she currently introduces him to Mam's three sisters, who congregate like the witches of Eastwick.

Dad's brother Davey creeps up beside me, startling me. 'All alone again, are you?'

'Looks that way, doesn't it.' I refuse to make excuses for Callum's absence. To a person with no knowledge of the situation, it might sound feeble. I know the truth, though it doesn't stop me glancing at the door for the hundredth time, praying for a miracle. I'd heard nothing since six o'clock, but at least he found his father. It would have been unfair to expect him to leave Jimmy after everything.

A few movers and shakers fill the makeshift dance floor already. The band plays lively covers from the seventies and eighties. I'd need to consume an entire bottle of wine before contemplating dancing, a prospect I haven't yet ruled out. The escalating noise level's all too much. I crave a breather and some fresh air.

Pinching a bottle of white wine from one of twenty positioned at the end of a long buffet table, I head outside with a fresh glass. The evening has dried up, and the temptation of a little solitude is too inviting to pass on. The full skirt of my black, knee-length prom dress swishes from side to side as I stroll pointedly through the reception and out the front door.

Several evening strollers nod at me as I cross the road to sit at a vacant wooden picnic table overlooking the Shannon. I tuck my pointed platinum stilettos under the table and squint at the fuchsia scene in the sky. The screw cap twists open easily and I slug a generous measure into my glass, enjoying the burn as it slips down my throat.

Birds sing carelessly and distant laughter echoes in the background. I close my eyes and allow the last of the evening rays to warm my face.

The wood stained bench bends suddenly under the weight of another body and my eyes fly open in surprise. Next to me, sits the very man that I'd been determined not to think about all day, the very man I used to dream with, in this exact spot.

Cream chinos and a khaki shirt hug his lean frame. His hazel eyes burn intently on me. He runs a hand thoughtfully over his short designer stubble. He's still attractive. There's no denying it.

'Abby.' My name had fallen silkily from that tongue a million times, yet it hadn't meant enough in the end.

'Sean, what are you doing here?' It wasn't a complete surprise. A tiny part inside acknowledged there was a chance he might arrive. It's a small town after all.

Did a part of me even want him to? With Callum's sudden departure and the nostalgia and familiarity of my hometown, I'm reminded of the life I had once before.

It had been a good life, one that I wouldn't have given up, had the decision been left to me.

'If my father catches sight of you, he's likely to skin you

alive.' I glance around, guilty by association, yet his presence here is almost fitting.

'Abby, please, there's so much I need to tell you.' He launches in, not even pausing to draw breath. 'I made the biggest mistake leaving you, but we were too young. The thought of forever freaked me out. Now I only dream of it.' He inches closer to me.

'Don't, Sean, just don't. It doesn't matter anymore.' Why does he have to rock the boat? I wonder, if I hadn't met Callum, would I take Sean back? Would he ever have resurfaced if it wasn't for Callum's role in my life?

'For years, I willed you to return. There was plenty that I wanted to say to you. Since I met Callum, I don't feel the need. There's nothing to say. It's over between us, it has been for years.'

My anger evaporates. A deep sense of sadness threatens to set in its place, sadness for what might have been, especially when I look at my parents. Thirty years married today. Will I ever have that with Callum? With anyone, for that matter?

It's time for Sean to go. I've moved on. Now he's here, I'm not even remotely interested in why he left me. Suddenly, none of it matters.

'I love you, Abby. I've spent the last four years regretting my decision, too ashamed to show my face, wondering what it might take to win you back.' He tries to take my hand, but I shrug him off.

'You're too late...' A salty tear slides down my right cheek. Tears for my family, tears for my younger self, certainly not tears for him.

Mistaking my emotion, Sean throws his arms around me, pulling me into a chest that feels all wrong.

'I'm so sorry, Abs.'

Furious footsteps approach from behind us. I break away

from Sean's embrace in time to see Callum swing a punch at Sean's face.

'What the fuck, man? Get your hands off her.' Callum towers over us in a thunderous stance.

'In case you didn't notice, she wasn't exactly pushing me away.' Sean smirks, twisting the knife. Nothing to lose and all to gain.

Passers-by gather to witness the heightening exchange, and I pray that Mam and Dad remain in the bar, oblivious to the commotion.

'One more word out of your poisonous mouth, and I will knock your head clean off your neck. Do you understand me?' Callum's voice's dangerously low, aware of our increasing audience.

'Does he talk to you this way too, Abs? She used to love a filthy mouth,' Sean taunts Callum further.

Red rage flushes Callum's cheeks. A vein throbs furiously at his temple. 'I'm going to give you three seconds to walk away from us right now, or I swear to God, I will not be responsible for my actions.' Callum's knuckles click. He clenches his fists, subconsciously preparing for a fight.

'I'll go when Abby asks me to leave. We were actually having a bit of a moment before you interrupted.' Sean looks at me with a silent, defiant question in his eyes: *Me or him? Now or never?*

I look between the two men. One I thought I loved, the other who taught me to love myself again, following the aftermath of the first. It's a no-brainer. I throw my arms around Callum's waist. I pick Callum. It'll always be Callum.

Sean reluctantly disappears into the distance, kicking a rock he passes as he leaves.

'Twice, I've had to witness his grubby hands on you.' Callum nuzzles into my hair. 'Don't let there be a third time...please.'

I tilt my head up to meet his gaze. His eyes look tenderly into mine. He's nothing like the man-whore I pegged him for in the early days, not when it came to me, anyway. If anything, it was my behaviour that was off. I should have pushed Sean away quicker.

'I'm sorry.'

Callum pushes his lips possessively onto mine, parting them gently with his tongue. Lust fuels me, I melt into his kiss, pressing myself against him, desperate to feel his body close to mine.

I break our kiss, remembering the reason for his absence. 'Where's your father?'

'Brian's staying for a few days until we can sort out a full-time carer.' He brushes a stray strand of my hair from my face.

'Thank you for coming.' I'm touched at the extent he had gone to get back to me.

'You might recall, I told you once before, you have no idea of the lengths I'd go to for you. You didn't believe me at the time.' Callum takes my hand and we stroll towards The Landmark together.

CHAPTER FORTY-FOUR

ABBY

Dad warmed to Callum before the weekend was out, with Callum promising VIP match tickets and a few pints afterwards. I'm newly optimistic with the prospect of blending my new life in Dublin with my old one in Carrick, no longer terrified of them crossing. So much so that I'm planning a show about it, something along the lines of, How To Embrace Your Past As Part Of Your Future.

Alicia and Mam wave us off with tears in their eyes, like we're heading to the other side of the earth instead of Dublin. I promise to return as soon as possible and am actually looking forward to it, keen to reacquaint myself with a town that I've been avoiding.

'You ok?' Callum places his hand on my thigh, giving it a gentle squeeze.

'I will be, once I get you back to my house.' There hasn't been a lot of time for intimacy while we've been away.

'I hear you.' He winks and accelerates.

I wonder for the millionth time in the last couple of

months what on earth I've done to deserve this man. It isn't something I'd ever have predicted. Then again, nobody did, not even Esmerelda.

The moment we enter my cul-de-sac, I realise there's a problem. Vivid flashing lights from an ambulance illuminate our private estate. Several neighbours hover excitedly on their doorsteps, observing the unusual commotion from the house next door to mine. Callum swings into my drive and motions for me to stay in the car. No chance. I get out and cross Mrs Boyle's perfectly tended to peonies.

The ambulance speeds off, lights flashing but no siren. Two plain-clothed detectives remain alongside two uniformed guards. Callum approaches one of the detectives, who apparently recognises us. His eyes dart back and forth as he makes the connection.

'What happened?' Callum asks.

'Is this your house?' The second detective quickly joins us.

'It's mine,' I confirm.

'Do you mind if we go in?' The first detective, who's older and heavier, gestures to my front door. I fumble in my handbag for keys and hand them to Callum to open the door, shaken by the commotion.

Callum shows them into the hallway. The guards take in every inch of my house as they follow us through to the kitchen.

'How well did you know Mrs Boyle?' The younger guard asks, removing a notepad from his breast pocket.

'She was a good neighbour. We had tea together a few times. She was nice, if a little nosy, God forgive me. She took the odd parcel for me. I checked on her if I hadn't seen her for a few days.' The words tumble out of my mouth in no particular order. I realise he referred to her in the past tense, and so had I.

'Is she dead?' I know the answer already.

'I'm afraid she is.' The older detective nods.

Esmeralda's words from weeks ago strike me with an unnerving clarity, instantly transporting me back to her crumbling cottage in Wicklow amongst the smell of the cats and chilling evening air.

She'd been right. About everything. Mrs Boyle was as close as a person could get, in proximity. She lived next door. I initially assumed that Esmerelda's prediction referred to a person I had a close relationship with, not the person I lived close to. Nevertheless, she'd been spot on.

The work opportunity. Then Karen's cancelled engagement. Now someone close to me had died. Is it wrong that I'm relieved that if it had to be anybody, it's Mrs Boyle, who I wasn't overly fond of, but lived fifteen feet away from me?

'What happened?' Callum questions as I stand rigid and quiet.

'We aren't a hundred per cent sure. One of her sisters called round for a visit this afternoon, and when Mrs Boyle failed to answer the door, it roused her suspicion. Initial reports indicate a stroke, but we're waiting on the coroner's report to eliminate foul play. We'll know more in the next twelve hours.'

Callum makes the two detectives coffee as they ask the usual questions: Where had we been this weekend? Had we noticed anything unusual lately?

This type of thing happens in movies, or to other people. I answer to the best of my ability, but I'm in shock. Ashamedly, not just because my next-door neighbour had dropped dead, but more so because it had been predicted with an unnerving accuracy by an elderly woman forty miles away. And it was only half an hour ago that I'd literally dismissed her predictions as nonsense.

Callum shows the officers out. The thought of his big strong arms around me, under the comfort of my duvet is something I selfishly crave while poor Mrs Boyle isn't even cold yet. Despite my physical desire for him, a wave of uncertainty penetrates my soul.

Would Esmerelda be proved right about everything?

This unnerving thought casts a whole new light on mine and Callum's relationship. Maybe it's destined to fail from the very beginning. A hollow feeling of desperation edges into my heart, contrastingly low against the highs of the weekend.

Callum climbs into bed next to me. His presence here feels so overwhelmingly right. Yet if Esmerelda's third prediction proves as accurate as her first two, it's all wrong. She distinctly told me, in no uncertain terms, that I would marry a man called Patrick, a fact which I'd laughed out loud in response to. It's no laughing matter now.

I fall into a troubled sleep, one where Sean Fitzpatrick lurks in every corner.

CHAPTER FORTY-FIVE

CALLUM

Abby took the death of her elderly neighbour terribly, sobbing at the funeral, as though the woman was her very dear and treasured grandmother instead of a mildly acquainted neighbour she occasionally had tea with. The autopsy confirmed she died of a stroke. It's been a week, yet Abby wears a permanently haunted look. I can't shake this horrible feeling that she is troubled by something closer to home.

Things should be looking up. I've secured a full-time carer for Dad, and he's actually enjoying the company. I've forged the foundation of a relationship with Abby's family. Noel has been in touch a few times. Harmless sporting exchanges, but it's a promising start. Then there's my best friend's upcoming wedding only a few short weeks away. Yet for some reason, Abby and I are paralysed in some weird limbo that I can't for the life of me understand. She answers when I talk to her, but there's a faraway look in her eyes. I can't remember the last time she initiated a conversation that didn't revolve around dinner.

She lands back through the front door, sweaty and flushed from a long run, the only thing she claims lifts her spirits. I'm yet to see it, but don't argue with her, trying not to take it personally that she can't gauge some kind of comfort from me. Little by little, she's becoming increasingly distant. I can't go on like this. Tact has never been my strong point. After breaking down all of her carefully assembled walls to get to where we are, if I don't pull her on it soon, the barricades will be rebuilt so high and wide that I might never successfully penetrate them again.

I open a bottle of chardonnay and prepare fresh salmon while she showers. I'm driving up and down to Carton House most days, afraid to leave her alone too long in this semi-fragile state. Yet the more time I spend here, the more distant she becomes. Maybe she needs space? I'm at my wit's end, in this weird state of nothingness.

Returning from the shower with towel-dried hair, she slips her arms around me, nuzzling into my back. Physically, things are better than ever between us. The wild, frenzied sex has progressed into something much more tender, yet equally enthralling. She reaches for me every night, and most mornings too, recently with a slower appreciation. But each time, I'm led to believe she's preparing for the last time. It's the only time I can connect with her. Mentally, she's withdrawing. Maybe it's paranoia, but it's like she's preparing to leave me. It's eating me alive.

'Abby.' I turn to face her, searching her eyes for the answers I live for. She squeezes them tight, leaning into my chest, closing off from me mentally, unwilling to talk.

'When you don't talk to me, I assume the worst. Something's changed between us. What is it?'

It's killing me, being suspended in mid-air waiting to see which way the ball will land.

She lets out an enormous sigh and takes a sip of her chardonnay, buying time while she assembles the words. 'You're going to think I'm crazy. And maybe I am,' she admits warily, taking a seat at the table.

'Well I'm going crazy as a result, so you're not alone. I need to know, Abby. Is it something I did? Or did somebody say something?' Maybe she'd stumbled across something about me that she didn't like. God only knows there's enough of it out there on the World Wide Web that I can barely stomach, let alone expect her to.

I sit in the chair opposite and take her hand, willing her to communicate with me. Her withdrawal reminds me of my mother's all those years ago. I swallow back the memories.

'Alright. I'll tell you. I'm sorry if I made you feel it's something you've done. It's not you. You're perfect.' She takes another mouthful of wine. I turn the cooker down and prepare myself for the 'it's not you it's me speech.' The wait is killing me. My breathing labours in a state of nervous apprehension.

'A few months ago, Karen dragged me to a fortune teller in Wicklow.' She pauses to look at me meaningfully. I try not to laugh at the absurdity, failing to understand the relevance.

'She told me three things. First of all, that I'd get an opportunity at work which I'd be successful at. Secondly, that somebody close to me will die.' She eyeballs the direction of Mrs Boyle's recently vacated property to the right of us.

Okay, I'll admit, it's a little eerie.

'She told Karen that she wouldn't marry Dan next year,' she adds. 'I never believed in any of this bullshit, by the way, but she's been proven one hundred per cent right about every single thing she predicted.'

I fail to see what this has to do with our relationship. I don't have long to wait to find out.

'The last thing she told me, before I left, is that I'd marry a man called Patrick,' Abby says quietly, sourly into her wine glass.

I sit back to process her revelation. Confused fog clouds my mind as I decipher what she's really saying.

'Let me get this straight. After everything we've been through together, you're withdrawing from me, because some old lady predicted you'd marry a man called Patrick?' It sounds absurd, even as the words tumble out of my mouth. If it wasn't so serious, it would be hilarious. Only as I speak aloud, does the real problem hit me like a tonne of shit.

The reappearance of Sean Fitzpatrick a few weeks earlier.

She's still thinking about him. Does she consider him 'the one that got away'? He's called Patrick. She picked me in Carrick, but maybe she's regretting it.

Now I've dragged the truth of the matter out of her, I wish I hadn't. I rise from the table, shoving half my fist in my mouth to prevent saying something I might regret.

Alarm spikes in her darkening eyes, confirming my worst fears. I've hit the nail right on the head.

'Have you been seeing him behind my back?' I have to know.

'Of course not. Not like that, anyway.' Her answer does nothing to appease me.

'Like what exactly then, Abby?' I don't want the answer, but forever left to wonder would be worse.

'He's still turning up in places where he knows I'll be. In the park, outside my work. He doesn't talk to me. He just stares.'

'Abby, you promised you'd get a restraining order. After everything that happened in Carrick, I honestly thought this was behind us. You lied to me.' Even if it's by omission.

I trusted her to take care of it. I wouldn't hesitate to do the same for her, had it been a woman from my past. She guiltily eyes the floor. Maybe she enjoys Sean pursuing her? Perhaps it soothes her battered ego in a way that I would never achieve.

I'm suffocating here, the lemon walls closing in. I'd opened up to her, given her my everything and now she's holding back, and for what? A stupid prediction or an old flame? Whichever it is, I'm done trying to work it out. I walk out the front door unable to say a word, leaving the dinner in the oven to burn or catch fire. Either way, I don't care.

I could fight for her. I could show her my passport or my driver's licence, if a simple word meant so much to her. Would it make a difference? My remaining shred of pride prevents me from finding out.

I can't fight for a woman who won't fight for me. I can't be with a woman that ultimately doesn't want me, regardless of my name.

CHAPTER FORTY-SIX

ABBY

Thirteen sleepless nights have passed since Callum walked out. Every time I dare to close my eyes, I relive his hurt, the look on his face. My body aches for the touch of his hands. I'm drowning in the empty overwhelming nothingness of my life, torn between the love I want to pursue and the pointlessness of pursuing it. For an educated, self-professed cynic, I've abandoned everything I previously believed in. I'm sorely tempted to drive the forty minutes to Wicklow and challenge Esmerelda on her predictions. She may have ruined my love life for no good reason. Yet, each of her prior predictions had materialised, not just for me, but for Karen, too. Which is why I battle, unsuccessfully, to park all thoughts of Callum to one side of my brain.

Alicia is in daily contact, but I can't admit the truth of my situation to her. I'm falling back into old habits, texting instead of ringing for fear my secret shame will be discovered again. Poor old Abby still can't keep a man. Am I destined to be alone forever? No. Seemingly, I'm destined to marry a Patrick, wherever he may be right now...

Thankfully the press haven't got wind of it yet. Our break-up's bound to make at least second, if not first page news.

Callum's keeping a low profile. I stalked his social media pages relentlessly until the early hours of every morning, but there has been little or no activity.

Part of me wants to drive to his apartment and throw myself at him, to beg for his forgiveness. But the sensible part accepts that the situation is fruitless. If we're destined not to have a future together, it's better to face the pain now rather than later. The longer Callum spends in my life, the harder it would be to overcome the loss of him.

However sceptical I had been about going to a fortune teller, she had been eerily right about everything. There's no denying it. And really and truly, Callum's bound to break my heart at some point, or I'm bound to drive him away. Far safer to quit while we're ahead.

'Bet you wished you hadn't given Sally No Soul those tickets to New York now.' Aoife interrupts my thoughts. We wait sombrely for the current track to finish.

She's the only person I've admitted the truth to. It's impossible to hide anything while trapped together in our tiny studio. I trust her. She depicts a steadiness that I've come to rely upon.

'I honestly couldn't give a shit about the trip to New York.' The thought of packing a bag and boarding a flight to a country that does not have Callum in it doesn't appeal to me. Though we're apart, I take a small modicum of comfort that he shares the same city as me. Most of the week at least.

'Good Lord, you have got it bad, girl. Pull yourself together; go and see him. He's bound to be as glum as you are. What will it take for you to see that you two are made for each other?' To Aoife, it's simple. Black and white. Yes or no. In or out.

'It isn't that easy. If it's ultimately doomed from the start, I'll only end up hurt all over again,' I admit.

'You're already hurt. But you know what you really are, Abby?' She's going to tell me anyway. 'You're scared. For the first time in years, you actually care. You sit here dishing out advice to the nation, yet you don't practice what you preach. Take a chance. What's the worst that could happen?'

The worst that could happen is what remains of my fragile bleeding heart could be smashed to smithereens, irreparably and permanently, along with my job and any remaining self-worth and preservation.

The track finishes. I resume my position an inch away from the microphone. If ever I felt unworthy of this job, agony aunt to the country, it's now.

'Good morning, that was Niall Horan with "Nice To Meet Ya". Thank you for joining us on this beautiful sunny day, it's almost eleven thirty, and you're listening to Ask Abby on Ireland Today 97.5 FM.' I clear my throat before continuing with today's topic.

'Last week I received an email from a girl called Jane, who wrote to us from Wexford looking for advice. Jane's boyfriend of six years recently proposed to her, and she is yet to give him an answer. Jane's asking for the insight of the nation before she commits. Which prompted today's show, How Do You Know? I'll read the email to you, then we here in the studio would absolutely love to hear your opinions on the matter.'

I'm especially reliant on public opinion presently. If poor Jane's relying on my romantic advice, she's fecked. I inhale deeply and read from the computer in front of me.

'Dear Abby,

'I listen to your show most mornings while at work in my local shop. I'd appreciate your advice.

'Last week, my boyfriend of six years proposed to me. Well, it was more of a suggestion than a proposal, as such. Is that enough to base the rest of our lives on? A suggestion?

'He claims it makes perfect sense to get married and listed the following reasons supporting his 'proposal'.

'We practically live together anyway, there's no point in paying two lots of rent.

'We aren't getting any younger.

'We've been together six years and his family is starting to annoy him.

'Is it silly of me to want a little romance? Or should I just be grateful to have a man that wants to marry me in an era of internet hookups?

'Please advise,

'Jane.'

I sigh deeply, forgetting I'm live on air. Aoife rescues me, as she's done so many times lately.

'That's one heartfelt letter. One that so many of us can relate to, especially in this current era of Tinder and Instagram photos that boast images of happiness, love and excitement. It makes us question ourselves, our lives, and if what we have, or what we are doing is enough...' She kicks me swiftly under the desk, a warning to concentrate.

'Absolutely, Aoife. It's a tough one. I can see Jane's dilemma. She has a man who seemingly wants to spend the rest of his life with her, but is it for the right reasons? Is it a proposal of convenience and practicality rather than the fact that he is in love with her?' I ponder aloud. My mind strays to Callum once again.

'We women need a bit of romance,' Aoife muses on air.

'I think it's more than just the romance.' I warm into the

subject. 'For a lot of people, it's about feeling desired, valued, a sense of belonging.'

A flashback of Callum sitting in Aoife's chair ploughs into my headspace at a hundred miles an hour: *If you don't have it in the beginning, you're not going to find it in your laundry basket ten years later.* He'd unearthed the crux of it. No wonder the ratings went through the roof. The unnerving clarity of the memory catches me off guard, raising rippling goosebumps on my exposed arms.

'We'll take some music while we assemble some advice for Jane. We'd love to hear from the listeners at home, anyone that may have been in a similar situation. This is Kygo, Whitney Houston with "Higher Love" on Ireland Today.'

'Call him, text him, visit him – do something, please, Abby. I've never known you to be so desperately miserable,' Aoife urges, with one hand on her small swelling bump.

Candice waves from the window. Her hawk eyes study the two of us briefly, and I force the jolliest smile I can muster. Today's T-shirt reads, Kiss It, Before You Miss It.

I wonder if there's a conspiracy. Everywhere I look, every single thing reminds me of Callum. Yet I hadn't given a single thought to Sean, or any other Patrick for that matter, since the blackest day of my life, the day Callum walked out.

Aoife makes me a coffee from the Nespresso machine in the corner of our studio while I scan the incoming messages from listeners with advice for Jane. Jane's a fake name, too coincidently generic.

'What're they saying?' Aoife squints over my shoulder as literally hundreds of messages flood the screen of the iMac.

Take it when it's offered. I've lived alone for the past twelve years, loneliness is a killer.

Jane should tell him to ask properly or piss off.

Jane should go with her gut instinct, it's never wrong.

Romance isn't all it's cracked up to be, you need to marry your best friend.

Welcome to the real world, Jane. Life isn't like the movies.

Tell him to sling his hook. You're worth more, Jane!

The phones are ringing off the hook next door, the tech team sift through callers looking for opinions that might add value to the show. I sip the scalding liquid and consider Jane's dilemma rationally and impartially.

Communication's the main problem here. If Jane had sat her man down and explained to him what she had explained to me in her email, then she'd more than likely receive her answer – if what they had was enough.

Why do humans avoid talking to the ones that we have the issues with? And instead, seek validation from external sources? But we do, it's programmed into us.

The thick fog of my own ignorance thins, parting the thunderous clouds that hover over me since Callum left. Clarity dawns painfully on me.

Communication is my problem, not just Jane's. I should have openly expressed my concerns the night that Mrs Boyle died, however daft they may have sounded. Callum would have talked some sense into me. We could have laughed them off together. Instead, I let them fester, unable to voice my irrational fears, resulting in them multiplying into something that I couldn't see past.

Why did I seek validation when it came to mine and Callum's relationship, from anyone, when I'd always previously believed that we determine our own futures? I never believed in fate before, so why had I started? Fear is the answer. I didn't trust my own judgement because I'd missed any clue of Sean's unexpected departure. It was easier to shun him now, hide behind Esmerelda's predictions and use that as the reason not to get any more involved and risk the momentous hurt of life without

Callum. I pushed him away purely so I could be in control of the pain inflicted on me, because I was the one inflicting it. Distancing myself was the only way I could take control of the situation, similar to the way in which I distanced myself from Carrick on Shannon when Sean left.

All Callum had seen was the increasing distance between us. He'd obsessed on my ex having a 'Patrick' in his name, which admittedly, I'd considered, but that was before I'd seen Sean again and reinforced that I no longer had any feelings for him.

My head hurts from the force of brutally decoding my erratic emotions.

Ten seconds left on the song, and I have the first live caller on hold. I exchange an amused glance with Aoife. The live callers are wild cards. They can go either way.

'Hi and welcome back to Ask Abby. Who do we have on the line?' I attempt to sound breezy, despite my internal duelling emotions.

'Call me B. You know, for the purpose of privacy,' a deep masculine voice echoes over the line.

'Ok, B, do you have a similar story? Or perhaps you have some advice for Jane?'

A low chuckle reverberates, and he pauses for a second before he begins. 'My story's a little different. I knew from sixth class who I would marry. Thankfully, she felt the same. We're married ten years next month and have two kids.'

'Congratulations.' A rare story in these days, it was one that I thought I'd have been telling.

'I think when you know you know. It's a gut feeling. It consumes you from the inside out. Once you've found that person, the thought of a life without them is unbearable.'

Wow. B is deeply insightful, different to our usual male callers.

'So what advice would you give Jane on the matter?' Aoife says.

'I didn't ring to give Jane advice. I really rang to offer it to Abby...' An amused tone enters his voice, a small frown burrows onto my face as I consider the identity of B, concerned Sean had convinced someone to ring in, especially with a tale of an everlasting childhood romance.

'I want to tell you about a guy I know.'

Here we go... Aoife's hand hovers over the red button in case we have to drop the call rapidly.

'He was a player, in every sense of the word. Women loved him, and he enjoyed their company, though he never had any real meaningful encounters.' This wasn't the start of the tale I was expecting, though it was oddly familiar nevertheless.

'Then, out of the blue, he met this woman, and everything changed. The guy I knew was gone, replaced by a more wholesome, fuller, better version of himself. He fell in love. And while it was enthralling and dizzying, it also made him vulnerable. He couldn't see straight. He imagined things that weren't there. Things that everyone on the outside could see were merely ghosts or shadows became the living, breathing boogeyman to him. And his fear allowed him to lose his new love. And now he's a shadow of his former self.'

B's overwhelmingly familiar story resounds deeply in my empty soul. I too have felt the highs of the roller coaster of dizzying love and the subsequent undercurrents of fear dragging me below the surface. A slow, heavy tear rolls from my face down onto the keyboard in front of me.

'Ring him, Abby. He will kill me for this, but it's already killing me to watch him suffer. He loves you. I should know. I'm his brother.' A gentle click signifies Brian's departure.

I scrape the chair back forcefully and grab my purse and phone.

'I have to go,' I announce.

'Candice will fire you one of these days, Abby. Highest show ratings or not.' Aoife eyes Candice's retreating back.

'Cover for me, please,' I beg. 'Tell her I've got the vomiting bug. With any luck, she'll think you aren't the only one up the duff. By the time she realises I'm not, she'll just be relieved she doesn't have to look for maternity cover for both of us.'

Aoife sniggers, relieved I've finally come to my senses. I'm not sure if I have actually come to my senses with what I'm about to do. There's bound to be an audience at training, in addition to the entire Irish rugby team. I could be building myself for a massive fall. For all I know, Brian could be wrong, Callum could have sought solace in the arms of one of his many previous conquests. Or a new one, for that matter. The man isn't short of fangirls. But if I don't go now, while I'm relatively brave on the back of his brother's words, I never will.

I have to get to Callum. I owe him an explanation. And an apology. I need to feel his arms around me. I need to look into his devastatingly blue eyes and tell him I know...because I do know, what we have is enough for me...regardless of his name. I pushed him, shut him out and let him leave, abandoned him. All the things I swore I wouldn't do. I pray to God I haven't caused a hurt that can't be forgiven.

CHAPTER FORTY-SEVEN

CALLUM

A cluster of midweek guests congregate to witness our training. While practice offers an immediate physical distraction, it does nothing to occupy my mind.

My brain persistently reminds me of all the reasons that Abby was different to any woman I'd ever met before. Her infectious laugh, her genuine impassive attitude to sport, her perfect combination of fierce and feminine rolled into one sensationally wrapped package. Her ability to remain calm when Dad loses it. Linda loved her, and she hardly takes to anyone. James approved. Marcus and Shelly adored her. Her family are borderline crazy but a rare wholesome breed of loyal. I'm batshit fucking crazy about her. Abby Queenan is wife material, and no amount of training or drinking will erase her from my head. Made doubly troubling is she clearly no longer feels the same way about me. Did she ever? I've heard nothing in two weeks.

She left me no choice but to leave, unable to sit back and watch things deteriorate between us any longer. It's impossible, competing with the ghost of her engagement. It seems I couldn't live up to the legacy that was Sean Fitzpatrick. I unwittingly tested our relationship and failed. Our relationship gave me more than I'd ever experienced with anyone, but she'd experienced this all before. It wasn't anything special to her in the end.

'If you drop that ball one more time, Connolly, I swear to God I'm going to fucking brain you with it,' Marcus promises me with a grimace.

'Head in the game, boys,' Coach urges, like it's the real thing, not just a practice.

There are no games until August. It's only July, and we still have James's wedding ahead of us before the season kicks off again. Thankfully, we had the foresight to combine his stag party with the end of Six Nations celebrations. The thought of swanning off somewhere with these rowdy fuckers for two nights does nothing for me right now.

Abby, Abby, Abby. I'd begun listening back to her show at night. Yesterday's was particularly entertaining as she hashed out the unwritten rules of a first date with Aoife. Even Candice went live on air to offer her worldly dating knowledge.

According to yesterday's Ask Abby, I managed to bypass most of the dating faux pas of the modern world, all except one, that is. Though technically, I hadn't outright asked her to sleep with me on the first date, but I undoubtedly made certain implications. It wasn't a real date. I'd just caught her on the hop, half-naked and mad as hell outside the sauna.

Abby sounded distracted on air. Only someone that knew her well would notice. As ever, she put on a good show. I wonder if she misses me at all. Or if she has taken Sean back. The thought floods me with a fresh riptide of rage.

Only now can I appreciate what a dick I've been to women all these years. I was never bad to them, but I certainly wasn't good to them either. I've since learnt what it is like to be left wanting. Though I can't bring myself to regret my past, or I wouldn't have been forced by the lads into pursuing Abby.

Surely, she hasn't seriously taken Sean back after everything? The thought of his hands on her body sends a fresh wave of nausea to my unsettled stomach. They have so much shared history, a lifetime together. Maybe she'd been able to rediscover the part of herself that she lost when he left. Though the thought of them together disgusts me, I'd never begrudge her happiness, merely wishing it was me that could have provided her that happiness.

I run fifteen feet across the pitch, and catch a glimpse from my peripherals of a slim blonde in tight skinny jeans rushing hastily toward the field. Her dishevelled hair's piled on top of her head in one of those messy buns. I'd recognise those long shapely legs anywhere. It's Abby. I pause to double-take at the precise moment Marcus passes the ball sideways to my careless hands.

The ball slips swiftly, soft like melted butter, through my fingertips, as my soul reignites with a tiny flicker of hope that she's willing to make amends.

The sound of twenty angry elephants charges towards me before I experience the weight of my teammates bundle. One by one, they leap on top of me, clambering over one another to make their point. My game isn't good enough. Someone catches me in a headlock. It's all fun and games, but to me, it was comparable to being trapped under a thousand stampeding animals

'Head in the game, you lovestruck fucker,' James calls through the mountain of arms and legs.

'You're not the only one with a woman. The rest of us can fucking multitask,' Marcus bellows.

'Wherefore art thou, Callum? I don't even recognise you

anymore.' Eddie thumps me on the arm as he lands arse first on top of me.

I count four more of my so-called teammates accumulating on my bending body. It's darker than the deepest scrum. I struggle to breathe under the pile of bodies suffocating me. The banter's in full swing, but I fail to distinguish anything coherent, wondering if these animals will ever get off me.

Abby's here, yet I can't see past these enormous floundering eejits on top of me.

Coach blows the whistle to break up the bundle. Just as the pressure shifts from my right leg, something or someone lands hard on my left. A sharp snap resounds through my soul, a split second before the hot white pain sears through my cruciate. An animalistic shriek escapes my lips and the boys scutter over themselves to free me. It's too late. The damage is done.

Piercing pain in my chest paralyses me, radiating the length of my left arm. I dizzily question if it's broken in addition to my leg. A smothering tightness in my chest envelopes, and blinding nausea overwhelms me as I struggle to secure unobtainable oxygen.

What's happening to me?

Someone takes my hand as I loll in and out of consciousness. Blue flashing lights approach in the distance. I can fight the darkness no more.

CHAPTER FORTY-EIGHT

ABBY

The putrid smell of disinfectant and death lingers heavily in the expectant atmosphere at the Mater Hospital. Callum's been in surgery for hours. His leg's in a bad way, but worryingly, it's his heart with the real problem. How ironic.

If the ambulance hadn't already been on its way, there was a terrifying possibility that we'd have already lost him, and he's not out of the woods yet.

Physically, Callum appears the least possible candidate for a heart attack, but that's exactly what he suffered. The consultant diagnosed a rare underlying genetic heart condition, previously undetected. Terrifyingly, the doctor called it The Widow Maker. The ambulance crew resuscitated him twice with a defibrillator, and he's currently in a critical condition undergoing surgery, in the hands of Dublin's best consultants.

Jimmy and Linda sit next to me in the family waiting room outside intensive care. Jimmy paces the floor relentlessly, and Linda sits in shocked silence, occasionally glancing up to check on her brother.

I alternate between praying Callum will be ok and hating myself for wasting the last two weeks away from him.

If he pulls through this, I vow to never leave his side again. That is presuming he'll still have me. The prospect of a world without Callum Connolly is a bleak possibility I cannot afford to contemplate. He has to pull through. I need him.

'Can I get you guys a coffee?' We've already had two. Anything to pass a few minutes, or to offer a tiny modicum of control, to pretend I'm doing something productive. Waiting helplessly is killing me.

'Thank you, Abby.' Linda manages a tight smile. It's been a long day for all of us, and it's far from over.

Jimmy says nothing, transfixed in his own little world.

Twice, he's had to be reminded why we are here.

I stand and stretch, pushing down that sinking nauseous sensation, determined to remain positive for Callum's family, if not for myself.

The vending machine's located on the first floor. I take the two flights of stairs down and bump straight into Marcus and James in the corridor.

'Abby. I am so fucking sorry. How is he?' Marcus is verging on tears, emotion crackles in his deep tone.

'Don't be. By all accounts, you guys did him the biggest favour of his life. Thank God the ambulance was only thirty seconds away.' I pat him on the arm affectionately and blink back my own threatening tears.

'Any news?' James asks, subdued and horrified with the events of the afternoon.

'It's a waiting game now, I'm afraid. He's still in surgery. As soon as I hear anything, I'll let you know.' I sigh a long low, frustrated hiss, unable to believe how quickly life as we know it could be ripped so cruelly from under our feet.

'Will he be okay?' James asks the million-dollar question that none of us possess the answer to.

'All we can do is hope.' A shudder rips through me as the fragility of the human form dances before my eyes once again.

'As soon as there's news, please let us know. We'll be here,' James pleads. Black sagging bags settle underneath his eyes, adding years to his previously youthful appearance.

They accompany me to the vending machine. I slot in a few euro coins and watch as the dark brown steaming liquid falls into cheap paper cups.

'You know he's mad about you, Abby,' James says quietly.

'The feeling's mutual. But for some daft reason, one that I don't even want to explain to you, I pushed him away. If one of my listeners rang in with the same story, I'd tell her she was behaving that way to test him. Or because she doesn't believe it will last. It was a way of taking control of the situation. Self-preservation. You'd think I'd know better, given the job that I do. Amazing how it takes something like this for the clouds to clear.' It's a relief to air the oppressive guilt from my chest, even if it is to two of the most unlikely candidates.

I hand James one of the coffee cups.

'Do you know how this all started?' Marcus tugs at the collar of his polo shirt uncomfortably.

'How what started?'

'We dared him to ask you out,' Marcus admits sheepishly looking at the ground.

'I know.' I smile wistfully. 'He told me. I'm so glad it was me you picked. I bumped into him earlier in the spa area that day. He gave me the total come-on and I shot him down immediately.' I laugh out loud at the memory of us arguing over the towelling robe.

'He never mentioned that, the sly fecker.' James grins, taking comfort in discussing simpler times.

'Not for a single millisecond did we ever think it would work out between you two,' Marcus confesses, seemingly wishing to lighten his own burden. 'I'm so glad it did. We've never seen him like this. Apart from anything, it's given us years' worth of piss-taking ammunition. But it's like he's bulletproof now. He doesn't give a shit what any of us say. You did that for him,' he acknowledges with a nod of respect.

James butts in then with a thought that hadn't seriously occurred to me.

'You never know...you two might give us a day out yet.' He attempts to lighten the mood as the two of them help me carry the coffee back upstairs to Callum's father and aunty.

'Abby?' A grey-haired woman dressed in turquoise scrubs calls to me as I walked past the nurses' station.

'Is there news?' I suck in my lower lip and wait with bated breath.

'Not yet, I'm afraid. But would you just sign this for me? Linda said you're his next of kin.' That can't be right, we've only been together a few months. I scan the paperwork she presents to me, private insurance documents. The black print blurs in front of my tired eyes, I rub and blink hard twice.

I can't take in the information on the page because there's one word printed in bold font at the top that I can't tear my eyes from – Callum's name. My heart skips a beat as I take a sharp breath. There it is, in bold black print, one tiny word that jumped directly from the page straight into my previously cynical heart: Callum Patrick Connolly. I'm torn between laughing and bawling crying. A rush of elation surges tingling through me. It's the final piece of Esmerelda's eerie prediction that I'd been unwittingly searching for.

We are meant to be together. I know it myself, but this tiny reassurance evokes a final burst of confidence that I need to believe it. There's nothing left to hide behind now. It's time to feel my fear and do it anyway.

I sign the paperwork and sink silently into my seat next to Callum's family. He could have told me this two weeks ago. Why would he choose not to? The answer springs to mind immediately – because he shouldn't have bloody well had to! I'm such a fool. Such a cowardly weak fool. I can only pray that he comes out the other side and I get my chance to make it up to him, to hold him in my arms, and to bollock him for not calling me on my bullshit, instead of letting both of us suffer.

Hours pass agonisingly slowly. I churn every mistake I ever made with Callum over and over, the enormity of the hurt I probably caused him only fully hitting me now. I silently beg the man upstairs to give me the chance to right my wrongs. To make Callum happy, to tell him how loved he is, how I will never leave him again if he only gives me the chance.

The door opens and the consultant approaches. His face is neutral, displaying no hint of Callum's condition. I rise from the chair, aware of the tightness in every muscle in my body, rigid in preparation of the news. I daren't breathe for fear it will be the last breath before my world is shattered for good.

'He's out of surgery. We fitted stents and are optimistic. He's being transferred to ICU shortly. You should be able to see him soon.' I have an overwhelming desire to fling myself at this scrub-wearing hero, kiss his surgical crocs and declare my eternal gratitude.

'Oh, thank God.' Tears of sweet relief flood my face, and I joyously throw my arms around a confused looking Jimmy, who pats me on the back and smiles.

'I'll tell the lads. They're all waiting downstairs for any news.' I run down the stairs and back up again as quickly as possible. When Callum wakes up, I want to be near.

An agonising eighty minutes pass before a friendly

looking nurse in her forties sticks a reassuring head around the door.

'Abby? He's asking for you.' She nods to a private room on the ICU unit, encouraging me to enter.

Linda sits quietly in the corner, fat grateful tears of sheer relief rolling gently down her cheeks, hands clasped together in a prayer-like statue.

I'm ecstatic he's awake, but my stomach balls with writhing nerves. I fire up a silent prayer that he still wants me, that things will work out between us.

There's no going back from this. I swore that if Callum pulled through, there will be no more daft doubts planted by some old lady in Wicklow, or by anyone else for that matter.

I push open the heavy clinical door to find him propped up in a semi-reclined position, tucked under the white starched sheets of the hospital bed.

Glazed medicated eyes light in my presence. Instinctively, he attempts to rise. I shoot a warning hand out to stop him. Copious amounts of wires and tubes would have had the same effect, but I'm done leaving things to chance. I slip my hand into his warm, strong palm and kiss him tenderly on the forehead.

'Abby.' My name falls from his lips thickly.

'How are you feeling?' I balance precariously on the edge of the bed, studying him intently. His pale face is shadowed with a greyish tone, but a determined strength emanates from within.

'Like utter shite. Not least because my sporting career is undoubtedly over. But you don't know how happy I am to see you.' A hundred emotions cross his face as he struggles to locate the appropriate words.

'You frightened the life out of us.' The pent-up tension in my chest releases in the form of a relieved, lengthy exhale.

'You came to practice?' His eyes flash to mine, searching for confirmation of hope.

'I should never have let you go, Callum Patrick Connolly. I'm going to spend every day, for however long you'll put up with me, making it up to you. I'm so heartfelt sorry.' I bring his intubated hand to my mouth and kiss it lovingly. It's the best I can do for now. 'There was never a question of me going back to Sean. Not since I met you. But why didn't you tell me your middle name was Patrick when I spouted all of that daftness that I was hiding behind?'

A slow sinking anxiety creeps into the pit of my stomach again. Had he wanted the break from me? Did I push him away? Do I bore him? He's used to a different woman every weekend. Had he taken comfort in the arms of someone else in the time that we'd been apart?

'I could have put you out of your misery a long time ago,' Callum confesses. 'But I needed to know that it was me that you wanted, regardless of my name. That what we have, is enough, regardless of any prediction. Because when you're in the limelight like we are, honey, there will always be someone making predictions about us. And most of the time, they won't be good.'

I plant a kiss firmly on Callum's dry lips. 'Don't you ever do that to me again,' I warn him.

'No. Don't *you* ever do that to me again,' he corrects. 'Don't ever doubt what we have.'

'I won't. I promise. Now rest. I need you in tip-top condition as soon as possible.' I blow him a suggestive kiss.

'Move in with me,' he whispers, clutching my hand like he never plans to let go.

'Are you crazy? Did you bang your head as well as everything else? Or is the anaesthetic talking?' I tease.

'I don't want to spend another night apart from you.' The

sincerity of his words are reflected in the silver glint of his iris.

'You move in with me. More room for the kids.' Many a true word is said in jest.

'Ok.' He concedes all too easily, exhausted eyes battling to remain open.

'Sleep.' I run my fingers through his silky hair. 'I'll be here when you wake.'

CHAPTER FORTY-NINE

ABBY

Almost two weeks have passed since the day that changed everything. Callum was discharged after six days, straight into my care. He made a relatively speedy recovery, but one thing's for certain, he will not be returning to a career as a professional rugby player. The consultant is optimistic for a full recovery, but it will take time. Time is something that Callum does not have on the pitch. I expected him to be devastated, instead, he was quietly accepting of his new fate.

It helps that he'd been offered an indecent amount of work for sponsorship. Ireland's bestselling brand of running shoes offered him an advertising deal. A huge tech company from America wants to use him to advertise a personal ECG machine that's currently selling like hot cakes on Amazon. Coach has offered him a position training the under twenty-ones. Callum will not be short of work, if he wants it. And if he is, Candice is still quietly hopeful that he may yet accept a position at Ireland Today.

Having Callum under my roof twenty-four seven is heaven

on earth. He slipped into my life as effortlessly as ever and takes care of me as much as I take care of him. The few hours I spend at work each day are torturous with the knowledge that he's at home in our bed waiting for me. Thankfully, his incident hasn't affected his libido. He still behaves as though he's a sex-starved teenager.

Alicia tells me that Sean remains in Carrick, working at his parents' garage, shifting teenagers in Finnegan's on Saturday night. I had a narrow escape there. Thankfully, it's none of my business.

'Are you ready?' Callum calls up the stairs impatiently.

At long last, the day of James and Nadine's wedding has rolled around. James was initially concerned that Callum wouldn't make it. Callum wouldn't have missed it for the world, even if it meant wheeling his hospital bed to the venue. Thankfully, there's no need for that today.

'Be down in two minutes.' I squirt a generous spritz of Chanel and give myself a last once over in the full-length mirror. OTT is not the word for it. But this is no normal wedding. It's the wedding of one of Ireland's most famous rugby players to his model fiancée. James and Nadine signed an exclusive deal with Hello Magazine to be their main feature next month, but the venue will be crawling with shameless paparazzi desperate to capture a few cheap shots.

A floor-length, backless bronze dress hugs my figure elegantly, and my hair tumbles in loose curls covering my shoulders. I cautiously tiptoe down the stairs in three-inch stilettos, and Callum lets out a long low whistle of appreciation.

'I feel sorry for the bride.' He admires me like I'm the only woman in the world. At least now, I'm the only woman in his world.

'I'll take that as a compliment. Though Nadine has no fear.' My smile extends to my pearl droplet earrings.

'Seriously, you look amazing.' He kisses me passionately on the lips, and I break away knowing that given half the chance, he will destroy my freshly applied make-up before we step outside the door.

I stand back to pay homage to him. 'You look good enough to eat.' His black tuxedo is tailored beautifully over his enormous shoulders. Suggestive eyes twinkle at my obvious approval.

'Careful. I might just take you up on that.' He wiggles his eyebrows and places a firm hand on the base of my spine, guiding me out of the front door into an awaiting limo. The driver opens the door, and I slide into the back first, holding my dress at my ankles. The cool leather seats are spacious and comfortable for the short journey ahead. Both the ceremony and reception are taking place at The Shelbourne Hotel on St Stephen's Green.

The sun illuminates everything it touches, but in true Irish style, it isn't overbearingly warm. Excitement churns in my tummy as the chauffeur pops a bottle of Moët and fills two crystal flutes before closing the door.

'Cheers.' Callum raises his glass to mine, before smacking his forehead playfully and attempting to pry the glass from my fingers. Confusion stirs within.

'Oh, sorry. I forgot you don't drink...' he jokes, reminding me of the white lie I told him that very first night in the Carton Hotel when he arrived at my room with the exact same tipple.

'Very funny. Someone must have driven me to it in the last few months.' I take the glass firmly back into my own hand and tap it against his with a wry smile.

'Funny you should mention it, but you have driven me to do an awful lot of things that I'd never done before...' Callum's tone is suddenly serious. He gulps a large mouthful of champagne.

'I like to think we've evolved together.' I lean in for one of his mind-blowing kisses, with no further concern for my lipstick, but he retreats, pausing an inch in front of my face.

Before I can fully comprehend what's happening, he's on two knees in front of me on the thick red carpet of the limo, presenting the most beautiful diamond ring I have ever laid eyes on. Three perfect glittering stones glare brilliantly at me from a tiny velvet box.

'Abby Queenan, my life meant absolutely nothing until the day you walked into it. Will you do me the enormous honour of becoming my wife?'

There is only one answer I can give him. It screams at me wildly from the deepest part of my heart.

'Yes.' His lips crash onto mine in the biggest win of both of our lives.

EPILOGUE

ABBY

FOUR MONTHS LATER

'Karen, I swear to God if she opens the door, I'm not listening to one word from her wrinkly mouth. I'll give her one hundred and fifty euro in order for her not to predict my future.'

We'd meddled enough the first time. Though it had worked out perfectly in the end, there was untold heartache along the way. No way am I going through that again. She had been spot on about everything. But it didn't make it right.

'Aren't you even curious?' Karen indicates off the motorway.

'No. Not one single iota. In fact, if Callum finds out you dragged me out here again, he'll cheerfully throw you into the Liffey.' I sigh deeply and look out the window in disbelief that she managed to drag me out here for the second time this year.

'It's supposed to be a bit of fun,' Karen chimes overly cheerily.

'Yeah, and look where that got us the last time.'

'She told me something significant would happen if I visited her again in six months.' Karen reminds me of the only reason that I agreed to accompany her again.

'The only thing of significance is that you're about to hand over another hundred and fifty euro,' I say with a resigned sigh.

I turn on the radio. Sally No Soul's slot has been taken over by Bobbie's 80's Bangers and so far seems to be doing relatively well. Following Sally's interview with M.O.D.E.R.N. she was offered a permanent position on a radio station in the Big Apple. Recent updates on her social media led me to believe she may even have a new man in tow. I'm delighted for her. I really am. I wouldn't swap with her for all the world.

We fall silent for the final part of the journey, both immersed in our own thoughts. It has been a crazy few months. Karen officially came out. Nobody batted an eyelid. Her parents were super supportive, simply relieved that she hadn't gone through with the wedding. Though she is yet to meet the love of her life, the one that Esmerelda apparently predicted would materialise this month. Time is running out, but I don't doubt the prediction will materialise. The old woman has been one hundred per cent accurate about everything else, which is precisely why there's no way I'm going in again. Ignorance is bliss. I can't spend any more of my life waiting on the materialisation of a stranger's predictions. I'm too busy living every day.

Instinctively, I place a hand over my tiny bump. Three weeks away from the twelve-week mark, I made Callum swear he wouldn't tell a soul until we have our scan. The excitement is bursting from both of us, an exciting new chapter awaits.

We arrive at the crumbling cottage. Apprehension tightens in my chest. I'm not comfortable being here. The sight of the desolate hanging baskets and dead flowers proves too much. I look away.

'I'll wait here,' I insist.

Esmerelda hadn't predicted anything bad for me, but the last few months would have been so much less stressful if I hadn't had the niggling expectancy of her prophecies. It isn't something I'll ever subject myself to again.

'Suit yourself.' Karen breezes out of the car and slams the door shut before the wind takes it from its rusty hinges. She's replaced the skirts for combats or jeans, no longer feeling obliged to put on a show. The headbands remain though. That's her quirky trademark, regardless of her sexuality.

Curiosity forces me to watch her navigate the cobbled path. She doesn't have an appointment. Esmerelda has been mysteriously uncontactable this time round, which only fuelled Karen's insistency on seeing her.

She knocks firmly, the wind carrying any sound to the depths of the Wicklow mountains behind. Several minutes pass with no response. I open the car door cautiously.

'Karen. She's not here,' I state the obvious, shouting against the wintery elements.

Disappointment forms on every feature of Karen's heart-shaped face. Her black bob blows wildly as she retreats back down the path, shoulders sagging in reluctant defeat. She slumps into the driver's seat disheartened. I wince as she bangs the door again. One day, it'll fall off. She inserts the key into the ignition and starts the engine. Out of nowhere another car pulls in behind us, it's full-beam piercing startlingly through the twilight.

A woman rushes out, adjusting her denim jacket and patting her cropped hair. We linger, curious as to who else would be this far out, in the arse end of nowhere. The woman approaches, tapping on the driver's side, she peers through the window with a smile. Karen gets out of the car to speak to her.

'Are you here for the viewing?' The woman sticks out a hand and introduces herself as Fran, the agent charged with selling the cottage.

Karen's visibly taken aback as the woman explains Esmerelda's family are looking for a quick sale following the untimely death of their mother.

Darting eye contact and multiple coy bob fluffing from Karen takes me back to the playground. Karen kicks a stone sheepishly, and though I cannot hear the exact words that are exchanged, I can hear the animated edge in both women's voices.

Karen reaches up and readjusts her headband, angling her head sideways in some sort of question. The woman reaches into her pocket and hands over a business card. Karen takes it, clutching it as though it's one of Willie Wonka's precious Golden Tickets. As she reluctantly opens the driver's door, I hear her promise to call the agent later.

With a resigned smile, Esmerelda's final prediction presents in the form of the parting human gift before us. I sigh in sweet relief, hopeful that this may be the start of Karen's well-deserved happily ever after. I place my hand over the tiny human inside my stomach and smile.

OTHER BOOKS IN THE PROFESSIONAL PLAYERS SERIES:

Love & Other Games

Love & Other Lies

Love & Other Forbidden Things

Love & Other Vows

OTHER BOOKS BY LYNDSEY GALLAGHER

The Seven year Itch

The Midwife Crisis

How Will I know?

LOVE & OTHER GAMES PREVIEW....

CHAPTER ONE

Emma

As I pace the varnished wooden floor of my new extension, I'm overcome with a sinking suspicion that I'm about to become single once again. There's no sign of Paul, and our taxi is due to arrive in ten minutes. I've called him five times. Desperate, you may say, and I'd completely agree.

I'm an expert at the unwritten rules of dating, and repeated phone calls are solidly up there with 'don't mention your ex' and 'never have sex on the first date.' I rarely make an exception to any rule, but today we have a plane to catch. I'm not prepared to miss the flight to Croatia for Abby and Callum's wedding.

Several scenarios flit through my mind as to why Paul isn't currently standing at my front door with his luggage. Perhaps he's been involved in a traffic accident? Or maybe a gang of delinquent teenagers mugged him for drug money while he was on his way?

My rose gold sandals thwack against the floor. Pacing is a bad habit, but at least it gets my daily steps in. However, it doesn't do anything to eradicate the niggle of worry that warns me I've done it again; come on too strong, scared yet another one away. I have no problem attracting men, but even with strict adherence to the unwritten rules, I just can't seem to keep them. The second I let my guard down, the second I get even a tiny bit comfortable and *dare* to admit that I'm looking for something serious, I'm dumped right back at square one.

The familiar bars of Beyonce's 'Single Ladies' erupt from my phone, startling the silence. My little sister Holly picked my ringtone. In her mind being single is something to celebrate. Where I have spent most of my adult life looking for my one true love, Holly is content looking for lots of love. But she has youth on her side, and being the youngest of three girls – zero family pressure. I'm looking for husband material, and not just because of my emotionally challenged mother's repetitive digs regarding my inability to bag one, and my ever-shrinking ovaries.

I tap the green icon and press the phone tightly to my ear. 'Paul, is everything okay?'

'Emma. I'm not going to make it.'

I knew it. Deep down, I knew this would happen. His absence has already spoken volumes.

'Why?' My heart lurches in my chest.

'I'm stuck at work. The deal we're trying to negotiate isn't going as smoothly as I'd hoped.'

'So you'll meet me at the airport instead?' I hate the uncertainty that creeps into my tone.

'No. I won't make the holiday. The wedding.' He clears his throat, and the silence that follows is uncomfortable.

'You are joking?'

'I'm deadly serious, Emma. This client is a big deal to me.

If I don't nail things down this weekend, another agency could swoop in and steal the deal from underneath my nose. You know how it is, babe.' His patronising tone ignites a suppressed fire flickering in the depth of my abdomen.

'This wedding is a big deal to me, Paul. I really wanted you to be there.' Swallowing down my irritation, I wait with bated breath to see if he might miraculously have a change of heart.

Silence from the other end of the phone. He's probably staring into his computer screen, waiting to get the predictable bollocking over with.

Maybe it's weddings, in general, he tries to avoid? If that's the case, he's going to be no good to me, because I want the works; the embarrassingly humungous white dress, the Cathedral overflowing with guests, 'Pachelbel's Canon' belting out from the organ.

'You wanted *me* to go to the wedding? Or you wanted *someone* to go as your date to the wedding?' Paul asks, a knowing arrogance weaves into his tone.

Huh. I can't believe he's trying to turn this around on me! Though...perhaps he has a point. For the previous few weeks, I've been ignoring that niggling inner inkling that perhaps we aren't entirely compatible, brushing it off, squashing it down. The air whooshes out of my chest at the worrying prospect of starting over again; scrolling thousands of meaningless faces, desperately searching for one that might demonstrate some sort of potential. Embarking on endless disastrous dates in the hope of eventually finding my very own Prince Charming.

Paul clears his throat. 'This isn't working, Emma. Your need to get a ring on *that* finger is painful. Life isn't like one of those crappy romance novels you read. You're a beautiful girl, even without the inch-thick make-up, but your desperation makes you ugly.'

His comments rip through me, tearing me up from the

inside out, twisting my intestines around my heart and temporarily winding me. My mouth moves, but no sound comes out.

What's wrong with wanting to get married? It's a normal ritual in society. And in the absence of it actually happening in real life, what's wrong with seeking solace in a bit of fictional romance?

Ten seconds pass silently while I gather the strength to end this conversation with my dignity intact, no mean feat when he's just scraped the top of a deeply etched wound. Frankie, my boxer puppy, stands at my feet protectively. His black eyes remain fixed on me, head cocked in concern. I rub his silky ear between my finger and thumb affectionately.

'You are right, Paul. This isn't working. I wish you all the best. I really do.' I force the words out of my mouth and disconnect the call.

'Another one bites the dust, Frankie. Six more months of my life wasted with the wrong man. Perhaps we are destined to be just the two of us?'

Frankie wags his tail and follows me into the lounge where I gather my luggage.

Though the relationship was more likely to lead me down the garden path than up the aisle, its inevitable end, and yet another rejection, stings.

Holly calls me Emma The Assassin because she swears I'm cutthroat. In or out. Do or die. She might be right when it comes to business, but when it comes to men she is sadly very wrong. Someone with transferable skills wouldn't be considering adopting four cats and joining the local crochet club. If I was any good at dating, I wouldn't have to be doing it at all, I'd be sitting at home binge-watching Netflix, with my charming, loyal husband, while our adorable children slept quietly upstairs.

Holly claims that when I meet a man that demonstrates

potential, I do this weird nail thrumming on whatever hard surface is available, be it a sticky bar top in an over-priced wine bar, the roof of a stationary car, or even once on the side of the kitchen tea caddy as I interrogated the architect planning the extension at the back of my house.

The finger tapping translates as my own private Morse code as I mentally list the subject's positive versus negative traits and potential suitability. It's kind of crazy, but it's subconscious. I'm not even aware that I'm doing it. Luckily for me, very few people have cracked the code. Only one, in fact, and thankfully that's my baby sister, who is one of my best friends and most trusted confidants.

Holly swears blind that if the beat sounds regular and solid, like 'We Will Rock You', they're in with a fighting chance. (The architect turned out to be gay, no amount of thrumming was going to change that. I was at the peak of Queen's famous resounding chorus before he less than subtly dropped in his boyfriend has a penchant for Pina Coladas and bottomless brunches).

If the tapping beat is faster, more impatient, it's already a resounding no. They're dismissed before they've had the opportunity to swipe right.

Another heartfelt sigh escapes my lips, but honestly, I'm far from distraught. Disappointed, but not distraught. I file Paul's comments amongst the murkiest parts of my brain to analyse and agonise over when sleep alludes me, unable to dwell on my latest failure at this precise moment. Though I am now dateless – I still have a plane to catch.

Hastily, I check I have everything; keys, phone, purse, passport, book, all tucked securely into my favourite Prada crossover satchel. Taking one last glance at my reflection, I use my new sunglasses as a hairband to tame my waist-length free-falling locks.

Make-up was my first true love; the bright popping

coloured lip shades, the glittering palates, promising glamour and sparkle. My own is immaculate. It has to be because it's my armour, my shield against the world. It gives me the confidence to pose as the successful businesswoman most people believe me to be. Doublewear foundation covers a magnitude of sins; skin pigmentation, an unhealthy sugar addiction, and my infuriating inability to get more than five hours sleep.

Beyonce's 'Single Ladies' pierces the air again. For a second, I wonder if it's Paul, if he's changed his mind. Too late, the damage is done, and I'm not one for giving second chances. A quick glance at the screen shows it's Sarah, the girl I entrust to manage my business empire for me in my absence.

'Emma, sorry to bother you when you are on holiday.' Sarah's tone is apologetic. She is my longest-standing employee and a good friend at this stage too.

'Ring me anytime. What's up?'

'It's not good news, I'm afraid. The solicitor has been in touch. There's been another bid on the Balbriggan property.' She pauses while I digest this disheartening snippet of information.

This is my new venture, my latest business baby; a luxury spa, which will provide a brand-new flagship, marking my fifth branch of Believe in Beauty in as many years. It's also heavily entwined with my newest and most costly investment so far.

'How much?' I hold my breath in anticipation.

'1.1 million euro.'

'Shit.' A low whistle rolls from my lips. 'Ring the accountant, see what we can realistically stretch to. If this goes into a full-on bidding war, we need to be prepared. I cannot lose this property. It stands for too much.'

'Okay. I'll be in touch.' Sarah hangs up.

The low thrum of an engine outside signals the arrival of

my taxi. I kiss Frankie goodbye and promise him my mother will be along to collect him shortly. She might be devoid of emotion when it comes to her middle daughter, but I reluctantly entrust her with my adorable fur baby, the most loyal creature on this planet.

Stepping out into the September sunshine, I pull my sunglasses from my head and slide into the backseat. The driver lifts my luggage into the boot, no mean feat considering it's crammed with ten shades of lipstick, fifteen dresses, six bikinis and a variety of wedges, sandals and stilettos. One can never be too prepared.

'Which terminal, pet?' The driver's voice is gentle, fatherly, reminding me of my own dad, who works out of the country more often than he is in it, no doubt chased away by my mother's coldness or indifference.

'South, please.' I run my fingers over the soft fabric of my maxi dress and try not to think about Paul's parting comments. Will he go back to banging Tammy-tits, his busty twenty-two-year-old PA? He assured me it was over long before he met me, but one look at her informed me she still had designs on him. Surprisingly, I don't care either way.

Dublin airport is only ten minutes away from my red brick house in Swords, and traffic is light. As the car passes the familiar landmarks, my thoughts turn to Abby and her upcoming nuptials. She's a radio presenter – the wedding will be full of Irish celebrities. Not only did she snag one of Ireland's most handsome rugby players, but they also have a beautiful five-month-old daughter, Casey. I don't begrudge her, on the contrary, she deserves every happiness, having had rotten luck in the past. But I can't help but wonder if I haven't had enough rotten luck now too? How many more frogs will I have to kiss before I find my prince?

I huff unwittingly, and the taxi driver glances back in his rearview mirror.

'You alright back there, love?' His unexpected kindness results in tears brimming, threatening to spill all over my painstakingly applied make-up. I swallow hard, pushing them back in place.

'Grand, thanks.' I lie. I need to pull myself together. I'm going on holiday. To witness the nuptials of one of my closest friends. I won't let Paul's parting remarks or anything else ruin it.

As the view of the city fades behind us, I contemplate how and when I will resume the husband search. If it's not Tinder, it will be back to scouring trendy cocktail bars on a Friday night. Serial dating is exhausting. When I was younger, I enjoyed it, filled with misplaced hope every single time I went on a new date. Each date offered a chance, an opportunity. After an epic amount of time wasters and appalling experiences, the prospect now seems worse than manual labour in forty-degree heat.

Shrinking ovaries aside, perhaps a lifetime of watching *Don't Tell the Bride* alone isn't the worst thing in the world? At least I won't have to share the remote. Imagine lying on the sofa in my pyjamas on a Friday night, eating whichever take away I choose, make-up free and bra-less. Though it doesn't even have to be a lifetime...even a few months would be an absolute treat.

The thought of a reprieve from the romantic rat race is overwhelmingly appealing, but the fact is, I'm not getting any younger.

Removing my phone from the satchel, I glare at the little square apps; Tinder, Hinge and Plenty of Fish. Deep down inside, I know that my heart and head can't take much more rejection. Not at this point anyway. I'm indifferent about Paul. It was the one before him that cut me the deepest. I have a tendency to jump from one man to another, almost frightened to be alone, trapped in my eternal quest of finding a man to settle down with.

Would a couple of months make that much difference in the real scheme of things?

In a moment of quick decision, I delete all the dating apps from my phone. Maybe I am cutthroat after all? If I take myself out of the game, I can't lose. An instant surge of relief ripples through me. Flicking my hair back from my face with a single-minded determination, I decide to devote my attention solely to the spa for the next three months. It might not keep me warm at night, but it will keep me busy. Business is the one thing that I excel at, so it's immeasurably safer to invest in, than risky gambles with matters of the heart. A three-month break will do me the world of good; recharge, reassess and restart from a stronger position.

Arriving at the airport with a newfound spring in my step, I pay the driver, humming away to myself, lighter than I've been in months.

Chapter Two

Eddie

I'm late as usual, I can't help it. It's one of my world-renowned failings. I shouldn't have gone out last night, but I needed a distraction from my latest, and most epic, bust up with Maria. She's hot, cold, hot, cold. It's finally over, and frankly, I'm glad to be shot of her mental games.

With Balbriggan beach only eight metres behind me, I inhale the familiar salt and seaweed scent as the waves of the Irish Sea crash against the shore. Dublin is sunny but breezy today, with that distinct nip in the air, the one that creeps in every year when kids start back at school.

I cross the narrow road and lean on the high bricked wall to wait for the estate agent. I'm not the only one that's late this morning. A man in his forties pulls up in a black Volvo. He hurriedly exits his car, smoothing down his crumpled suit and wipes his hand on his jacket before reaching out to shake mine.

'Eddie Harrington?' He checks, although by the awestruck way he's staring at me, he already knows who I am. 'It's a pleasure to meet you. I'm Tim O'Rourke, the agent charged with selling this property.'

'Tim, I don't mean to be a dick, but I'm in a massive rush today. It's Callum Connolly's wedding in four days, and I have a plane to catch. Can we make this quick? I'll make it easy for you. I'm ninety-nine per cent sure I'm going to purchase this property for my brother. So if we could just have a quick look inside, I'll get a formal offer sent across to you from my solicitor before I board my flight.' I'd already viewed five others, all of which claimed to have a sea view, which might be true if you stood on the kitchen table, jumped up and down in the air and craned your neck. When this place suddenly came to auction, it felt like fate.

'Great. Wonderful. Though the bidding is technically open until Tuesday, and there is a lot of interest. Properties such as this rarely come up for auction. But I'm sure we can arrange something.' Tim gives me a conspiring 'boys together' type of wink, and I have to fight my eyes from rolling in my head.

He pulls out the key from his trouser pocket and unlocks the door with shaky fingers. Following him into a spacious corridor, I note the stairs are wide enough to fit a stairlift. The house is very similar to the one I live in myself, five doors down. Having bought that property fifteen months ago, I then spent the first nine months renovating. It's the ultimate bachelor pad with a bar area, a games room, thick carpets, expensive decor, and enormous triple-glazed windows which open out on to a sea-facing balcony. I haven't put a hot tub in yet, but it's on the to-do list. The fact of the matter is that I'm away training more often than I'm in it at the moment.

'How's the rugby going?' Tim interrupts my thoughts, determined to make conversation despite my aforementioned time constraints.

'Grand thanks. If I'm successful with this property, I'll send you two match tickets to a home game.' It's a sneaky bribe. Anything to seal the deal.

I take in the double doors, high ceilings and wide corridors. It will be perfect for my wheelchair-bound brother and his family when they relocate from the States next month. The back garden is completely paved. Another bonus – minimal maintenance will be required. Opening the sliding doors, I'm greeted by the rhythmic sound of the waves again. I hope the seaside location will soften the blow for Matthew, sweeten the fact that he has no choice but to return home.

'I'll take it,' I tell Tim, retracing my steps out to the front door.

'Don't you want to know what the current bid is?' A frown burrows on Tim's bushy eyebrows.

'My solicitor will deal with everything. She'll be in touch with a formal offer within the hour.' She's actually my older sister. Keira takes care of all of my finances, but Tim doesn't need to know that.

'The auction closes on Tuesday morning at ten a.m. The highest bidder must be available to sign the paperwork that day. This property *is* in great demand,' he repeats.

They all say that, though, don't they? It's a direct quote from The Salesman's Handbook.

'I'll send you those match tickets.' I couldn't be any more obvious, but I don't care. The property is perfect for Matthew. I have to have it.

I jump into the taxi that awaits me, five doors down. The

driver chews noisily on a piece of gum as we begin the journey to Dublin airport.

My mind drifts to Matthew again – he's never far from my thoughts. He will hate me for buying him a house. He will assume it's guilt. Maybe it is, but we all want to ensure his transition back to Ireland goes as smoothly as possible. I'll find a company that manufactures stairlifts and get one fitted the second I sign that contract.

Temporary traffic lights on the motorway add forty-five minutes to the journey. I throw the driver a fifty, grab my holdall and rush towards the Aer Lingus check-in desk.

'Dubrovnik.' I tell the twenty-something girl, clothed head to toe in the familiar shade of green.

'Cutting it fine.' She observes with a raised eyebrow. If she recognises me as the Irish rugby team's current hooker, she doesn't show it.

I leg it towards security, skidding to an abrupt halt at the back of a long line of unmoving holidaymakers. What is the hold-up? I glance at my watch pointedly and bite back the 'for fuck's sake' that's on the tip of my tongue. If we don't get moving soon, there's an acute possibility that I might miss the flight to one of my best friends' wedding. My size twelve Nikes tap against the dirty floor impatiently, for all the fucking good it does me.

A woman's outraged voice travels the length of the queue. I can't make out a word that she's saying, but the passengers in front of me are nudging one another and sniggering. I side-step to get a better look.

A tall, curvaceous brunette stands with her back to me, berating two guards, who are currently rifling through her small suitcase. She flicks her long dark hair aggressively with the back of her hand, and her tanned arms fly frantically around in exaggerated gestures. Dresses line the metal surfaces. Brightly coloured bikinis and numerous lone shoes are strewn across the floor. Whatever the security guys are looking for, they haven't found it yet. If her case is overweight, I'll happily pay the difference for her trouble, if she'd just get the fuck on with it and quit holding everyone up. I debate calling out to her with my offer.

The woman's tone becomes increasingly irate as a black lace bra drops to the floor. I'm temporarily distracted from my own concerns, entranced by her picture-perfect hourglass figure captured in a slim-fitting, floor-length dress.

After what feels like an eternity, the brunette locates what she's been looking for. She triumphantly thrusts a flashing, vibrating electric toothbrush in the guard's face and tilts her head defiantly. His shoulders sag, and his reddening face drops to the floor.

I can't help it. An explosive rumbling laugh erupts from the depth of my gut as I realise the extent of the situation. The brunette spins swiftly round on her heel to locate the source of the amusement. Her glinting emerald glare penetrates me like a bullet. My laughter lodges in my windpipe as I absorb her familiar features; it's Emma.

Now it's me that looks to the floor, though I raise one arm casually in a greeting which I hope conveys I'm apologetic and not just for laughing at her current misfortune. I haven't seen her since *that* night. Or morning, should I say. That's not to say I haven't thought about her, though. Quite the contrary, in fact.

The line moves again. I remove my belt and shoes in preparation for the metal detector, keeping my eyes fully focussed on Emma's rapidly disappearing silhouette. Obviously, she's going to Callum and Abby's wedding.

I have tried so hard not to think about what happened last year, about what might have been, but if I'm brutally honest, she's never far from my mind. For a split second, I imagine the two of us travelling together, like the couple everyone was so sure we'd become. But like everything else in my life, I fucked it up.

I breeze through security with a nod of acknowledgement from the two guards, who are clearly in no doubt about who I am. I scan the televisions for directions to my gate and jog towards it, slinging my holdall over my shoulder. I wonder if I'll be anywhere near Emma? If her glare was anything to go on, it's probably safer if I'm not.

ACKNOWLEDGMENTS

This is my fourth book baby, and similarly to labour, each book takes months of blood, sweat, tears, and self-doubt before its exhausting yet triumphant arrival. Although with the year that was in it, writing Abby & Callum's story provided the perfect lockdown escapism. Thank you for reading it.

Thank you to my beta readers, especially Vikkie, aka Little Miss Book Lover who has come to be a great friend as well as reading partner, and to Aoife who has a fantastic eye for detail.

Thank you to all my crazy, lovable, supportive friends who (possibly unknowingly) help me create some wacky yet endearing characters.

Finally, and most importantly, thank you to my husband who has the patience of a saint, listening to my endless ideas and offering his never-ending support as I pursue my dreams.

If you enjoyed Love & Other Mushy Stuff, please consider leaving a review on Amazon or Goodreads and follow my Instagram and Facebook pages for updates on my latest books @lyndseygallagherauthor

ABOUT THE AUTHOR

Lyndsey Gallagher is an eternal sucker for a swoon worthy, happy ever after. She lives in the west of Ireland with her husband, two small children and a boxer puppy. When she's not writing, Lyndsey can be found curled up in front of the fire with a good book and a G&T.

www.lyndseygallagherauthor.com

Printed in Great Britain
by Amazon

12683195R00171